RUN ROBBIE RUN

Jon Pepper

NORTH COVE PRESS

Coconut Grove

For Dee: my cover designer, critic, editor, and inspiration.

Contents

PART ONE

Dewey or Don't He?

1. Look Alive

The once and possible future leader of the free world snored loudly on his sofa, engulfed in a dream where he was having cocktails with *The Golden Girls,* an aged sitcom playing on his big-screen TV. Bea Arthur and her cronies were admiring Dewey Fenwick's astonishing physique, his smarts, his dazzling smile, and asking if they could become part of his cabinet when he assumed office once again.

Dewey laughed and barked out, "You like me, don't you?" He arched his back, expelled a low, rumbling fart, and mumbled incoherently before lapsing back into a dreamscape of dewy Dewey meadows where golden girls frolicked.

Former President Fenwick, eighty-seven years old, was his party's presumptive nominee at the convention in Chicago in less than a month. He hadn't been outside of his rickety mansion in Beachville, Maryland, in weeks, and his translucent skin looked it. He wore a headband and workout gear, but the getup was less than convincing. Gaunt, frail and pale, Dewey and his campaign were running on little more than hatred toward the bombastic incumbent, President Roland I. Platt, and a lack of viable alternatives who were under the age of eighty and politically to the right of Mao Tse-Tung.

The Fenwick campaign's intern, a postdoc from Georgetown University named Dinda Bigley, wrung her hands in agony. "I don't know how much more of this I can take," she complained to the campaign chief, Ned Witherspoon. "If he doesn't wake up, we're going to blow the interview. He'll lose the race, and I'll never pay back my student loans."

Ned cupped his hand on her shoulder and looked her in the eye. "Get him elected and you won't have to pay back anything. Taxpayers will pick up the tab."

She took a deep breath and nodded hopefully. That was as good of a plan as any.

Ned turned away. "What's the time?"

"Eleven twenty." Dinda sighed, as she looked at her watch. "He's barely moved in a week. Boof and Skeeter will be here in, like, thirty minutes."

Ned apprised Dewey's outfit. "Why's he dressed like Richard Simmons?"

"I wanted to put him on the treadmill before Boof and Skeeter got here," Dinda said. "I figured I'd get his blood circulating. That's why I had his nurse put that stupid workout gear on him. I thought it would show… Oh, I don't know. I think it might have been a mistake."

Ned calmly waved her off. "Forget it. I've been through this drill many times." Ned moved in close to the former commander-in-chief and gently jostled his bony shoulders. "Mr. President… Mr. President, sir." Fenwick briefly opened his eyes before his head lolled back on his shoulder. Ned tapped him again and spoke more sharply. "Mr. PRESIDENT!"

Dewey stirred. "Wha…?" He licked his lips and peered at Ned. "Who the hell are you?"

"It's Ned, sir. Ned Witherspoon."

"Oh yeah," he said. "You're that young fella who… I dunno. Did somethin'."

"I was your deputy chief of staff when you were in the White House," he said. "You remember the White House."

"Of course I do, dummy." Dewey coughed. "It's over on whazzit… Ocean Drive." He chuckled to himself. "See? I know what time it is!"

"Sorry, sir. I'm talking about the White House in Washington, DC."

"Oh. That old barn," Dewey grumbled. "Huh. When we goin'?"

"Going where?"

"The White House. Jesus *H,* man*!* Are you *dense?"*

"We'll get there soon if you can just… look alive." Ned glanced over at Dinda, who appeared as if she would collapse in tears. Ned shrugged, then addressed Dewey as if he were speaking to a child. "As I'm sure you remember, sir, I'm directing your campaign for president. We're getting ready for the convention in Chicago in three weeks. You have famous visitors coming to interview you this morning and I'm sure you'll want to be at your best to meet them."

Dewey shook his head. "Tell 'em I don't want any."

"Any what?"

"Whatever crap they're selling." Dewey barked. "Where'd they go anyway?"

"Who?"

"The ladies."

"What ladies, sir?"

"The *goddamn ladies who were just here*, you nincompoop! Bea Arthur. Betty White. All them chicks. They were about to take their tops off and you scared 'em away." He pointed toward the TV, which was playing a commercial for laundry detergent, but his gaze shifted toward Dinda, who turned away, aghast.

"What's wrong with you people?" Dewey asked.

Ned sighed. "You may have been having a dream, sir. We need to get you up now."

Dewey worked his creaky jaw back and forth, trying to get the hinges loose.

Ned looked at him in dismay. *What did he want? An oilcan?* "Let's get you up on the treadmill for a few minutes and we'll put a little jump in your step. Okay, sir?" He took one hand, Dinda took another, and with a one-two-three and a heave-ho, they rocked him back and forth and got him to his unsteady feet.

"There you go Mister President," Dinda said as she helped him stagger to the treadmill.

Dewey grumbled, "Where's my damn thingamajig?"

Dinda called over her shoulder. "Brittany! Are you there? Grab his Yeti!"

Brittany, a part-time aide, sauntered in, brushing her long hair off her face. "I thought you didn't want me to touch him."

"His water bottle!" Dinda replied, exasperated.

"Oh." Brittany retrieved the giant Yeti emblazoned with a presidential seal from the coffee table and brought it over to the treadmill, where Ned dialed in a leisurely pace for the aged warrior.

"There you go, sir," Ned said. He hoisted Dewey up onto the treadmill, where he began moving at an almost imperceptibly slow pace. Dewey gripped the handrails, whitening his knuckles as if he were on a terrifying rocket ship ride into space.

Dinda held the bottle for the president as he took a swig, dribbling a wet stream onto his shirt. "Mm," he mumbled. "That tastes good." He took another sip and fixed a glassy stare at Dinda. "What do you call that stuff?"

Puzzled, Dinda replied, "Water?"

"Well, it's okay, whatever it is. Keep it handy. I might want another shot." He looked over and winked. "I'll need it working this hard."

"Yessir," she said, patting his shirt dry. She put the Yeti on the floor while Dewey took a couple of deep breaths and trudged ahead, loosening his ancient joints and connective tissue.

"You're doing great, Mister President!" Ned called. He looked at Dinda and rolled his hand in a circular motion, suggesting she chime in.

Dinda nodded. "Oh yeah! Totally a-*maz*-ing!" she crowed.

Dewey chuckled. "Where am I goin' anyway?"

Dinda laughed, then whispered to Ned, "That's a joke, right?"

Ned shook his head. "Back to the White House, sir!" he called out. "You're an inspiration! Hope I can go that fast when I'm eighty-seven." He turned back to see the television, where the moldy *Golden Girls* rerun had come to a merciful end. God forbid Dewey caught sight of them again. The excitement might prove too much.

"Keep an eye on him, will you?" he whispered to Dinda. He walked over to the coffee table, picked up the remote and switched the channel to FFS. There, Finn Tingleberry offered the latest breaking news on President Roland Platt's continuing tiff with Canada.

"President Platt today announced a naval blockade of Nova Scotia until Canada removes its steep tariffs on salmon," Tingleberry said. "The president said US battleships were steaming north toward Halifax and would remain there until Canada 'freed the fish.'" The video cut to Platt standing in front of a helicopter on the White House lawn. "If Canada continues to make salmon unaffordable to the American people, then we will retaliate with tariffs on bear claws and shortcake. And I can assure you, their economy would crumble in very, very short order…"

"Dinda!" Ned called. "Are you hearing this?"

Dinda noted that Fenwick was safely strolling at a geriatric pace before she rushed over to Ned's side. "What now?"

"Platt's sending battleships to Canada," he said in a tone of wonderment.

"Good grief!" she cried.

"Something about fish and pastries and —"

Behind them, Dewey's pace began to falter, and his breath came in gulps. He fumbled for a dial to slow down the newfangled treadmill, but he hit the wrong button, making the track incline. He pounded the controls to make the treadmill stop, but it only moved faster. The speed sent him tumbling off the treadmill onto the floor, where he cracked his head on the Yeti bottle.

"Oh, *no!*" Dinda shrieked.

She and Ned rushed over, where Dewey was splayed grotesquely on the floor, with his mouth open and his eyes closed, his knees and arms pointing in different directions. "Mister President! Mister *President!*" She gently shook him, then put both hands to her face in horror. "He can't be dead! Oh, please God! Not now!"

Ned kneeled down and put his fingers next to Dewey's carotid artery. "He's got a pulse."

Dinda scanned him. "I don't see any blood," she said, hopefully.

"I don't think he has any," Ned muttered.

Brittany appeared in the doorway at the bottom of the stairs. "Boof and Skeeter are here."

"Fuck, fuck, fuck, fuck, *fuck!*" Dinda muttered. "Get them coffee or something!" she called. "And hold them." She turned to Ned. "Should we cancel?"

"Now? And tell 'em what?" Ned gravely shook his head. "We can't do that. I invited them in to put a stop to Platt's claim that Dewey was…" He looked to Fenwick, "…this."

"I don't see how we convince them now," Dinda said.

Ned scoffed. "He's not dead yet."

"That's not a good campaign slogan," Dinda said. "What are we going to do?"

Ned sighed. "We can either draw a chalk outline around him or get Dr. Feeley."

"Isn't that pretty much the same thing?" Dinda asked.

"Let's find out."

2. Quack's Like a Doc

Ned quietly slid out the patio doors toward the beach, then walked up a grassy knoll to a back door into the garage. From there, he accessed a pantry inside the rambling mansion and a service stairwell to the second floor. He knocked lightly on the door to the bedroom suite of Dr. Franklin Feeley, the former White House doctor. The doctor had followed Fenwick into his retirement and became the family's exclusive private physician at the behest of the former First Lady, Janice Fenwick, for whom Feeley was rumored to administer daily check-ups.

"Come in," the doctor said.

Ned entered to see the physician in an easy chair across from the television having a smoke as he watched the emergency room drama, *The Pitt*. Feeley had a pen in one hand, and a notebook in his lap. "I'll be with you in a moment," he said. He picked up his remote and paused the action to read the subtitles, before scribbling notes, talking quietly as he wrote. "Dr. Robby says… five-hundred milligrams… IV drip… " He paused and tapped the pen on his chin. "That's interesting."

Ned approached the doctor. "The president's taken a fall."

Feeley didn't bother looking up. "He takes a fall every day."

"We think he may be hurt."

"May be, could be, might be…" Feeley muttered. He stubbed out his cigarette and issued a cough that sent a phlegmy pinball rattling around his chest, hitting every cushion on its way down. "The man takes more tumbles than a Romanian gymnast. He always gets up."

Ned balled his fists on his hips. "Maybe not this time. He went down hard. I mean—*splat*. And he's not getting up."

Feeley yawned. "Give him a minute." He pointed toward the TV with his thumb. "Show's almost over."

Ned grew heated. "Show's over for all of us if he doesn't come to." He grabbed the remote and snapped off the TV, annoying Feeley. "Damn it, Feeley. This is urgent. We have media in the house *right now*. They need to see him alive and well and on top of his game."

Feeley scoffed. "They should have come twenty years ago." Feeley rose and stuck a finger in Ned's chest. "I'm a doctor, not a magician. You want to make him out to be some sort of Adonis."

"I would settle for him looking alert."

"Show him some porn," Feeley suggested.

"He just finished watching *Golden Girls*," Ned replied.

Feeley was baffled. "That normally does the trick."

Ned implored, "Just help me get him through the day, all right?"

Feeley waved him off. "This is all bullshit and you know it. Sooner or later, the public's going to realize what's going on." Annoyed, Feeley made a notation in his diary. "I'm charging my time to the campaign."

"Go ahead. We're out of money anyway." Ned nodded toward a console where Feeley's medical bag was perched. "Bring your bag of tricks. You might need 'em."

Feeley threw a handful of syringes in his bag and followed Ned, who retraced his steps outside, careful to duck under windows to avoid detection by Boof and Skeeter. Ned and Feeley shuffled down the knoll and through the patio doors into the president's lair. There they encountered Dewey in the grotesque heap on the floor.

Feeley looked down in astonishment. "Oh, my word! I can't believe it!"

"You get it now?" Ned looked at Feeley and wagged a finger. "I tried to tell you..."

Feeley carefully stepped over the prostrate president and picked up the Yeti bottle. "Is this a Yeti?"

"Yes, it is," Dinda answered brightly.

"Interesting," Feeley said, studying the bottle. "I was thinking of getting one of these. Does it work like they say?"

Dinda nodded. "It sure does! It's great for the beach, and..."

Ned cut them off. "Dinda! Doctor!" he snapped. "*Please!*" He pointed to Dewey. "Can we do something with this?"

Feeley handed Dinda the Yeti, and sniffed, indignantly. He kneeled next to Dewey and checked for a pulse. "I'll say one thing: the man takes a lickin' and keeps on tickin'. We should all have his constitution."

He turned Dewey's head from side to side and said, "Hmm. Don't like that." Then he reached up to Dewey's face and pulled open one eyelid, then the other, revealing unmoving eyeballs staring blankly into space.

Feeley stood up. "Well, I'm sorry to tell you this. But, in my opinion, there's no question about it."

"What?" Dinda demanded.

"This man needs to see a doctor."

Ned rolled his eyes. "What are you?"

"Of course, *I'm* a doctor, dumbass," Feeley said, pulling out a cigarette and lighting it.

Dinda interceded. "Then what are you saying?"

Feeley looked at the sorry spectacle of Dewey Fenwick. "He needs a doctor with all the equipment for a complete examination. That means CAT-scan, x-rays, bloods..." Feeley said, brushing off his hands. "There's only so much I can do in this haunted house. He should go to the hospital. ASAP, in my view."

Dinda looked at Ned. "Well, he can't. He's scheduled for an interview."

"An interview?" Feeley chortled. "Are you out of your mind? He's unconscious."

Ned sighed. "He's done it before."

"He can't even talk, man!" Feeley said.

"Can't you just shoot him up with something?" Ned asked. "B-12, maybe?"

Feeley thought it over. "That might give him a jolt, but I've got to tell you: his old chassis is like an electric car. Eventually, he runs out of range. I can't very well run a cord up his ass." Feeley rested his smoking cigarette on the side of the coffee table, dipped into his medical bag and pulled out a capsule of amyl nitrate. He broke it in two and took a whiff, which jolted his head back. "Oh, yeah. This might do the trick." He took another sniff. "Anyone want a hit?"

Ned shook his head. "Feeley... honest to God."

"What?" Feeley asked.

"The *president*."

"He's not the president, you know," Feeley said as he kneeled.

"He was before. And he will be again," Dinda insisted, folding her arms across her chest. More quietly, she said, "He has to be."

Feeley waved the capsule under Fenwick's nose, but it produced no reaction. He tried again. "This is not promising."

Ned looked at his watch. "We're running out of time, doctor. What if we just prop him up on the couch?"

"You honestly think that will fool them?" Feeley asked.

"Their show is on MSDOA, doctor," Ned said. "It's practically owned media."

"Got it," Feeley said with a nod. "But I am not going to be in the room. This is on you."

Ned gripped the former president under his armpits, Feeley picked up his legs, and Dinda supported his bottom from below and they carried him over to the sofa. "*Oof,*" she muttered. "He's heavier than I thought."

They dropped Dewey into the cushions, arranged his arms and legs so that it looked like he was sitting comfortably, then folded his hands together over his stomach.

"Headband!" Ned called.

"Got it!" Dinda replied with increasing panic. She rushed over to the treadmill, tripped over the Yeti, and fell to the floor. She scrambled to her feet, retrieved the headband, and handed it over.

Ned slipped it over Dewey's crown and arranged it at a jaunty angle, then threaded his thinning white hair around it. Dinda furiously pinched Dewey's cheeks to bring some color into them, then dashed over to the countertop to grab his aviator sunglasses. She returned to place them on his head.

"Dang," she said, stepping back. "He looks… I dunno. Fit."

"I probably wouldn't let him drive," Ned said sardonically.

"You think they'll buy it?" she asked.

Ned nodded and patted her shoulder. "Good chance. Dewey is Santa Claus to these people. They want to believe in him."

Feeley snapped his medical bag shut. "Call me as soon as you're through. I'll arrange for transportation to Agnew Memorial. We'll keep it quiet for now."

Brittany appeared as Feeley left. "Are you ready for your guests?"

Dinda took a deep breath and glanced forlornly at Dewey.

Ned smiled. "It's showtime."

3. Useless Idiots

L. Robertson "Robbie" Crowe III drained the last drops of his oat milk latte and looked past his witless staff assembled around the conference table toward the dreary fog hanging over the Hudson River. The fourth generation scion of the great American industrialist Homer Crowe had spent nearly an hour at the Crowe Institute for the Greater Good searching in vain for a project that would (A) change the world, (B) afford him the respect and adulation he deserved for getting his ass out of bed every morning, and (C) rid him once and for all of the tags "nepo baby" for being a spoiled rich kid, and, worse, "nappo baby," for his habit of falling asleep at his desk. Yet Robbie's path to achieve his goals looked as murky as the low-hanging clouds obscuring the Jersey City skyline across the water from Manhattan. *I can't believe I'm still wasting my time on this shit…*

Robbie had already spent a small chunk of the Crowe family fortune backing losers over the past five years. Not one of the projects he had supported since he was deposed as chair of the Crowe Power Company could be called a success. A sustainable fast-food restaurant chain in California that served super high-fiber sanitized compost sounded promising. Who knew nobody would eat it, even when it was drenched in graywater gravy? An elaborate ventilation system that converted flatulence from corporate conference rooms into usable energy appeared to be an innovative idea. It could cut utility bills by 15 percent! But no company wanted to admit that farts were often the only reliable product developed in their staff meetings. Then there was Obese-a-Tea, a beverage made from the eye of newt and toe of frog or some bullshit that was supposed to melt pounds away and solve the diabetes crisis. Research showed — only *after* he had committed his money! — that its name was far too embarrassing for fatties to buy the product at the store or even order it online.

"All I see here is crap!" Robbie bellowed. He looked around the table at the glazed eyeballs of his nerdy staff and fumed. Why did he bother paying these overeducated Ivy League morons? He should fire them all!

"What the fuck are you people thinking?" He glared. "I want ideas for world peace! Curing cancer! You give me a tire recycling project in…" He glanced at his print-out. "Maseru? Where the fuck is that?"

A trembling aide named Kyle or Kevin or something cleared his throat. "It's in Lesotho, sir."

Robbie seethed. "And I'm supposed to know where that is?"

"It's in southern Africa," the aide replied.

Robbie leaned over the table. "What?"

"It's the former Basutoland, if that helps."

Robbie spoke in a low rumble. "Oh yeah. That helps a hell of a lot, Kyle."

"It's um, Kevin sir."

Robbie flushed red. "Well, listen, *Kevin*," he hissed. "When you wake up from your wet dreams of Africa, think about where I might actually want to travel for a check writing ceremony. Paris? *Oui oui.* Rome? *Molto buono.* You pick a project in Unga Bunga, I'm sending you. All right? One way."

Robbie picked up the sheaf of papers before him and flung them across the table. "A hundred monkeys with laptops could find better projects than these!"

He pushed back from the table, muttering to himself, and stood up as he scanned the faces in the room. How was it that nobody in this organization — *people that somebody must have hired!* — could play at his level? All of them were tops in their class from Columbia, Harvard, and Penn. Maybe the problem was their majors were in Intifada Planning and Advanced Vandalism. How was he supposed to win the Nobel Prize with these nincompoops as his support team? Abraham Lincoln had a team of rivals. Robbie had a team of mopes and dopes.

"Mr. Crowe? Sir?" Kevin stammered.

Robbie glared at him. Kevin was coming back for more? "What?" he seethed. *"What?"*

"Hate to bring this up," Kevin said, "but you do know there is an issue with our rating from the Standards Board?"

Robbie raised his chin defiantly and peered down his nose at the impudent moron. "An issue?"

Kevin looked around the table. He knew Robbie well enough to know an issue that could reflect poorly on the king should not be discussed in front of the serfs on the staff. "Sir, perhaps this is best discussed privately."

Robbie sat down and smirked. He'd show this wise ass. "No, no. You brought it up. Sock it to me."

"Right," Kevin said. "Well, see... The board noted that our foundation is spending far more on administration expenses than it is on projects."

Robbie shrugged. "So what?"

"Unless this is remedied, we will lose our accreditation," Kevin said. "And if we lose our accreditation, we will get no more donations. We're already down as it is."

Robbie flushed red. Another failure due to incompetent underlings! What in God's name were these jackasses doing all day? "Why was I not told of this?"

Kevin coughed to clear his throat. "Mr. Crowe, the Standards Board warned us in a letter sent to you a month ago. It said that if we did not comply with their guidelines, we would be dropped from their list of recommended philanthropies."

Robbie slowly shook his head in disgust. "And you didn't think you should bring this to my attention?"

Kevin stammered. "I have tried for several weeks to get on your calendar to discuss their questions." He paused, fearing another explosion. "Of course, we all know how busy you are."

Staffers snickered into their sleeves. Robbie did next to nothing all day, and they knew it.

"What questions?" Robbie asked.

Kevin pulled the letter from a folder and shifted uneasily in his chair. "They wanted to know about employee compensation."

Robbie deflected with a wry smile. *Aha!* "Apparently they realize some of you are overpaid."

Kevin blushed. "They were asking specifically about you, sir," he replied. "The average salary for the president of a non-profit is one-hundred and fifty thousand dollars. They noted that you were paid eleven million dollars last year."

Robbie gulped. How could the Standards Board criticize him? He knew their trustees! He went to school with them and frequented the same clubs! Their kids went to the same schools together! Weren't they supposed to cover for one another? "Well, that's just bullshit," Robbie declared. "You get what you pay for."

"I told them that," Kevin said.

"And?"

"They asked, 'What is that exactly?'"

Robbie had never considered the question that bluntly, largely because he never thought anyone would have the temerity to ask. He was paid what he was paid because that's what he wanted to be paid and his name was on the shingle, which was a license to do whatever the hell he wanted. Obviously, he lent prestige to the organization. And of course, it benefited greatly from his grand vision to make the world a better place. Still, his mouth went dry as he felt all eyes in the room were on him, witnessing his discomfort over this insult. He had no response, but he did come up with a plan to extricate himself from the delicate situation.

He shot to his feet. "I've got to take a call."

He bolted from the room and approached Matilda, his matronly administrative assistant. She was busy going through mail at her desk, consisting of bills for business credit cards, forms from the State of New York, and lunch promotions from El Vez, a Tex-Mex joint across the street. *Hmm*, she mused. *Boss might like a nice taco...*

Robbie gestured toward the conference room with his thumb. "Get in there and fire them."

"All righty," said Matilda, picking up a note pad as if she were taking a coffee order. "Which ones?"

"All of them."

The steady Matilda didn't blink. "Yes, sir. That's ten people?"

"Whatever it is, yeah. Let them all go. Except for that cute girl in the back," Robbie said. "What's her name?"

"Amy?"

"Amy. Yeah. Keep her." He wouldn't mind working with Amy in private on whatever it was she did. "She might be of use."

"Anyone else?" Matilda asked.

"Keep Kevin. I might need him." Robbie required at least one person to cuff around. Kevin seemed to take abuse better than most. After all, he kept coming back for more.

"Do you want to offer severance?" Matilda asked.

"Oh, hell no," Robbie said. "We're already over budget. These guys have been spending like drunken sailors." He turned toward his office, then reconsidered and turned back. "I'm going to lunch. Have Serge pull up out front right away."

"Shall I make you a reservation?"

"Santi in Midtown. Call Harry and tell him I'll meet him there in twenty minutes," he growled. "And text me once the coast is clear. I don't want to see any of these sad sacks when I come back. I hate crying in the office."

"That's because you are a humanitarian, sir," Matilda said.

Was she being a smart-ass? He looked at her and realized that no, she was just sincerely stupid. "That's exactly right," he said. "See you in a bit."

4. Top of His Game

For media stars Boof Bellamy and Skeeter Donlan, scoring an exclusive audience with former president Dewey Fenwick was a major coup. Surely, it would boost the sagging ratings of their MSDOA morning show, *Boof & Skeeter in the A.M.*, which had fallen behind reruns of *Full House*, *Sabrina the Teenage Witch*, and the paid program, *Were You in a Car Accident?* More than that, an interview with Dewey Fenwick handled in just the right way could restore their standing with their media colleagues. *We're still on the team!*

Not that it was ever seriously in doubt, but there had been concerns about Boof's party loyalty after he interviewed the detestable President Platt and failed to sniff, sneer or even roll his eyes at him. When the round concluded without scoring a knockout, or even landing any jabs, questions began to circulate: Was Boof going soft? Was he straying from the consensus understanding that every effort must be made to attack and expose Platt's evil doings and evict him from office?

Boof heard the criticism and it stung. All Bartholomew "Boof" Bellamy ever wanted was to be considered one of the cool guys, yet it had been a lifelong struggle. His nickname was derived from the trademark bouffant hairdo he had worn since the fifth grade in Oklahoma City, where he was roundly abused on the playground with a daily dose of noogies and wedgies. With no one to play with after school, he taught himself guitar and banjo, recorded a CD, and made a hundred copies. It failed to sell but it did make a shiny target for skeet shooting. He pressed on to break into the glamorous world of broadcasting by working graveyard shifts from Bemidji to Baton Rouge before breaking into the big leagues.

Co-host Skeeter Donlan had scaled the dizzying heights of local weather and traffic reports in Memphis to become host of the *Howdy Houston* morning show, then a substitute news reader on *Way Before Daybreak* in Los Angeles, which ultimately led to a pairing with Boof on MSDOA's show *Wake Up, Slobs!* Boof was smitten from their first show together. That he could even get a smile from such a beautiful celebrity—she did shampoo commercials on the side! —made him feel he'd arrived.

Their pairing proved a hit, as they came together onstage and off, with each dumping their respective spouses for another march down the aisle. They found their ratings groove during Dewey Fenwick's first run for president, when their unnamed sources deep inside the campaign (namely, Ned) made them Dewey's virtual megaphone, dependably spouting the Talking Points of the Day for other media to pick up and amplify. Sadly, their groove became a rut when Dewey declined to run for reelection and Platt rose to power. With tensions rising on the set and at home, Boof and Skeeter desperately needed Dewey Fenwick to complete a comeback.

This was the chance to save their show, their marriage, and their standing among colleagues. No competitors had scored an audience with the elusive former president, running for a second time on his highly successful Subterranean Strategy: lie low, say nothing, and let Roland Platt do all the talking. While every sound bite from Platt was washed, rinsed and spun by the opposition media as further evidence of his tyranny, Dewey's image remained pristine. But with rumors circulating on social media that he was failing physically and mentally, the campaign was pressured to reassure the public that he was A-OK. And so Ned turned to his dependable mouthpieces, Boof and Skeeter, to spread the word.

As they entered the room for their discussion, Boof marched over to shake Dewey's hand. "Mr. President!" he exclaimed.

Ned quickly placed a hand on Boof's back and guided him away. "You'll excuse the president if he doesn't shake your hand right now, Boof. He's a bit of a germaphobe these days," Ned explained. "You understand."

"Of course," replied Boof, credulous as always. "Great to see you, sir."

Dinda followed with Skeeter, her blond hair perfectly coiffed, befitting her continuing gig as a model for Miss Hair-Do shampoo *and* conditioner. "Don't you worry, Mr. President! I won't even try to shake your hand," she said with a reassuring smile. "I'm just delighted to see you looking so well."

Ned invited them to sit down in easy chairs opposite the sofa while he and Dinda sat on either side of what was left of the great man. Ned stretched his arm along the back of the sofa within sufficient range of the former president's head to assist in the event it listed in an unfortunate direction.

"Before we get started, I just want to say how thrilled the president has been to see you," Ned said. "Dinda can attest to that."

"For sure!" Dinda crowed. "Talked about it practically nonstop all morning."

"Nonstop!" Ned echoed. "In fact, he talked himself hoarse. Terrible timing, but he's developed laryngitis. So, you know…"

Skeeter drooped. "He can't speak?"

"Not a word," Ned chipped in.

"Oh," Skeeter said.

Boof regarded Dewey quizzically. *He doesn't look so hot…* "That's disappointing," he allowed. "But of course we get it. I mean—" *What?* He couldn't think of anything to say.

"We're just glad for the face time," Skeeter said.

"Face? No worries there," Ned said, jovially. "We've got lots of face for you."

Dinda added, with a nervous giggle. "He might lean a little light on the banter today, but he has lots and lots of face."

Skeeter and Boof both stared at Fenwick, who hadn't moved since they sat down. Then they looked at each other. *Dewey better be okay.* They were counting on it.

Ned sensed their concern and jumped in. "I know what you must be thinking: He's not quite as animated as usual. If he could talk right now, he'd admit it. But it's the darn laryngitis."

"That can be so debilitating," Dinda noted.

Skeeter nodded sympathetically. "That would get anyone down," she acknowledged.

Ned added, "I can assure you he's perfectly fine. In face, I'd say he's at the top of his game."

"Oh yes," Dinda said. "Tippy top."

Ned nodded vigorously. "You should have seen him in tennis this morning." He raised his right hand as if he were being sworn in to testify. "Kicked my butt."

"Really?" Skeeter asked.

Dinda laughed. "Made Ned look like he was playing with the wrong hand! I've never seen such a clod. He—"

Ned squinted at Dinda. "I think they get the idea."

Skeeter scribbled in her notebook. "I'm so impressed! That's really incredible."

"Eighty-seven years old!" Ned said in wonder. "Hope I'm as with it as he is at this age." Turning to Dewey, he added, "You really are amazing, sir."

Dewey remained as stiff as a side table. There was dead silence for a moment before Ned slapped his thigh with his free hand. "So…" he said to the reporters. "You need anything else?"

Boof looked at Skeeter, then back to Ned. "That's it?"

"What?" Ned asked, a touch of irritation in his voice. "You need more?"

"Well," Boof said, apologetically, "we were hoping to ask a few questions. You know, to get the inside dope."

"You do know how busy he is," Ned said sharply.

Skeeter nodded, deferentially. "Of course," she said. "Just one or two questions, perhaps?"

"The man can't talk," Ned protested.

Dinda pointed to her throat. "He's got the thing…"

"Right, the thing," Boof said with a sigh. "What if it's just a simple yes or no question and he can—I don't know—nod his head?"

Ned looped his little finger inside Dewey's headband. "What do you say, Mister President. Does that work for you?"

Ned pulled on the headband, which gave Dewey the appearance of nodding. "Appreciate that, sir." Ned turned to Boof and said, "Fire away."

"If there's any elaboration you need," Dinda added, pointing back and forth between her and Ned, "we're right here for you."

Boof smiled and jumped in, fixing the unconscious potentate in his sights. "Okay then, Mr. President. Roland Platt noted that you would be ninety-two at the end of your term. He's also been calling you names like Dyin' Dewey and our Ex(Lax) President. Have you heard these insults?"

Ned looked at Dewey and tugged the headband, moving his head up and down twice. "I think that's a yes," Ned said triumphantly.

Skeeter leaned in. "Would you like to offer a response to Platt, sir?"

Ned looked at the frozen Dewey, then turned back to Skeeter. "Apparently not."

Skeeter persisted. "Nothing at all?"

Ned said, "Feel free to attribute this to him: he won't dignify such course language by engaging in name calling with a complete asshole."

"Very dignified, indeed," Skeeter said approvingly as she jotted some notes.

"Admirable restraint, sir," Boof said. "Would you mind if we fired back at him on your behalf?"

Ned, feeling more confident in his puppetry, decided to try moving Dewey's head from side to side by tugging on his ear. It proved a serious miscalculation, as Dewey flopped face down into Ned's lap. *Whump!*

"Guess that's a 'no,'" Ned said drily.

"Oh my God!" Skeeter exclaimed.

"Now, now," Ned said, picking up Dewey's head. "No worries. Please. It's just from the medication for his throat. Makes him drowsy sometimes. He'll come to…" He glanced at Dewey. "…eventually. Dinda, can you give me a hand?"

She jumped from her seat and helped Ned pull the former president back into a seated position, albeit with his mouth agape, his sunglasses askew, and his headband tilted like a ring around Saturn. Dinda pushed his jaw shut and sat back down.

Boof looked concerned, but trudged ahead, wanting to squeeze every dollop of history out of this moment. He asked, "Maybe just one more question?"

"Okay," Ned said. "But we're running a little late for his bike ride."

"He's going to ride a bike today?" Skeeter asked in astonishment.

"Oh, yes," Dinda replied.

"Even with his… thing?" Skeeter pressed.

Dinda chuckled. "He doesn't have to talk on his bike."

"Right," Skeeter agreed, "but… doesn't he have to pedal?"

"The man's a warrior," Ned insisted.

Boof turned to Skeeter. "Why don't you go ahead…"

"Okay then," Skeeter said brightly as she smoothed her skirt and faced the inert candidate. "Mr. President, some have said you have stayed off the campaign trail because you're in poor physical condition. Have you heard these criticisms?"

Ned didn't want to chance signaling 'no' again. He tugged on Dewey's headband to signal yes, which unexpectedly snapped his head back, then forward. Dewey's chin fell to his chest before he tumbled in slow motion, twirling off the couch in a tight somersault before sticking his landing on the carpet. *Plop!*

"Bravo!" Ned cried.

"Well done, sir!" Dinda added.

***

Dinda and Ned escorted the reporters out to their idling Cadillac Escalade and offered them hugs as their driver opened the rear doors, sending a whoosh of chilled air into the humid atmosphere.

"He loves you guys so much," Dinda said, pulling Skeeter close. "We love you, too."

"Same," Skeeter replied. "So great to see him. And you, too, of course."

"You did yourselves proud in there," Ned said, as he handed them each a sheet of key talking points on behalf of the former president. "He jabbers incessantly about how much you helped the campaign last time. That's why he trusts you. He knows you've got his back, and he appreciates it."

"Back at you," Boof said as he offered Ned a fist bump. He stuck a skinny leg into the SUV before turning back. "Gotta admit. He seemed a little, I don't know… off, maybe? Answers weren't quite as crisp as usual."

Ned stared at him. Was Boof wandering off script?

Boof noted the hesitation and worried he was treading into apostate territory. "But, given his age…"

"That's not an issue," Ned insisted.

Dinda added, "I think the throat thingy kind of sapped his energy."

Boof nodded. "Makes total sense. Sorry to even bring it up."

Ned said, "As you could plainly see, he's fit as a fiddle."

Boof nodded, as he shook hands with Ned. "Well, as they say, I don't care if he's eight or eighty, blind, crippled or crazy. He's better than the alternative."

"Damn straight!" Ned exclaimed. "Keep your eyes on the prize!"

"Right-o!" Boof agreed.

"We can't have another four years of Platt!" Ned reminded them.

"No, sirree!" Skeeter said.

Dinda said, "I'm sure President Fenwick would say exactly the same thing, if he were… um—"

"Able to talk?" Boof said.

"Yeah," Dinda replied.

Their vehicle exited the gravel driveway in a cloud of dust, with Ned and Dinda smiling and waving a cheerful goodbye. Through the side of his mouth, Ned told Dinda, "Let's talk about Plan B."

5. Eating Crowe

Tucked away in a corner banquette of a bustling Midtown Manhattan restaurant, Robbie picked indifferently at his asparagus salad as he strained to hear his financial adviser over the din. He would ask Harry Crenshaw to speak up, but there was good reason to speak low. What Harry was saying was not for general consumption.

"The Standards Board is the least of your foundation's problems," Harry said. "My guys have been looking over the books, Robbie. And I've gotta tell you: it's not good."

Robbie's mouth went dry and he reached for his iced tea. "How bad is it?" he asked.

"We can go over all the particulars if you like," Harry said, "but the bottom line is this: unless you raise money fast or decide to plow some of your own dough into the fund, you're gonna be out of business by the end of the year."

Robbie slumped in his seat and eyed his lunch companion. Harold "Hacksaw Harry" Crenshaw had enough credibility in New York's financial world for Robbie to take him at his word. Harry asked his team to review the books as a favor to Robbie—a token of appreciation for managing more than seven-hundred million dollars of Robbie's money in a hedge fund at an eye-watering commission. The cash funneled through the Crowe Foundation for the Greater Good was chump change by comparison.

"I don't understand how that could happen," Robbie said.

Harry looked around him, then leaned across the table. "Platt cut off all the funding you used to get from the Fenwick administration," Harry said. "Feds gave you money for every lunatic social experiment they could think of. Migrant recruitment centers in Venezuela. 3D penis printing for transgenders. And, of course, there was the infamous Midnight Checkers."

Robbie nodded vaguely. "I, uh... Midnight Checkers? What was that about?"

"It was a plan to replace cops in domestic disputes," Harry said. "Instead of police carrying guns, they sent in social workers from Barnard

College armed with board games. They tried to calm things by saying, 'How about a nice game of checkers? Or maybe Parcheesi?'"

Robbie nodded approvingly. "Not the worst idea I ever heard."

Harry scoffed. "It's in the top two. I guess you didn't see the results."

Robbie grew indignant. "Nobody tells me anything."

"A bunch of these so-called violence interrupters were beaten up, stabbed, shot, or attacked by dogs. Six people were killed, three people got rabies, and one's never gonna walk again. When Platt came in, all those programs went away. So did your stream of funding. And with your payroll expenses as high as they are—"

Robbie interjected. "Not anymore," he said, triumphantly. "I fired a bunch of them this morning."

Harry paused. "Who?"

"The staff," Robbie said.

Harry blinked rapidly. "That doesn't fix the problem."

"Of course it does," Robbie insisted.

Harry took a deep breath. "What about your salary?"

Robbie scoffed. "Somebody's gotta mind the store."

Harry backed up. "Of course," he said soothingly. "But if there's no store, what are you minding?"

Robbie glanced around the room, where the restaurant's white-coated chef was walking among the tables, checking in on his high-powered guests. Did any of them have to deal with the kind of bullshit that was served up on his plate every single day? In all the endeavors he had led in his adult life, he had been undermined by poor performers on his staff. Every damn time!

"I trusted my employees and they turned around and screwed me," Robbie groused. "They're just dead on their ass. You know that, right? Nobody wants to work anymore. They don't even want to show up at the office, as if that's an imposition on their personal life. They have to stay home because they have to walk the dog! They have to go out for a run! Maybe they need some cuddle time with their who-knows-who. I dunno, Harry. Has there ever been another leader in all the world's history that's had shittier followers than me? I'm fucking cursed."

Harry tried to rouse some sympathy as he sorted through a plate of prawns. "You've had a tough run, for sure," he said. "Maybe you should try a little staff development with the survivors of your purge. Provided there are any, of course."

"A couple might make it."

"Then maybe you do some coaching and counseling? It might help to impart some of your wisdom on how to succeed in business without really trying. They could learn something. After all, you do make it look effortless."

"Oh please!" Robbie muttered. "They're beyond help. I treat them exactly the way I wanted to be treated—like grownups. I leave them alone and expect them to do their job. If they do it, they stay; if they don't, they're fired. That's my management playbook in a nutshell. I don't believe in bossing people around. If they need help, they should ask me. My door's always open."

"Right," Harry said slowly. "But—and I don't mean to be blunt— you're never in there."

Robbie winced. "Whose side are you on?"

"Yours, of course," Harry said.

"Then you know they could find me if they really wanted to," Robbie said.

"Not with Broom Hilda at the front desk," Harry claimed.

"Matilda?"

"She's a fucking sphynx," Harry said. "She never tells anyone anything."

"That's what I like to hear," Robbie said.

"Yeah. Well, I may as well ask the Secret Service where Platt's sleeping tonight. I might have a better shot at getting information."

Robbie resumed picking at his food. "She's the one employee I have who knows what the hell she's doing," he said. "I don't need snoops poking around my business." He pointed toward the windows. "Who knows where I might be? I could be in the park, thinking big thoughts. Nobody needs to know that."

"Or maybe you're just getting laid."

"Whatever." Robbie stabbed a caper with his fork and studied it. "What the fuck are these things?"

"I don't know," Harry said. "Pods of some sort. Can we finish this business about your foundation? I think you need an exit plan."

Robbie tossed his napkin down on the table. "You seem to have all the answers," he said. "What do you suggest?"

"I'd put out a statement. Declare 'mission accomplished' and shut the damn thing down."

"Then what?" Robbie asked.

"I don't know. What do you want to do?"

"Something. Anything." Robbie looked cross. "Help me out here, will you?" he pleaded. "Look at my resume. I bet it tops anyone in this room."

Harry looked around and shrugged. "Maybe so."

"Nothing 'maybe' about it," Robbie said. "I worked my way up to the top of a Fortune 100 company. I'm the leader of a global foundation making the world a better place. Maybe I should write a book."

Harry couldn't imagine Robbie's attention span holding long enough to write a page or two, much less an entire book. "A book about what?"

Robbie laughed. "As Pavarotti used to sing: *me-me-me-me-me-me!*"

"A memoir?"

"Why not?"

Harry studied Robbie with wonder. What in the world would Robbie say about a lifetime of failing upward? No matter how many mistakes Robbie made in his career and his personal life, his name and his fortune insulated him from the consequences of his own ineptitude. And, where others might have given up from embarrassment, Robbie's colossal ego and penchant for blaming others for his failings kept him going. Robbie always landed on his feet, often on a higher rung, and Harry supposed he always would.

"How do you suppose such a book would end?" Harry asked.

Robbie sat back in his seat. "That's what holds me back. I need, like, one crowning achievement that brings it all together."

Harry chuckled. "I don't think you have to worry about opportunities, Robbie," he said. "They always seem to find you."

6. Democracy Inaction

Ned stepped out of a cab on F Street in Washington for an emergency meeting of the National Committee. He pushed through the revolving door of a drab office building that served as home to the Hands Up Foundation, the philanthropic arm of the party's finance chair, the uber wealthy investor Benedikte "Bennie" Barbu and his son, Marius.

Ned scanned his ID at the front desk and took the stairs up two at a time to a conference room, where Bennie and other leading players of the National Committee were assembled to discuss contingency plans should Dewey Fenwick continue to falter.

"You realize that if Dewey is no longer a candidate, there are factions in our party that are going to demand we pick the nominee through an open convention," said Worth Talmadge, a prominent DC lawyer and chair of the committee.

Eleanor Winthrop, director of the activist group Democracy by Any Means Necessary, emphatically stabbed the conference table with her index finger. "And throw our party into chaos? No, no. Not on my watch."

"You realize critics will insist we follow a democratic process," Worth replied.

"Hate to be indelicate, but tough poopski, as my grandmother used to say. If we have to suspend democracy in order to save it, so be it," Eleanor declared. "You know that I would defend to death the right of all delegates to have a vote under normal circumstances. But, where Roland Platt is concerned, the circumstances are never normal."

"I'm on board with that," insisted Meredith Worthington Duke, cultural anthropology professor at Columbia University, and board member at the George Floyd Center for Racial Justice. "I think I speak for all Black people when I say an executive decision by this committee is in their best interests." Untroubled by the fact that no Black people were present, she noted, "After all, I've studied and worked among them all my life."

Bennie, sitting quietly at the head of the table, had hoped to avoid complications so late in the game. He turned to Ned. "Any chance Dewey can finish the race?"

Ned offered a hopeless shrug. "He's in a coma."

Bennie asked, "Is he expected to come out of it?"

Ned winced. "Not vertically."

Bennie gripped his son Marius's arm and sadly shook his head. His dear friend Dewey was dying—and so was his plan to once again run the government through an addle-brained chief executive.

Marius asked, "Do reporters know about Dewey's condition?"

"Our sense is that many of them suspect something is up, but they're no threat to report it. Their hatred of Platt is so visceral, they're doing all they can to pump up Dewey, regardless of his condition," Ned said. He nodded toward a TV in the corner of the room, which was playing MSDOA. "We had Boof and Skeeter out to Beachville yesterday."

"Tough interview?" Marius asked with a wry smile.

"You have no idea," Ned replied.

Bennie slid the remote across the table. "Let's hear what they have to say."

Ned pointed the remote control at the TV and turned up the volume. All heads in the room turned toward the screen, where Boof and Skeeter were boasting about their exclusive visit with the former president.

"Dewey… Horatio… Fenwick," Boof intoned somberly. "The man, the myth, the marvel."

Skeeter shook her head in wonder. "They say still waters run deep. We saw proof of that yesterday, didn't we, Boof?"

"You betcha, Skeeter. The man was completely still!"

"And so deep!" she claimed.

"He doesn't say a whole lot, but he doesn't have to," Boof contended. "He listens. He thinks. He makes you just feel these, these, these—what am I trying to say here? These vibes. These *awesome vibes*."

"Yes! Vibes!" Skeeter added.

"The vibes communicate in ways that words never could," Boof claimed. "Wisdom. Truth. Compassion. The kind of decency that once graced the White House but has disappeared under Roland Platt."

Skeeter chuckled. "I wish our viewers had seen how he responded to Platt's insulting comments about his health. A perfect rejoinder, didn't you think?"

"'Dyin' Dewey,'" Boof spat. "The man executed a perfect somersault—right before our eyes! *Boom*, daddy!"

"Absolutely incredible," Skeeter added with a smile of wonderment. "He stuck that landing like a lunar module in the Sea of Tranquility. Eighty-seven years young!"

"You know what that told me?" Boof said, waggling his finger at the camera. "Anyone who claims this man is too old to become president again ought to try telling that to his face. Pardon my French, but he'll kick your ass from here to Beachville!"

Ned muted the sound and sighed. "No, he won't."

"My goodness," Bennie said with dismay. "Are those people on TV as gullible as they seem?"

"Pretty much," Ned said.

Bennie sighed. "So where does that leave us?" Bennie asked. "Have you sifted through our alternatives?"

Ned connected his phone via Bluetooth to the computer screen on the other side of the room. "Yes, we've run the data, talked with our consultants, and winnowed the field down. Ultimately, I ran our criteria through Poindexter, our AI program. No matter how I framed the question, Poindexter kept turning up the same name." He hit a button, and a photo appeared on the screen. "L. Robertson Crowe III, otherwise known as Robbie."

Bennie looked like he'd been stricken with gout. "Robbie Crowe? Why him?"

"I'll tell you what our research told us," Ned said, glancing at his notes. "Robbie's the anti-Platt. He's a businessman like Platt, but not a good one. He's a billionaire, but he feels guilty about it. His speeches always make references to creating a better world, but he's light on the details. And he's got a household name, but nobody's quite sure why. We have an opportunity to define him with very little time for scrutiny between now and the convention. Problem is we don't know how long Dewey might linger."

Bennie squinted. "I knew Robbie Crowe's father years ago, so I've watched Robbie from a distance. He hasn't exactly set the world on fire," he said. "In fact, I've never seen anyone do less with more."

Marius piped up. "What do you mean, pop?"

Bennie glanced over the printed bio. "He was handed the chairmanship of the Crowe Power Company by his family. He booted it. He's even worse at running a foundation. From what I understand, it's nearly out of business. He made the front page of the *New York Post* for assaulting a company shareholder who publicly criticized him. He testified against his family's own company in a lawsuit while cavorting unwittingly with a Chinese spy." Bennie laid aside the bio. "Any success he's had in life could be attributed entirely to his ancestor Homer Crowe, his former CEO Walker Hope, or his ex-wife, Lindsey, who rescued their company after he nearly drove it into the East River."

"All true," Ned said. "He's probably the least deserving billionaire in America."

Marius smiled. "In other words..."

"He's perfect," Bennie concluded.

"Exactly right," Ned said, nodding vigorously. "Robbie Crowe has bungled every opportunity in his life and blames it on the system. He gives cover to every moron in America."

Bennie turned to his son. "How does he score in our rewards program?" he asked.

Marius tapped the side of his smart glasses and paused, reading. "He's top tier. Lots of good intentions, even if the results are abysmal. The main thing is, I think we can work with him." Marius looked at Ned. "Bring up the graphic, would you?"

As Ned hit a button on his phone, Marius walked up to the screen, showing a huge pie chart. "Our biggest opportunity is with this huge voting bloc we call Bitter Losers. They're twenty-nine to forty-five, largely male, holding useless degrees in Jungle Sex Rituals and Football Studies and paying down debts for student loans through shitty jobs. They're ready to hold somebody accountable for their failures. And, of course, that somebody is Platt. He stubbornly refuses to forgive the loans they took out for stupid majors." He pointed to a second large slice of the pie. "The second biggest voting group is Guilty Winners. This group is mostly female, forty-six to sixty-five, weirdly miserable about their comfortable lives. They tend to have had bad experiences with men but still long for a mate they can berate."

"They're looking for a pussy?" Bennie asked.

"Essentially," Marius said. "These women record their rage on TackyTalk, go to rallies with their pals, and hold protest signs while they sit in lawn chairs by the side of the road, listening to banjo music and yelling at traffic. Robbie could appeal to them in a big way. He's a—quote-unquote—nice boy."

Worth said, "I've known Robbie since prep school in New Hampshire, and I can tell you: he comes as advertised. Personable, charming when he wants to be, and a complete and utter fuck up. He's easily distracted from any task before him and will find any excuse not to work. He was too lazy to copy my papers in school, even when I offered them. He only graduated because his dad built the school a power plant."

Bennie turned to Dr. Kristi Kramer, the North Carolina-based campaign consultant, noted TV commentator, and celebrated author of best-selling business books. "According to the dossier, Dr. Kramer, you accused Robbie Crowe of sexual harassment some years ago."

Kristi blushed. "I did indeed."

"What did he do?"

"Well, let me think," she said. "First he kinda went like this." She stroked her thigh. "Then he sorta touched this—" She said, moving a hand toward her breast.

Bennie interrupted. "Those details are not necessary," he said.

"I wouldn't mind hearing them," Marius protested.

Bennie looked him off. "Perhaps in the interest of time, Dr. Kramer, you could summarize?"

Kristi nodded. "Yes, of course," she said, sitting up and batting her eyes. "I can tell you he did exactly what people in powerful positions sometimes do. He used his position to extract favors of a prurient nature."

"In other words, he's a guy who's led around by his dick," Ned said.

"To the extent he gets around at all, yes."

"Did he ever apologize?" Ned asked.

"Of course he did," she acknowledged. "In fact, I wrote his apology for him. He needed something to run in the *Times*."

Bennie looked at her with astonishment. "*You* wrote it? Weren't you furious with him?"

"Well, yes. Of course!" Kristi chortled. "He paid for it. And the fact is you don't stay angry with Robbie for long. He can't help himself. He was born so rich, he never learned life had boundaries. He regards everything he sees as his personal property."

Bennie stood up to shake off the numbness in his feet and restart the circulation in his aging legs as he pondered the possibility of Robbie Crowe leading the ticket. Would Robbie help Bennie reach his objectives?

A Romanian national who grew up poor on the streets of Bucharest during the Soviet occupation after World War II, Bennie rose from poverty to make a fortune betting against the currencies of Western democracies. He increased his odds of profiting from national failures by working with the CIA to funnel foreign aid through his foundation to create social disruption and chaos in countries he was shorting. The strategy worked so well in central Europe, Asia, and Africa that he turned his sights on the biggest prize of all: the United States, a nation he had deeply resented since childhood for its failure to push the brutal Soviets out of Romania. He swore then that he would give America a taste of communism if he ever had the chance by financing niche political parties that could prove powerful in local elections, supporting radical candidates to run on their tickets, and paying activist groups to foment mayhem in the streets, and spur voters to respond.

By sending US taxpayer money back through non-governmental organizations like Democracy by Any Means Necessary and the George Floyd Center for Racial Justice, Bennie promoted voting rights for pre-teens, drug injection sites in public schools, and Name, Image and Likeness rights for political assassins—any crazy idea to roil his opponents and take their eye off what he was really up to, which was a complete reordering of the system.

His strategy worked perfectly until Platt came along.

"I'm sorry to hear about my friend Dewey," Bennie said. "He was a dependable ally for a long time." He grimaced as he walked, then reached down to message his right leg. "Is there no chance for Evita?"

Ned scanned the other faces in the room. Everyone knew that Bennie had a special affection for the glamorous Evita Manolo, the Socialist Sensation, leader of the Girl Guerilla Caucus. The progeny of a wealthy Manhattan bank president and a professor of Sexual Healing at Bartleby College, Evita managed to fashion herself as a hero of the working class because she slaved part-time one summer at a convenience store in Westchester, experiencing firsthand the life of the downtrodden working for minimum wage. Now a charismatic force in the party, she had nearly one-hundred percent approval rates in pockets of New York, San Francisco and other urban centers, and next to nothing in the heartland, where she was feared as a communist and loathed as an ignoramus.

"We don't believe she can win on her own," Ned said. "Poindexter says the country's not ready for a socialist president. Her only way in is on the coattails of someone a little more mainstream, and a lot less threatening."

"Like Dewey," Bennie acknowledged.

"Or Robbie Crowe," Ned said. "If we can keep the focus on the top of the ticket rather than the bottom, Evita could conceivably slide into the White House through the back door."

Bennie nodded agreeably. "Ned, keep me apprised of Dewey's condition," he said. "Dr. Kramer, are you still on speaking terms with Robbie Crowe?"

Kristi cagily replied, "Oh, I'm pretty sure we speak the same language."

"Good," Bennie said. "See if you can get him down here as soon as possible. I would like to meet this prospective leader of the free world."

7. Destiny Calls

Robbie returned from lunch and slouched gloomily through his foundation's reception area, where a TV stream showed President Platt holding a press conference. He paused to watch Platt announce he was rescinding his executive order that forbid wearing masks in public demonstrations. He insisted they be put back on "ugly people."

"Many of these protesters are very, very homely," Platt lamented from the Oval Office. "People say they've never seen anything like it. Frizzy blue hair. Nose rings. They should wear masks covering their entire face. They should probably wear hats, too..."

Hmm, Robbie mused. With his foundation failing, maybe he should call Platt, whom he knew a bit from his New York days, and see if he's got something down there for him to do. Secretary of something or other? Energy, maybe? Commerce? What was the Department of the Interior about? Decorating? Whatever... It didn't really matter what the job was if the position as long as it was no lower than cabinet level. A man of his background and breeding deserved to be in the Situation Room when the big decisions were made or at least hang around for the group photo. Who had more of a stake in America than he did? Hell, his family practically built the place!

Robbie thought of his last trip to DC. He loved how cabinet secretaries got a police escort when they roared up Pennsylvania Avenue in their caravans of black SUVs. Wouldn't he look smart strutting around the capital with a phalanx of babes-de-camp, furiously clicking their high heels on the Capitol's terrazzo floors to keep up with his fast pace and remarkable energy. Wouldn't they love to joust for a little private time with the boss? He'd pause in the corridors of power only to sign an autograph or address the press, maybe with some reading glasses as a prop that he could slide down his nose to make him look super smart. And wouldn't he tell the media a thing or two, given the chance! The thought of a new life was exciting, thrilling even. *Whew!* He needed to sit down and rest his fevered brain a moment. Yessir. A little shut eye was in his future!

He entered his expansive suite and paused at Matilda's desk for a report on the firings.

"They're gone," she assured him.

Robbie breathed a sigh of relief. God forbid he should have to face those losers on a day when they would hate him even more than usual. He waltzed past Matilda and entered his private office, closing the door behind him. He settled into his cushy office chair, leaned back, folded his hands over his stomach, and closed his eyes. No sooner had he punched his ticket on the express train to Napville than his trip was derailed by a buzz on his intercom. *What now?*

"Mr. Crowe," Matilda said, "I've got Dr. Kristi Kramer on the line. Would you like to take the call?"

Robbie felt a surge in his loins. Something about her honey-drippin' Carolina drawl, not to mention the memory of her sensational collection of body oils, summoned Little Robbie to rise in anticipation and urge him to take the call. Kristi had been Robbie's consultant when he was running the show at Crowe and had proven smart, capable, and a dervish in the sack. While their association resulted in an unfortunate controversy that loosened Robbie's grip on his job, their dangerous liaison was not without its redeeming moments.

"Put her through," Robbie said.

A half-second later, Kristi was purring on the line, "I miss you!" *Yee-eew...*

"It's been a minute," Robbie acknowledged, as he smiled for the first time all day. He thought back to that hotel suite in the Bay Area and the matching bathrobes and the session on the sofa and... *yow!* He'd sure like to see her right about now. "Where are you? Please tell me you're in Manhattan."

"Oh, no, darlin', I am in exile in Washington *Dee Cee!*" she said. "Ever since that stinker Roland Platt took the oath of office, my DEI business has dried up like an old prune. I can't get a contract to save my life. And neither can any of my friends. We're all livin' in the Land of Cancelled Retainers. And I must tell you: it is not *fun!*"

Robbie could think of some ways they could have fun together but sensed that's not what this call was about. Kristi only called when she wanted something. And what she usually wanted more than anything was money, or a way to get it. "Wish I could help, but I don't know what I can do about that."

"Oh, don't be so modest," she said. "There's plenty you can do."

"I may regret asking… but okay," Robbie said. "Like what?"

"Like get your cute little butt on a plane and come on down and see me. I've got a proposition for you that will knock your socks off," she said. Then, in a near-whisper. "Maybe your pants, too."

Ooh. This was serious! "What is it?" Robbie asked, excitedly.

"As you may know, I'm on the leadership committee for the presidential campaign? And I've gotta tell you, there is no party in this party right now. It is all doom and gloom." *Glew-um!*

Robbie sensed he was about to be hit up for a massive donation, a concept that curbed his enthusiasm. "I haven't really been following it," he claimed.

"Well, no, you wouldn't, because the press won't report it. They say everything's hunky dory and that ol' Dewey Fenwick is sharp as a tack," Kristi said. "But I can tell you from the inside—and this is *deep* inside— that Dewey Fenwick is in no shape to run to the bathroom, much less run for office. They're keepin' him together with spit and Scotch tape and I don't know what all, but I'm afraid the glue is not gonna hold. The question we're strugglin' with is, 'Dewey or don't he?' We're thinkin' he don't."

Robbie sighed. "I don't see how more money can help that."

"This is not about money, dodo. This is about a contingency plan," Kristi said. "If ol' Dewey meets his maker—or even worse, falls behind in the polls—the nomination would default to Evita Manolo, who's just to the left of Castro, or to Hiram Fry, who runs for president every four years just to remind people he's a total loser. If either of those two get the nod, we'll get creamed like chipped beef on toast."

"Yuck," Robbie said.

"So now we're desperate. The convention's three weeks away and we need help."

"You want suggestions on an alternative? I can go through my contacts," Robbie said, scrolling on his mobile phone. "There's Jack—"

Kristi interrupted. "Am I not bein' clear, darlin'? The alternative is you." *Yew-ew!*

"*Me?*" Robbie laughed. "Oh, bullshit. Now you are pulling my middle leg."

"Only if I get a chance!" she cooed.

"Stop!" Robbie said. "You can't be serious!"

"Serious as a lost earring," she said. "Why do you think I'm calling?"

The idea was preposterous. "I thought maybe you wanted me to head down there and have dinner with you."

"Well, of course, I'd love that, too," she said. "But I'm thinkin' breakfast. Like tomorrow. Can you get on that little ol' jet of yours and meet me down here first thing in the mornin'? I want to show you something."

Robbie cooed, "I'd like to see it."

"Oh no you don't!" she said in her most coquettish voice. "I'm talkin' about leadin' you on a tour through the poll numbers, not through the valley of *love*. When it comes to recognition, Robbie Crowe is a household name. You are *known*, sir!"

It sounded ridiculous, but Robbie's curiosity was getting the better of him. Two hours ago, he was thinking he would soon be out of a job. Now, it was an actual possibility that he could get the biggest job in the world? He was back, baby! All in the space of an afternoon! Maybe it was true that he led a charmed existence.

He looked at the blank calendar on his laptop, where there was nothing but white space as far as the eye could see. "I think I can squeeze something in."

"Don't I know it," she purred.

Robbie growled. "Ten a.m.?"

"This is breakfast, darlin'. I want your legs under my table by nine."

Robbie thought about it and figured: president's kind of a big job. Maybe he should get up early. "All right. You're on."

"Wonderful!" Kristi cried. "Robbie Crowe, come on down!"

8. Plane to See

Robbie knew one thing for certain. If he were president, he wouldn't play the part like some bland Eisenhower type, freaking out over military-industrial complexes. What was that even about anyway? Places where generals and CEOs lived? What a waste of time! Robbie would go full-blown JFK, with the Saratoga shades, sailboats around Cape Cod, a gangster moll for a girlfriend and… whatever he wanted. Who's to stop him? Robbie would be king of the world! Like Jack in *Titanic*, standing on the prow, throwing his fate to the wind, embracing his destiny as it rose to meet him. True, it was an iceberg that got there first and Jack's boat sank in a ghastly fashion, but still… They got a hell of a song out of it. Could Celine Dion sing about him at the inauguration ball even if she's Canadian? So many questions!

Robbie was dizzied and dazzled by the possibilities unfolding before him. This could be his magnificent revenge tour. Becoming the president, or even just the nominee? That's a whirling, twirling look-at-me-now-motherfuckers moment if he ever heard one! Take that, ex-wife Lindsey! And that, Crowe family dolts who voted him out of the company! You, too, investment bankers who said he didn't know his ass from a gopher hole. Not to mention the idiots at the foundation who stared at him all googly-eyed yesterday at the staff meeting. What would they think when they see the monument the country creates for him in the capital. The L. Robertson Crowe III Memorial! It could be like Lincoln's, but bigger. Still, he wondered: would he have to be dead for them to build it? Or could they start right away?

As Robbie heard the landing gear descend from the fuselage, he was jolted back to reality. If this gig required more hours than nine-to-five, or even ten-to-three, that could be a deal-breaker. He was at an age when his pace should be slowing down, not ramping up. Three hours a day was practically killing him as it was. He'd probably need a million minions to do the heavy lifting, to the extent there was any. Maybe he should ask to see a job description. He ought to at least get a sense of what was required before he decided to give it a go.

A black car picked up Robbie on the tarmac, crossed the Potomac River, and deposited him at the storied Hay-Adams hotel. He was met by a concierge at the door, who checked him in through a handheld device, summoned a bellman to take his bag to his suite, and directed Robbie to the Lafayette Restaurant on the top floor. It wasn't quite nine a.m., but the elegant room, with its windows overlooking the heart of the capital, was already thick with poohbahs and potentates.

Robbie was guided to a table by the window overlooking Lafayette Square, where he met Dr. Kristi Kramer's warm and aromatic embrace. "You look good enough to eat!" she cooed, flipping her long, frosted tresses over the shoulder of her Chanel suit.

"Leave room for dessert," Robbie suggested with a laugh.

"Oh, you," she said, playfully slapping his shoulder.

The Matre'd held a Chippendale chair for Robbie and helped him scoot up to the linen-clad table where he could gaze directly into Kristi's aquamarine eyes and sneak a peek at the shiny pearls nestled in her breasts. Oh, he'd love to be a pearl right about now!

A busser asked Kristi if he could clear away the extra place settings, but she declined. "Leave one," she said.

Surprised, Robbie blurted, "Table for three?"

She took a deep breath. "We're having company."

Robbie's disappointment was obvious. His face fell along with another body part. "Oh."

"Don't look like you just found your goldfish swimmin' backstroke," Kristi said. She leaned across the table and patted the back of his hand. "This is good news, sweetie-petey. It's someone you know." She looked over to the host stand at the entrance. "Here he comes now."

Walking their way was the exceedingly tall and expensively tailored Worth Talmadge, powerhouse attorney at Clifford & Starr and chair of the National Committee. Worth was a presence who turned heads even in a room of power brokers, a player among players, widely regarded as one of the biggest and dickiest of the capital's big swinging dicks. He also happened to be one of Robbie's oldest chums from prep school.

"Worth, you son of a bitch!" Robbie exclaimed as he rose to meet him.

"Lester... Robertson... Crowe... *the Third!*" Worth offered a perfectly manicured hand. "Take a second and roll this around on your tongue, you asshole. President… of *the United States of America!*" He clapped him on the back, winked at Kristi, then looked back at Robbie. "I hear trumpets, man. Ruffles and flourishes."

Worth took a seat, unfurling a linen napkin as if it were the star-spangled banner.

"I have to admit," Robbie said. "It sounds intriguing. And I'm sure I could do it, of course. But… man, this is big." He looked at all the power brokers around him, busily crafting new ways to fleece the citizenry. Then he glanced out the window, where the virgin White House poked its head up just over the trees, beckoning. "It's not exactly my comfort zone."

Kristi acknowledged, "It *is* kind of a big job. Leader of the free world, and all."

"Let's think about that while we eat, all right?" Worth said. "I did a TRX workout this morning, and… damn. If I don't get some protein in me soon, I'm going to keel over."

Worth signaled a waiter—*chop, chop!*—who took their breakfast orders and left them alone to update one another on their personal and professional activities.

Worth recounted how he had glided through the capital's clubs, cliques, and corridors of privilege with effortless ease until Platt was elected, leaving him on the outside looking in. The great-great grandson of Virginia slaveholders, Worth fathered twin boys who matriculated from St. Alban's School and now played lacrosse at Duke. His daughter, a star in field hockey, would start her senior year at Holton Arms in the fall before heading off to William & Mary. And his wife, Marilyn, was spending her summer playing singles every morning at the Chevy Chase Club and throwing down doubles poolside every afternoon. With his family safely occupied, Worth needn't bother to see them anymore, especially given his pressing duties as chair of the National Committee.

"Our country can't continue this way," Worth opined. "All the chaos and disruption and personal vendettas and backroom deal-making. It's a disgrace." Worth cocked his head. "Did you hear Platt wants to sell Hawaii to Japan?"

"No," Robbie said. "That's awful."

"He said we need to monetize Hawaii because all we're getting is pineapples, puka beads and poi. I guess he's got something against poi." Worth shook his head. "Do you know the most disgusting part?"

"Poi?" Robbie asked.

"I'm not in on the deal!" Worth exclaimed. "If we get another four years like this, everything we've built will be destroyed."

"Meaning… what, exactly?"

"My hourly rate, for one. It's falling faster than my balls." He sighed with regret. "I might have to sell the beach house on Martha's Vineyard. Cutest little cottage you've ever seen. Seventeen rooms. Wrap-around veranda. It's been in Marilyn's family for a hundred and fifty years. She has her own wing, and she never has to see me. Better yet," he said, looking across at Kristi, "I don't have to see her. My helicopter doesn't even have to land on her side of the house."

Robbie noted the chumminess between Worth and Kristi and couldn't help wondering whether it was something more than professional collegiality. He got a clue when Kristi recounted her own tale of woe.

Following the death of George Floyd, Kristi said, she had enjoyed a highly lucrative run helping big corporations unearth their long-cherished values and reminding them how they were committed to racial justice, this time for real. Through her boutique agency in Chapel Hill, Kristi had recruited a dozen Chief Diversity Officers for Fortune 500 companies. They in turn rewarded her with fat contracts to tell them what they were supposed to do. Then Platt was elected, the money was cut off, the diversity officers were fired, and the corporate consciousness business was over as fast as it began.

"It wasn't so much me he hurt. It was all the little people out there," Kristi said, pointing vaguely toward Georgetown.

They took a moment of silence to mourn their deceased contracts before Worth spotted a senator from Maine walking in. He excused himself to cross the room to say hello, leaving Robbie and Kristi alone.

"I didn't know you had such an interest in politics," Robbie said.

She leaned across the table to avoid prying ears. "I don't," she said. "In fact, I couldn't care less. I took this gig because it was all I could get."

Robbie shrugged. "No offense, but why did the National Committee hire you when you didn't have any experience?"

"Now, don't you go tellin' anybody this," she said as she cast a glance around her first. "I said on the application that I was transgender."

Robbie fell back in his chair laughing, prompting Kristi to shush him. "I told you—"

"Don't worry," Robbie said, returning all four legs of his chair to the floor. "It's just that I am familiar with the original equipment."

Kristi said, drily, "Fortunately, I didn't have to drop my pants in the interview."

"You did when I hired you," Robbie reminded her.

"That was different."

Robbie nodded toward Worth. "Was it?"

Kristi smirked. "Not much."

Worth returned as their food arrived, and it was Robbie's turn for an update. In his telling, the Crowe Institute for the Greater Good was a smashing success, as evidenced by the many awards he won. If he had any problem at all, it was that his foundation was *too* good. In Robbie's quest to create a more perfect world, he had invested in a few too many programs that were simply ahead of their time. Someday, the world would come around to see the virtue of beach volleyball leagues in land-locked Afghanistan, gender education dolls for preschools in Minnesota, and drag queen dance competitions in Islamist countries where first prize was still, sadly, to get launched off a rooftop. Despite the challenges, Robbie was feted at numerous black-tie dinners for his humanitarian efforts and awarded the prestigious Good Intentions Peace Prize for blowing gobs of money that produced no results.

"Let's be real about running for president," Robbie said. "Much as I hate to admit it, I do have some baggage."

"Oh, darlin', stop!" Kristi said with a laugh. "So does everybody in this room. How do you think they got here?"

"I've got a dossier on every one of them," Worth bragged.

Robbie laughed. "I suppose you have one on me, too."

"Of course I do," Worth said, drily. He stabbed his Eggs Benedict with a fork, squirting a burble of yolk over his English muffin.

Robbie stopped laughing. "Oh."

"Fortunately," Worth said, "you're on the side of the angels. As long as you stick with us, you have nothing to fear. We can handle your baggage like Sardine Airlines handled mine last week. You'll never see it again."

"Or..." Kristi said, "we make your baggage work for you."

Robbie was puzzled. "How so?"

"It's like I told you a long time ago," Kristi said. "The only thing people love more than the downfall of the rich and famous is their redemption. Once you've been humiliated in public, you have the opportunity for a comeback. Now, in your case, you've managed to be humiliated many, many, many times."

Robbie winced. "I don't know if it's that many 'manys'."

"Look at the Clintons, brother." Worth dabbed the corner of his mouth with a linen napkin. "They've had every scandal known to humankind, and what did that prove? People have come to expect horrible behavior from politicians. It's their superpower." He reached out and patted Robbie's shoulder. "You'll fit right in."

Robbie blew out his cheeks. "Well, you know, there's my ex… She could cause trouble if she wanted to."

"Lindsey? Nonsense," Worth scoffed. "She runs a heartless power company. Just give her a contract to power a data center or two. That should shut her up."

Robbie winced. "I don't know."

"Dude. Do *not* overthink this," Worth said. "What got Roland Platt elected? He's *authentic.* An authentic jerk, but so what? Everyone knew what they were getting, for better or worse. No apologies for insults. It's the Popeye strategy—'*I yam what I yam.*'" He jabbed a finger in Robbie's direction. "You are what you are. You've had some fuckups? Own 'em. Leave the critics nowhere to go. Bennie thinks your record is an asset. It makes you relatable."

"Who's Bennie?"

"Bennie Barbu," Worth said.

"He's the money," Kristi added. "And that's something you'll desperately need."

Robbie sat back. "You know, this is all fascinating. But… I'm not sure I'm ready for this. I need some time to think."

Worth leaned across the table and spoke urgently. "They've got Dewey Fenwick over at Agnew Memorial right now. They're running tests to determine whether he gets a bed or a slab, and I'm betting on the latter," he said. "If he croaks, we'll need a replacement fast to head off Evita Manolo and Hiram Fry."

"Evita finished second in the primaries, right?" Robbie asked.

"Yes," Worth said. "They love her on the coasts, but she polls like boll weevils in the South. If she heads the ticket? Our loss is catastrophic. We'll lose every down-ballot race in middle America. We won't even have enough votes in the House to impeach Platt."

"Impeach him for what?" Robbie asked.

"Does it matter? Pick any announcement he makes, like this morning," Worth said.

"What was that?"

"He said he was building a ballroom for his bomb shelter under the East Wing. Said it gets lonely down there in the bunker and he might want to have events for survivors if the country is nuked," Worth said. "It's completely unauthorized, of course. People in our party are totally pissed off, but they're pissed off pretty much every day. The important thing is if he's reelected, I'll be sleeping out there under a tarp."

A commotion near the host stand caught Kristi's eye. "Don't look now, Robbie..."

Robbie looked anyway, as did everyone else in the place. And there she was, the glamorous Evita Consuela Manolo y Garcia.

Robbie's jaw dropped as he was instantly smitten. Kristi noticed.

"Are you okay?" she asked sharply.

Robbie nodded vacantly. "Yeah."

"Then put your tongue back in your mouth," she commanded. "You might attract flies."

Robbie turned to Worth. "I hate to say it, but I think she's kind of..." His sentence tailed off into a grunt.

"Kind of what?" Kristi demanded to know.

"*Caliente?*" Worth chided.

Robbie grinned. "*Si, senor*! Hot, hot, hot!"

Kristi shook her head in disgust. "Lord have mercy. Do men ever think with anything besides their penises?"

Worth shrugged. "The science says, 'no.'"

The three of them watched Evita offering air kisses to ninety-five-year-old Senator Slim Winston, whose shrunken visage resembled a turtle retreating into its shell. "Slim's last erection was a statue of Robert E. Lee in 1956. Now look at him," Worth marveled. "His table's levitating." Worth turned away. "What is it about commie cooze that makes guys swoon?"

"I wouldn't have a clue," Kristi said, indignantly.

Evita paused her gladhanding to look their way, causing Robbie to squirm. "Won't she object if I cut the line in front of her?"

Worth shrugged. "It depends."

Robbie was puzzled. "On what?"
Worth said, "On your powers of persuasion."

9. Final Exam

Ned hunched over his phone in the waiting room at Spiro T. Agnew Memorial Hospital, scrolling through dozens of congratulatory notes from the party faithful giddy over the morning's TV coverage. *Boof & Skeeter*'s glowing endorsement of Dewey Fenwick's fitness for office bought Ned time—but not much. Suddenly, he was in the same position he had been in less than a year earlier when he was scratching around for a candidate. Finding no great options, he suggested the party lure Dewey out of retirement to make another run for president.

Dewey was selected despite his pitiful record of debt, disorder, and dementia. By the end of his first term, he couldn't remember his policies, his talking points, his wife's name, or whether he was president of the United States or Mexico, where he once owned a time share. That left his overmatched vice president, the vacuous Shrika Fugazi, as the default nominee, and she was swamped by Platt's red wave.

Three years later, Ned convinced party leaders they'd made a mistake in letting Dewey mosey out to pasture. Even in his decrepitude, he was far better for them than Roland Platt, who took a sledgehammer to their magnificent creation: a cultural and political establishment centered around a sprawling government bureaucracy, with universities, media, entertainment, and NGOs connected by intertwined financial interests. It was a well-oiled machine, its gears lubricated by taxpayer sweat and tears, and it stamped out an endless array of goodies for a self-perpetuating blob.

Ned's strategy called for the doddering old Dewey to glide to the nomination without ever uttering an unscripted word. The election would be a referendum on Platt, with the nation's media pressing the case that he was an unhinged lunatic, which he helpfully impersonated from time to time. The plan's potentially fatal flaw was that it depended on Dewey staying alive, at least through the election.

Dinda burst through the waiting room door. "Lady Janice is on her way up."

Ned blew out his cheeks. "Fasten your chin strap."

"Dr. Feeley's with her," Dinda noted.

Ned sighed. "Do they have their clothes on, at least?"

Dinda's mouth dropped open. "You think they get *naked* together?"

Ned rolled his eyes. "Let me put it this way: don't ever enter Feeley's office without knocking."

"Not that I would, but…" Dinda pointed an index finger down her open mouth. "Yuck. I thought Lady Janice had better taste than that."

Ned blinked. "I honestly have no idea why you'd think that."

Lady Janice was to Dewey what Geppetto was to Pinocchio: She made him. As a young beautician at a strip mall salon in Beachville, she recognized Dewey's star potential when he dropped in for haircuts during his first term as a congressman. Known then as Janice DiNucci, she implanted hair plugs so that Dewey's new hairline was not too far forward —*no Eddie Munster look for him!*—nor too far back. She selected a shade of white for his tooth caps so bright it could be seen from outer space. And to finish his makeover, she picked his spray tan color to resemble a toasted marshmallow, a metaphor more apt than she realized.

Lady Janice admired the results of her work so much that she couldn't relinquish the final product. After Dewey romped to a win in his first run for senate, she prevailed upon him to dump his first wife, Myrtle, and take on an exciting new running mate—her. Since then, she had become notorious for zealously guarding Dewey's image, propping him up when he failed, and exhibiting zero tolerance for jibes about his gaffes, infirmities, and imaginary tales of derring-do. She had enjoyed the status of her first stint in the White House so much that she insisted on being called Lady Janice ever since. Nobody was going to stand in the way of her triumphant return, not even Dewey.

She arrived in the waiting room as tightly coiled as a cobra, but perhaps more dangerous. Ned cautiously hugged her and noted that her hair smelled like Camels, suggesting that her time preparing for the worst was spent in the doctor's care.

"How is he?" she asked breathlessly.

"He's getting a brain scan," Ned replied.

Lady Janice wrung her hands. "Oh dear."

"Don't worry. They won't find a thing," Feeley said, drolly.

Lady Janice slapped his arm. "Stop that! He liked you. In small doses, anyway."

Feely offered to check on him, but Lady Janice grabbed his arm. "No, Franklin," she commanded. "You stay here with me. I need support, too, you know." She pulled him close. She knew how it looked but her nerves were raw, and she didn't particularly care what anyone thought. Staff drones like Ned and Dinda were in no position to judge the queen bee.

The waiting room door opened, and a doctor entered. "Mrs. Fenwick?"

"Yes," she said.

"I'm Dr. Nabob, Chief of Neurology here at Agnew," he said. "May we sit down for a moment?"

Dr. Nabob guided Lady Janice and Feeley to a couch in the corner. Nabob pulled his seat close to them so he could speak privately.

Ned and Dinda watched from across the room. "This can't be good news," Ned said, covering his mouth with his right hand. He and Dinda saw Lady Janice's face go ashen as Feeley patted her arm to comfort her, which touched off heaving sobs. After a moment, Dr. Nabob stood up, offered a few words of solace, and left the room.

Lady Janice looked up with watery eyes at Ned and Dinda, who approached slowly.

"He's brain dead!" she croaked.

"Oh, no," Ned sighed.

"Apparently, there's nothing they can do to revive him," she continued, before choking out another sob. "A ventilator is all that's keeping him alive."

"I'm so, so sorry, Lady Janice," Ned said, as he offered another hug. "He was a great man."

"Beachville's best!" she replied through more tears.

Ned thought that sounded like a brand of tanning lotion but kept it to himself. "Such awful timing. I know how much he was hoping you two were going back to the White House."

She stood and regarded Ned with disbelief. "And…?"

Ned was confused. "And what?"

"What are you saying, Ned?" Lady Janice asked sharply.

"Well," Ned fumbled, "obviously, that's off."

She laughed bitterly. "No it's not! Didn't you hear what they said about him on TV this morning? He's fit as a fiddle."

Ned regarded her with disbelief. "You're buying that? It was Boof and Skeeter, for Christ's sake." Had she not processed what happened?

Her husband was virtually gone. Once the machines were turned off, so was he. "There's no way this campaign can continue."

She looked at Ned as if he had just dropped in from Mars and sprouted deely bobbers. "You're going to let a little brain death get in the way? What's the matter with you?" She grabbed Ned by his shoulders. "He's still got a pulse, you know. And I'll be damned if I'm pulling the plug when we've come this far. I'm on the cover of *Glamourpuss* next month. You want me to call them and cancel it?" She turned to Feeley. "Franklin, there must be some way they can keep Dewey alive four more years. We could have body doubles, impersonators… something!"

Feeley opened his mouth, but nothing came out. How does one run for president when one is completely incapacitated? "You know, Ned, they have Lincoln impersonators walking around Gettysburg talking to tourists. I've seen them. They're rather convincing."

Ned rolled his eyes. "Right, doc. But nobody thinks they're Abraham Lincoln. They kinda know he's dead."

"You don't even need real people!" Lady Janice claimed. "You've got computer graphics! Artificial intelligence! Anima—what do they call those things? Animatronics!"

"Holograms can be very realistic," Feeley added.

"So's a Dewey Fenwick blow up love doll," Ned said sarcastically.

"Yes! I've got one at home!" Lady Janice proclaimed. "We can do this, Ned!"

Ned drew the line. "I am *not* doing a Dewey Fenwick love doll."

"You're just not thinking creatively," she insisted.

Ned sighed. "Look, Janice—"

"*Lady* Janice!" she snapped.

"*Lady* Janice," Ned conceded. "I know this is all quite a blow. I'm sure you're still in shock." He spoke in his most soothing tone. "But… you do realize he can't move. He can't talk. He can't even think."

Lady Janice laughed bitterly. "You know as well as I do he got through the first term that way." She shook her head. "As far as I'm concerned, we've worked hard for a second term, and he deserves to get it. And I'm sure as hell not going to be the one to deprive him of his chance."

"*His* chance?" Ned asked pointedly.

"Absolutely," she snarled. "That was his dream, and I intend to make it happen for him, brain dead or alive."

Ned looked at her blankly. *Was she insane?*

"Listen to me, Ned," she pleaded. "Dewey's our ticket back to the White House. All he has to do is win. Once he's in, that's it. We'll run things for him again, just like we did in the old days. That autopen still works, right? I don't care if he is a vegetable —"

Feeley interjected, "Vegetables are good for you."

Ned replied, "As president?"

"Why not!" Lady Janice fixed Ned with a piercing glare. "Just get off your ass and make it happen. Dewey Fenwick is going back to the White House. And so... am... I." She bared her ferocious canines and went full Beachville moll. "*Capisce?*"

On the television screen behind them came breaking news from Washington: President Platt announced he would order the Coast Guard to fish for cod in the waters off New England to make up for lost salmon from Canada. "We are going to make more fish sticks than the world has ever seen before," Platt promised. "Nobody thought it was even possible."

Lady Janice pointed to the TV. "Dewey's last words to me were that man must be stopped!"

"A guy in a coma isn't the one to stop him."

"He's *absolutely* the one to do it," Lady Janice said.

Feeley added, "All he needs is —"

Ned heard enough. He clapped his hands together, hard. "Snap out of it! Both of you! We ran a poll! You hear me! A dead Dewey loses to a live Platt in a landslide! Fifty-six, forty-four. If his corpse could win, I'd go for it, believe me. Nobody wants to win more than me. But the polls show death is a disqualifier, even with his base. You may think that means people just aren't open-minded enough, but that's where we are." He let that sink in a moment before continuing. "We all need to face the facts here. Dewey Fenwick, great man that he was, cannot continue to run for president. I'm sorry, Lady Janice." He took a deep breath. "It's over."

Her resistance finally broke with a cascade of tears.

Ned put his arms around her. "Let's just get through this as best we can, okay?" he said quietly. "Maybe there's a way to make something good come out of this terrible tragedy."

Lady Janice's tears suddenly evaporated as she looked up at Ned's face. "Yes, and that something is a dream I've had for a long, long time."

"What's that?" Ned asked.

"A beach house in Martha's Vineyard," she said. "When Dewey's gone, so am I. I'm done with this hick town and that ramshackle firetrap of a house. I want to be with my peeps, where I belong."

Ned shrugged. "I don't what I can do about that."

"Buy it for me," she said.

"We don't have money like that," he said.

"Then find someone who does," she said, stabbing a finger in his chest. "Dewey's not leaving for his next destination until I get my ticket punched for mine."

She looked over at Dewey hooked up to machines keeping him alive and staggered backward into a wall as the finality of the situation finally hit her. Feeley approached and put his arm around her to comfort her.

"This is so Dewey," she whimpered. "Just when you've got something good, he fucks it up. Damn, damn Dewey."

10. Dew or Die

After breakfast at the Hay-Adams, Robbie followed Worth and Kristi outside to H Street, where Washington's humid summer air smacked him like a wet pillow. Advised it was a ten-minute walk to the War Room in the Willard Center, Robbie was gripped by the sudden terror that his carefully coiffed hairdo could wilt like a head of lettuce. It was time to make his first executive decision as a possible commander-in-chief.

"We'll take my car," he insisted.

The three of them piled into Robbie's hulking black SUV and strapped in for the three-minute ride, with Kristi up front and the boys in the back. Worth flipped through the messages on his phone and sank into his seat, while Robbie looked out at the park and at the White House through the trees. After a moment, he leaned toward Worth and spoke quietly. "Can I ask you something?"

"Shoot," Worth replied.

"This may sound like a trivial concern," Robbie said, "but what does this gig pay?"

"President? I believe it's four-hundred thousand."

Robbie winced. "Per month, right?"

"Per year."

"That's it for a whole *year?*" Robbie huffed. *Well, that sucks.*

"I know. Pay's terrible," Worth said. "But here's the deal. You come out way richer than you were going in."

"How does that happen?"

Worth smirked. "Nobody knows."

Kristi glanced over her shoulder. "Nothing like public service for making a private fortune," she said. "Look at Congress. They have more houses than Zillow."

"Uh-oh," Worth said as he scanned his texts. "Here we go."

"What is it?" Robbie asked.

Worth looked up and nodded toward the driver, whom he did not wish to overhear. "Wait until we get out."

The driver blasted past crossing pedestrians, tour buses, carriages, and taxicabs, cut off delivery bikes with aggressive swerves, and pulled up to a building entrance on F Street to deliver his VIP passengers. Worth, Kristi and Robbie emerged from the vehicle and huddled on the hot sidewalk. "Just got a text from Ned," Worth said. "Dewey's brain dead."

"Duh," Kristi scoffed. "Look at his record."

"Well…" Worth said, "It's official now."

"Does that mean he's out of the race?" Robbie asked.

Kristi looked at Robbie and slowly shook her head. "You know what's truly ridiculous? That's not a stupid question."

Worth shrugged. "Ned says he doesn't think Dewey could even get past the fact-checker at the *Post*."

Kristi absorbed that news. "Lord of mercy. I guess that's it then."

Worth shoved his phone in his pocket. "Ned and Dinda are on their way over." He looked at Robbie and put a hand on his shoulder. "It's game on, my friend."

Robbie took a deep breath. Despite his breeding, education, and long record of near-achievements, Robbie harbored a nagging suspicion that deep down, the dipstick never touched anything of substance, at least for a job this big. Running for president could reveal him well out of his depth.

All his life, Robbie had struggled to keep self-doubts at bay by staying within confined social circles, where upper crusty friends reassured one another they were the very best of people because they hung out with swells like themselves. That allowed him to avoid the scrutiny of the hoi polloi in mysterious outer boroughs, suburbs, and alien lands like New Jersey and whatever was on the other side of that. If push came to stumble, he reminded himself he was a Crowe, and Crowes were special people, obliged to lead the poorer classes of dumb bastards to a more enlightened way of living where they cared about their fellow man from a safe distance. What such a world would look like if he were to become president, he hadn't a clue. He'd probably have to start with an inspiring vision to rouse the masses from their miserable existence. He leaned over to Worth. "If I do this, I'm going to need help," he conceded.

Puh, Worth muttered. "Trust me. You'll have more help than you can stand."

"I could use someone to, you know… gather my thoughts?"

"Don't worry about that," Kristi said with a snort. "They'll gather all your thoughts for you. You won't even know you had them."

Worth nodded. "If I'm being completely honest with you, Robbie, they're already gathered."

"By whom?" Robbie asked.

Worth shrugged. "The committee."

Robbie shuddered. That sounded ominous. If he was going to act like a candidate, he needed a script with his own point of view once he figured out what it was. "Can I at least get a speechwriter?"

"I'll get you fifty of them, if you want," Worth said. "You can't throw a bagel in a DC coffee shop without hitting one."

Robbie considered his options as he followed Worth and Kristi through the marble lobby of the Willard Center and took an elevator up to the lobby of Liddy & Cox, the national polling firm.

A receptionist eyed them through the window, nodded to Worth, and buzzed them in. Worth led his companions down a hallway to a locked door, scanned a card, and entered the War Room. It was pitch dark, with its drapes tightly closed to prevent snooping. Worth found a panel of lights and flicked them on, illuminating desks strewn with computers and printers, walls filled with print-out charts and graphs, sheets of handwritten paper tacked to the walls, and portraits of various candidates and famous people.

On one prominent panel, between photos of Charles Manson, Bernie Madoff, a La-Z-Boy recliner, and a Krispy Kreme cruller was a portrait of Robbie.

Robbie walked over to the display, studied the grouping, and shook his head. "I give up," he said. "What's this?"

"You all score 83 percent!" Kristi chirped.

"What?"

"Name recognition! You. The criminals. The recliner. The doughnut. You all get the same number according to our survey," Worth explained, as he put an arm around Robbie's shoulders. "Eighty-three percent of the people in America know who you are. 'Robbie Crowe' is right up with some very big names."

Robbie winced. "But... Charles Manson? How is that a good thing?"

Worth shrugged. "Fact is, Robbie, Manson polls better than Dewey, especially with Gen Z. Unfortunately, he's dead, so you're in luck."

Kristi noticed Robbie's discomfort and grabbed his arm. "Don't get your panties twisted around the dirty details. It's like I told you: you're *known*," she said. "That's half the battle right there. It doesn't matter what you're known for, just that they recall your name. Who cares whether you're ranked up there with a mass murderer or a recliner? It's notoriety that counts."

Worth agreed. "Remember," he said, "being a sociopath is a bad thing only if you let it. DC's the sort of the place where people can put their horrible defects to work for them and make a great career."

Robbie sensed such reasoning was supposed to be reassuring, but somehow it wasn't. The door creaked open, and Ned and Dinda walked through, bearing cardboard trays of coffee cups and pastries from a coffee shop next door. Introductions were made, and everyone grabbed a beverage or a scone and took a seat around the conference table. Ned stood at one end and filled them in on the scene at the hospital.

"The good news is Lady Janice realizes the gig is up," Ned announced. "The bad news is she wants to keep Dewey on ice a while longer."

"How much longer?" Worth asked.

"She said that if she can't live in the White House, she wants a summer home in the Vineyard. She says we owe her that much."

"Owe her for *what?*" Worth asked sharply.

"Years of selfless service, I guess," Ned replied.

"Our campaign is practically broke," Worth noted. "We can't spend donor money on another house for her. How many does she need?"

Ned backed up. "I'm only telling you what she told me. If she doesn't get what she wants, she threatened to let Dewey linger until November. I told her she's going to have to take it up with Bennie."

Worth flushed red with anger. "Even if Bennie agreed, this, this *extortion*, for lack of a better word—"

"No, that's the right word," Ned said.

"—could take time we don't have," Worth fumed. "We've got three weeks until the convention. If she doesn't pull the plug on Dewey soon, I'll put a pillow over his face myself."

Dinda was visibly distressed by the discussion. "I am really uncomfortable with this," she said, shifting in her chair. "We're talking about a man's life."

"Yes: mine," Worth snapped. "I've lost half my income."

Ned sadly shook his head. "I can't even pay my club dues." He hung his head. "I'm drinking in shame."

"It hasn't seemed to stop you," Worth pointed out.

"Well, no," Ned said with a shrug. "But it could, theoretically."

Dinda simmered. "Look. I get it—probably better than any of you," she said. "I'm freaking destitute, okay? I'm taking home leftover pastries from the War Room every night for dinner in a cruddy studio. But this is Lady Janice's husband we're talking about."

"Yes, and it's my wife," Worth snapped.

Ned scratched his head. "What does your wife have to do with it?"

Worth shrugged. "I can't afford to dump her until my income improves."

Robbie watched the back and forth with alarm. Was Dewey going to die on time or not? This was his future, too! Maybe he'd have to get involved somehow. He knew a guy who could handle the job. "If I choose to run," he said, "how do you explain why I became the nominee? I mean, you had primaries. Won't the other candidates be upset?"

Kristi piped up. "Why, darlin', it was Dewey's dying wish. He wanted his trusted friend Robbie Crowe to pick up the torch and carry it forward."

Robbie yelped, "I never even met him."

"You sure have!" Kristi insisted. "You were lifelong friends."

Ned nodded vigorously. "I thought somebody told you."

"Uh… no," Robbie whined.

"Well, that's our story and we're sticking to it," Worth said.

"Would anyone believe it?" Robbie asked.

Worth had enough of the kvetching. "Look, Robbie. None of this matters until you say you're ready to run. And the fact is, we need an answer or we'll have to move on."

Robbie didn't know what to think. They were talking about marketing him like a doughnut and flat out lying about pretty much everything. Robbie fancied himself as a skilled prevaricator who had honed his craft to a fine art form, but this was deception on an unprecedented scale. Was that something he could pull off? What if he agreed to run then lost the election—yet another humiliation in a lifetime that was already over quota? "Give me a second, will you? I need to clear my head."

"Of course. Take all the time you need," Worth said. He checked his watch. "Just let us know in the next five minutes."

Robbie discreetly grabbed his briefcase and hustled down the corridor to the men's room, where he found a stall and sat down. At times of momentous decisions, some people pray. Others meditate, talk with their loved ones, consult the stars, or climb mountaintops for perspective. Robbie scoffed at such weaknesses and superstitions. He had his own time-tested method that had been reliable since his childhood, when his absentee father, tired of being pestered on the rare occasions he was home by questions from his annoying child, gave Robbie a device to consult whenever he needed an answer. And so Robbie opened his briefcase and pulled out his pop-by-proxy, a scuffed black Magic 8-Ball. He placed the revered toy atop the toilet paper dispenser, closed his eyes, and asked his question silently. *Should I run for president?*

He paused a moment to give the plastic ball a chance to thoroughly consider the issue. Dreading the answer, he opened his eyes slowly, reached up, pulled the ball off the dispenser and turned it upside down. At last, he peered into its mystical window to receive its wisdom.

MY SOURCES SAY NO

What the fuck? This stupid toy! He wanted to smash it on the tile floor and teach it a lesson. Instead, he simply stared at it with disbelief. Maybe the ball didn't quite get the question. He decided to give it another chance by putting the ball close to his mouth and asking again, this time in a whisper, "Should I run for president?" He then shook the ball, turned it upside down again and looked for the answer.

OUTLOOK NOT SO GOOD

Piece of shit! How ignorant could a Magic 8-Ball get?! It was dumber than his employees at the Greater Good foundation! Could this plastic soothsayer not see the kind of quality candidacy Robbie would bring to America? If not, his first executive order would be to slap tariffs on the company that made this crap—even if it was in the United States.

He decided to give it one last chance to come up with the right answer before he smashed it on the porcelain and flushed the pieces. This time, he asked it loudly, *"Should I run for president?"* He heard a toilet flush nearby.

Shit! He didn't know anyone else was in here! A stall door down the way banged open and a man's voice said with a chuckle, "Go ahead, jackass."

Robbie gritted his teeth and waited until he heard the man walk across the tile, a faucet turn on and off, the kerchunk of a paper towel dispenser, and the creak of the restroom door. Safely alone, he turned the Magic 8-Ball over for its answer.

WITHOUT A DOUBT

Yes! Clearly, the dependably wise ball at last heard the question! And it was no bullshit this time! This was the most positive answer the Magic 8-Ball ever gave, an unreserved and resounding "yes." That was good enough for Robbie. He put the ball back into his briefcase, emerged from the stall and walked toward a run at immortality. With a surge in confidence, he strode down the corridor back to the War Room. Upon his re-entry, he placed his briefcase atop a credenza, turned and faced the team—his team now, and broke the news with a grin.

"Let's do this thing."

11. Called to Serve

Marty McGarry perused the morning news on his phone as he sat at a counter overlooking Broadway on Manhattan's Upper West Side, the spiritual home of the city's burgeoning socialist paradise.

Marty, a communications adviser to Crowe Power Company chair Lindsey Harper Crowe, was finishing his Bolivian Breakfast Burrito at Café Che when an alert popped up announcing the latest BREAKING NEWS from the Platt Administration.

PLATT GIVES GREENLAND BACK TO DENMARK
President admits: "Weather's terrible up there."
Scraps plan for Igloo Golf Dome
Turns attention to Bermuda: "They charge too much for shorts."

Marty rolled his eyes, shoved his phone in his pocket and looked around the restaurant, known as Commie Coffee for its celebratory posters of the Latin American revolutionary Che Guevara, patron saint of the city's radical leadership.

Marty regarded the store's urban guerilla vibe as a clever corporate marketing pitch, but the youthful clientele took it quite seriously. Angered by their meager rewards from capitalism, the young professionals scattered around communal tables and benches glued to their laptops and headphones had become entranced with the idea of communism taking hold in their city and showering them with freebies. The exciting prospect of equal outcomes shared by one and all regardless of race, gender, or criminal status struck them as a rightful comeuppance for people who had rocketed past them to become successful through a system that failed to recognize their own brilliance. It was time for the card-carrying members of Café Che's *Counter Culture* loyalty program to rise up with their soy lattes in one hand and seize the means of production with the other.

Marty noted a poster on the wall featuring a Warhol-style portrait of Karl Marx "To each according to their needs." It reminded him of his need: he was just one mochaccino away from a free Fight the Power Snowberry Smoothie, which helped customers lose weight through convulsive vomiting.

He slowly rose from his stool to discard the refuse from his breakfast and approached three receptacles colored blue, black and green. A sign over the bins urged the proletariat to THINK ZERO, a concept Marty believed this clientele had proven beyond doubt in the last election.

Using illustrations over the bins as his guide, Marty dutifully dropped his banana peel and a few bits of burrito into the receptacle labeled compost. He tossed a clamshell container into the bin for mixed recyclables. Sadly, there was no place to put his plastic utensils other than the bin called landfill, where his fork, knife and spoon were dispatched for all eternity to a dump in New Jersey.

Planet-saving duties complete, Marty dusted the crumbs off his hands and turned to find a headphone-wearing busboy hauling a clattering tilt truck across the tiles to the refuse containers. To Marty's dismay, the busboy emptied each of the bins into his cart, reuniting the discarded banana peel, burrito bits, and utensils in a single container.

"What are you doing?" Marty asked.

The annoyed busboy pulled up one side of his headphones to hear Marty. "What?"

"You dumped everything into one cart," Marty protested.

The busboy shrugged. "So?"

"It's supposed to be separated."

"Chill, dude," the busboy scoffed. "Somebody will sort it out."

"Somebody already did," Marty said, heatedly. "Me."

Sensing a minor revolt from an obvious bourgeois, a Commie Coffee apparatchik in a red beret, black t-shirt, and jackboots approached. His badge identified him as Comandante Justin, Store Direktor. "Is there a problem?"

Marty pointed to the bins. "Your guy —"

The coffee commander held up his hand. "Whoa, whoa, whoa. Hold it right there. Don't refer to them as a guy."

"Them?" Marty asked, glancing around.

The busboy claimed, "I've got, like, six genders."

Marty looked the magical busperson up and down. "Of course you do."

Justin squared up to Marty. "So, what's the problem?"

"I had three different piles of refuse," Marty complained. "I followed the directions on your signs and put them in separate bins. Then he—*they*—comes along and dumps all the bins in one cart."

"Yeah. And?"

Marty nodded toward the signs. "What's the point?"

"We're saving the planet," Justin claimed.

"No, you're not," Marty said. He leaned close and whispered. "It's just pretend."

Justin bristled. "What kind of asshole are you?"

Marty shrugged. "Garden variety, I suppose."

Justin seethed. "Are you a card-carrying member of the *Counter Culture* rewards program?"

"*Si, comandante.*"

"Let me see your card," Justin said.

Marty pulled out his wallet, retrieved his card, and handed it over, thinking Justin might offer him that mochaccino as compensation. Justin inspected the card and scowled. "You have committed a C3 violation of our community standards."

"Does that mean the death penalty?" Marty asked mockingly.

"It does for your membership." Justin held up the card in front of Marty's face and ripped it into little pieces. Then he handed it back. "Stick this in any bin you like."

Justin turned his back and walked to the counter, leaving Marty to consider this humiliation. Kicked out of the *Counter Culture* club? How low can you go?

Marty grabbed his coffee and a bottle of water and backed into the door leading to Broadway, roaring with morning traffic and stinking of marijuana. As he felt his phone vibrate in his pocket, he looked for a place to set down his coffee. Fortunately, a junkie in a fentanyl fold—bent over at the waist and frozen in place—made a workable coffee table. Marty set his coffee down on the man's perfectly level back to yank the phone from his trousers. The readout said LINDSEY.

"We've got a big problem," she said.

"We who?" Marty asked, as he retrieved his coffee.

"Me. My family. My company. Our country." She took a deep breath. "Robbie called last night."

"I thought you weren't speaking."

"I wish we weren't," Lindsey said.

"Uh-oh."

"He wanted me to know I could have been First Lady."

Marty laughed. "I don't think you were his first lady."

She paused and took a deep breath. "He's running for president."

Marty wasn't sure he heard that right. "President of what?"

"The United States."

"Of *America?*"

"What other United States do you know of?" Lindsey sighed. "Apparently, a deal has been cut. He's going to be the party's challenger to Roland Platt."

Marty roared with laughter. "C'mon! That's got to be a joke. President Robbie Crowe? Wow. We are even more fucked than I thought." Marty leaned back against a bus shelter, where he watched young men climb aboard the M11 bus and take turns beating the driver as it pulled away from the curb. "Who said the gods have no sense of humor?"

"I'm not laughing," Lindsey replied.

"I have to or I might start weeping," Marty said.

"Well, don't laugh too loudly," Lindsey said. "It's all hush-hush for now, but Robbie says Dewey Fenwick is on death's door. The party bosses are scrambling for a replacement to stop Evita Manolo or Hiram Fry from getting the nod. And for a variety of reasons—and I'm not sure I believe any of them—they recruited him."

"That can't be," Marty scoffed. "He's been a failure at everything he's ever touched."

Lindsey guffawed. "Apparently, they see that as an asset. They want someone with a household name—but one who's human, authentic, maybe even humble."

Marty paused. "Okay. Now you are talking about somebody else, right?"

"This is his spin—not mine," she said. "As for his opponent: do you want to know Platt's latest?"

"I heard. He's going to bomb Nova Scotia or something."

"No, no. That's yesterday's news." she said. "Today Platt is signing an executive order to bring back 'Eskimo Pies' and serve them with every school lunch. He's found a few Eskimos to help him make the announcement at an ice cream social on the White House lawn. And—lucky me—I'm invited."

Marty scoffed. "You're not gonna go…"

"Are you kidding? I have to," she said. "I'm building a powerhouse for a data center in Virginia that Platt could kill with a snap of his fingers. If he thinks I'm on Robbie's side, my plant's in big trouble. Two billion dollars goes down the drain."

"But you wouldn't even vote for Robbie."

"I know that," she said. "And you know that. But Platt doesn't know that. And I can't tell him because he would gladly spill the beans on social media. I'm stuck in the middle, and it's not a good place to be."

Marty ducked into the doorway of an empty storefront. "I get it. You have to walk a fine line."

"Fortunately, you don't."

Marty paused as he processed that comment. "What does that mean?"

"I volunteered you."

Marty held his breath. "Please tell me you're kidding."

"Sorry, Marty. But Robbie needs you," she said.

"For what? A punching bag?"

"Robbie needs a speechwriter, someone he can trust," Lindsey said.

Marty stammered. "Well, he can't trust me! He told me so a million times. Do you know how many speeches he balled up and threw at me?"

Lindsey sighed. "He says nice things about you."

"Does he now?"

"I don't know why, but for whatever reason, you've aged well in his memory," Lindsey said. "He told me you're the only speechwriter who ever 'got' him."

"Yes. I got high blood pressure. I got an ulcer. I got a pit in my stomach every day I worked with him. And—bonus round—I got a divorce from Jill, who couldn't stand how miserable I was when I came home from work." He sighed. "Why are you pushing this? I thought you liked me."

"I love you, Marty. You know that," she said, quietly. "But I need someone inside the tent. What he says out there on the campaign trail or what he might do in office could have enormous consequences for the company, and for my family. I need someone to watch over him. You've done it before. Please tell me you'll do it again."

"It sounds like a babysitting job."

"I'll pay you an extra fifty cents an hour," Lindsey said. "Just make this whole thing less of an embarrassment than I'm sure it would be if he were left to his own instincts."

Marty rubbed his forehead with his free hand. The happiest day of his career was the day he was fired at Crowe Power and handed a bag of money to go away. To work with Robbie again? That was a big ask.

"I can't make him behave, you know," he said.

"I get it," Lindsey replied. "He's an adult."

"Let's not get carried away."

"Will you do it?" she asked.

Marty sighed. "You know I can't say 'no' to you."

"Thank you, Marty," she said. "You're doing me a huge favor."

"Yes, well. Not so sure this is helping our country."

"Can you start tomorrow?" Lindsey asked. "He wants you in DC in the morning."

Marty shook his head and looked at the chaos around him. Was Washington DC any worse than New York, sinking into a socialist abyss? "All right," he sighed. "I'll do what I can."

"Great. He wants you to stop by his apartment tonight and pick up a shirt and his headphones." She paused. "Oh, and some running shoes."

Marty sighed. "Fine. I'll pick up a bottle of bourbon, too."

"He drinks scotch."

"It's not for him."

12. Railroaded

By late morning, Marty was on the Acela train wobbling down the tracks toward the capital. The train's jostling made reading the news on his iPad out of the question. So was eating lunch: a vulcanized rubber hot dog from Café Acela that may have been left over from Harry Truman's whistlestop tour in 1948. He pushed it aside and looked out the window as the train rumbled past Philadelphia's rowing clubhouses on the Schuylkill River and the city's majestic art museum.

As they pulled into Baltimore Marty marveled at block after block of abandoned row houses. How, he wondered, did thousands of policy makers shuttle between Boston, New York, and Washington year after year and fail to do anything about such blight? Maybe as they nestled in their rolling steel cocoon, catching a snooze or the news, they simply chose not to notice.

It made Marty wonder: *What would Robbie do differently?* As he thought back to his years of working with him at Crowe Power, Marty knew the answer: *Nothing.* He'd fit right in with a political class that considered good intentions the mark of their leadership. Results were of no consequence.

Robbie, in his telling, got booted from the chairmanship of Crowe Power because the broader Crowe family failed to appreciate his grand vision for the future—not because he brought their hundred-year-old company to the brink of bankruptcy. His twenty-four-year marriage to Lindsey collapsed because she was unyielding in her demands on his valuable time, not because he spent his evenings with paramours in Manhattan hotel rooms and a suite at the New York Athletic Club. Between disgruntled shareholders, failed partnerships, and alienated lovers, the aggrieved parties in Robbie's wake made a large pool, especially compared to his puddle of achievements. How was the National Committee going to turn him into a viable candidate for president?

Marty reflected on his own recruitment at Crowe Power, when he saw the side of Robbie that often appealed to strangers: warm, charming, self-deprecating, and in no hurry to get to work. Pushed to perform tasks he didn't like, or confronted with unpleasant truths, he was known to find an excuse to disappear or throw a tantrum that would do a toddler proud.

Marty arrived at Washington's Union Station and caught a cab across town to the global headquarters for the National Committee and Bennie Barbu's Hands Up Foundation.

"Marty! Hey!"

He turned to find the buoyant version of Robbie Crowe emerging from an SUV grinning from ear to ear, brimming with renewed confidence.

"Thanks for helping out," Robbie said with a grin. In a low voice, he added conspiratorially, "I can't believe this is happening. Fucking surreal!"

Robbie introduced Marty to Ned, Worth, and Kristi and they made their way up to Bennie's office at the foundation. A receptionist led the group down a hallway to a conference room and offered refreshments. She left them on their own to view the gallery of black-and-white photos from Bennie's childhood in Soviet-occupied Romania.

"Those were the days, my friend."

Team Robbie turned to see Bennie Barbu shuffle into the room wearing baggy suit pants held up by thick plaid suspenders, an open-collared shirt, and a two-day stubble. One of the richest people in America, Bennie still wore the schlubby garb that suggested he was days away from living on the streets again. By contrast, Bennie's thirty-something son, Marius, who stood at his side, sported a Saville Row suit, a buff physique, perfect glistening skin, oversized black rim glasses, and hair that was cut with microscopic precision, befitting America's new breed of sleek socialists, who were indistinguishable in their style of dress, their social status, and their net worth from the country's most successful capitalists.

After they shook hands and introduced one another, Bennie nodded to the framed photograph of an old theater in Bucharest from the 1940s. "One day, my country was aligned with the fascists in Germany and Italy; the next, we were under the thumb of communists from the Soviet Union," Bennie said with wistful resignation.

He jabbed the picture frame with his index finger. "This theater is where I found refuge," Bennie continued. "I would sneak in through a side door and watch the show from backstage." He smiled at the memory. "My uncle Constantin had a sketch making fun of the Soviet soldiers' theft of our clothes and cars and watches. It was great fun for us, but the soldiers failed to find the humor."

"What happened?" Robbie asked.

"They bundled Constantin into the trunk of a car, and we never saw him again." He sighed. "I learned a lesson about authoritarian regimes."

Robbie gulped. "What was that?"

Bennie offered a sly smile. "It's better to ride in the front seat."

They took chairs around the table, and Bennie folded his hands over the top of his belly while Marius took the seat next to him. "It is a pleasure to meet you, Mr. Crowe," Bennie said. "I've watched your foundation with great interest. Of course, I am also familiar with your work at your family's power company, which I see is now run by your wife."

Robbie blushed. "Ex-wife," he corrected him.

"Ex," Bennie acknowledged. "Now I understand our party has enlisted you to run for president of the United States. I presume you have a comfortable existence in New York and your other homes around the world. Why would you want to dive into the messy world of American politics?"

Robbie squirmed in his seat. None of the reasons he was considering the job—power, prestige, babes—could be uttered out loud without sounding like a jerk. What could he say that sounded more public spirited than, "I want to get laid"?

"I want to change the world," Robbie claimed.

"Right," Bennie said. "How?"

"Well…" Robbie paused, thinking. "For the better, I suppose."

"I would hope so." Bennie leaned over toward Robbie. "The question is: In what way?"

"You know… better than we have now."

Bennie rolled his eyes. *This is the best we've got?* "No need to go on, Mr. Crowe," he said. "I understand your instincts. You want to stay vague about your intentions. Throw out a few meaningless platitudes and let our Platt-hating media tell the public why you are the best choice for America."

"I'm sorry if I wasn't more specific," Robbie protested. "I—"

"Don't worry," Bennie assured him. "You're making progress. You've been here three hours and you're already sounding like a politician. Dewey Fenwick won one election after another for fifty years with a line of bullshit like that."

Was Robbie coming off as a bullshitter? Bennie fixed him with such a stare that Robbie feared he was flunking his audition before he could even take the stage. Bennie, renowned for being a hard-nosed investor, did not bet to lose. In a panic that his candidacy was over before it began, Robbie recalled advice Marty once gave him about how to handle difficult questions from the press. *When you don't have an answer, ask a question.*

"If you don't mind, I'd like to ask you something," Robbie said. "What do you think our country needs?"

Bennie smiled. "Interesting you asked, since I've given it a great deal of thought," he said. "I think it starts with a candidate who appears to be authentic, someone who can say to the American public, 'I didn't always get things right. Born with every advantage known to humankind, I still managed to bungle a great many things.'"

Robbie tried to figure out where Bennie was going with this line but decided it was best not to beat him to the punch.

"These times," Bennie continued, "cry out for a genuine… what's the word?"

"Fuckup," Marius offered.

Bennie patted Marius's arm and winked. "That's it. A fuckup."

Robbie fumbled for a response. Were they serious? Robbie laughed uneasily, "Well, I've certainly made my share of mistakes—"

"Don't be so modest. You're world class," Bennie said sharply. "And under these circumstances, that could be a very good thing. I believe a genuine fuckup such as yourself could connect with all the other fuckups out there and lead them to an inevitable conclusion: it's time to step aside from the mess they've made of their lives, stop making stupid decisions, and let our team of experts provide direction that works not just for them, but for everybody." He watched Robbie carefully to see how that landed.

Robbie, to Bennie's surprise, pushed back. "Respectfully, Bennie, I hear what you're saying, but I'm not sure more government's the answer," he said. "People don't want their lives run by the Post Office or the DMV."

"Of course not. That's the old model," Bennie replied. "Think of something more associated with going places, like a hotel chain or an airline." He reached a hand across to his son's shoulders. "Marius spent his early career working for Sardine Airlines and Hotsy Totsy Hotels. And he has applied his learning to our commercial properties. Now we want to take it further. We believe what America needs today is a loyalty program."

Loyalty? To what? And to whom? "Are you serious?" Robbie asked.

"Of course," Bennie replied. "Marius, why don't you show Mr. Crowe what we have in mind?"

"With pleasure," Marius said. He bounced out of his chair, pulled out his phone, punched a few buttons, and a screen illuminated on the wall next to him. A photo showed the storefront of a Café Che in New York City. "Perhaps you are familiar with our family's retail chain. It's very popular where you live."

Robbie nodded. "Of course. Commie coffee. That's what we call it."

Marius chuckled. "Everyone does. Which is fine, in our view. We think it's helping to give communism a positive rebranding—Commie Lite, if you will. People don't think repression and bread lines. They think lattes and scones and hip decor."

"Better than gulags, I suppose," Robbie said with a nervous laugh.

Marius smiled with pride. "Our *Counter Culture* customer rewards program at Café Che is our model for the federal government. We're going to give out points!" he said. "Instead of a free burrito for your points like you would get at our restaurant, the government might give you fifty bucks cash back on your taxes or a free night at a Hotsy Totsy hotel. Rather than a large latte, you get your federally backed mortgage approved at one of our affiliated banks. Or maybe we'll allow you to turn on your air conditioner during a heat wave through your local utility."

"Wow," Robbie said, trying to sound impressed.

"At the highest level," Marius said, "we approve dental insurance for a root canal before your toothache kills you. Different levels of participation get different levels of benefits. And our concierge service will work with our corporate partners to direct people to the right behaviors twenty-four/seven. There should be no more indecision for people wondering whether they're doing the right thing. They'll know."

"And, of course," Bennie added, "so will we."

Marius nodded agreement. "China has an evolving social credit system that tracks people throughout their everyday life, and it works beautifully. Our program does them one better: the best of both worlds— private and public, American and Chinese, Stalinist and Maoist, but with a twist that is uniquely American."

Marty glanced at Robbie: Was he buying this *shit?* He had the urge to bolt from the room but couldn't be sure they wouldn't shoot him when he reached the barbed wire.

"It's certainly… innovative," Robbie allowed.

"Yes, it is," Marius said. "That's why we're giving it a great big marketing push at the convention." He hit a button, and a logo came up on the screen, with the logo underlined by a red, white and blue swoosh. "Ta da!"

AMERICA'S JUST REWARDS
Get the Life You Deserve

Underneath were five tiers of rewards progressing from "Deep Red" at the bottom, which provided no benefits. "Pinkish" offered a modest improvement. "Whitelisted" gave upgrades. "Purple Power" allowed near-premium service. And a top level called "True Blue" was essentially first class. As a bonus, it provided entry into America's Just Rewards Clubs in major cities throughout the country, offering all the comforts of an airport lounge: a line to get in, a worked over buffet, and agents at the door who couldn't help you with anything.

Marius explained, "You enroll in the program online and check a little box listing the terms and conditions of our—quote, end quote—Privacy Policy."

Ned roared with laughter. "As if!" he chortled.

Marius smiled. "It's forty pages long but we're thinking of adding a note: anyone with enough time on their hands to read this whole thing will have points deducted from their account," he said with a laugh. "No matter. Once you check that box: congratulations! You've just agreed that we can track every activity in your life and make sure you get all the credit you so rightly deserve."

"Or don't," Bennie added.

Marty wriggled nervously in his chair. "How do you earn points?"

Marius said, "What are you saying on social media? Do you complain about our program or are you saying nice things? What are you watching on TV or your streaming service? Anything subversive, like some of these podcasts spreading misinformation? Are you driving a gasoline-powered car? Or do you make the more responsible choice and take the bus? How many children are you having and are they exhaling too many greenhouse gasses? And, for that matter, are you over the limit for children in your demographic group? We think it's important to pull back on the production of whites."

Bennie became increasingly animated. "We'll know through hospital records, digital currency, credit cards and cash transfers exactly what you're up to. And the best part is this: Unlike the old Soviet system, this one is totally voluntary—no coercion involved. You don't have to earn the points if you don't want them."

Marty looked at a wide-eyed Robbie, who meekly raised his hand. "Who decides what's a good way to spend and what's bad?"

"Our team of experts from business, academia and government working right here in this building with our corporate partners will determine what's for the greater good," Bennie said. "Isn't that what you've always wanted?"

"Of course," Robbie said, clearing his throat. "But that was just a— you know— general idea. This is quite specific."

Bennie massaged his arthritic knee. "Marius, give them an example of how it works."

"Say you have a sore knee, like pop," Marius said. "You see a doctor who decides you need a knee replacement. He checks your America's Just Rewards account. Are you Deep Red? He gives you a cane or a stick, and you hobble away—maybe after he whacks you with it." He laughed at the idea. "Pinkish, you might get a used wheelchair you can push yourself. Whitelisted—this is where the benefits start to really kick in—your wheelchair is electric. And if you're Purple Power? Whoa! You've been a very good boy or girl or whatever gender you prefer. You've earned a complete knee replacement."

"That's fantastic," Worth said.

"Yeah," Robbie said, nodding. "I'm warming to this."

"What if you're True Blue?" Marty asked.

Marius said, "That's best of all. You get an anesthetic before we operate."

Marty struggled to catch his breath, while Bennie smiled with the beatific countenance of a lizard. Marty imagined his tongue might dart out to snatch a fly in the air.

"The beauty of this program is that it's self-directed," Marius said. "Nobody forces you to get a knee replacement. Nobody demands you heat or light your home. It's only if you want it."

Marius sat down next to Robbie. "We understand some people might complain at first," he said. "We had a young staffer who objected to our program, claiming it was a dystopian nightmare." He laughed. "I told her, 'Look sweetheart, this is all about choice. You can just shut the fuck up and do your job, or we can give you a ride to the airport. Your call.'"

"What did she do?" Robbie asked.

Marius shrugged. "Last I saw, she was getting in a car."

Marty asked, "In the trunk?"

"I think it was the back seat," Marius said. "Wasn't it, pop?"

Bennie scratched the stubble on his chin. "Not quite sure."

Marius focused on Robbie. "Please understand something, Robbie. This is not a radical concept. It's the direction our country is already heading. People have signed off their rights to privacy and personal choice many times over. Everything they do is tracked, and it's not only here. It's everywhere around the world. We're just bringing all the information together under new management and accelerating the timetable for complete knowledge of our people in real time."

Robbie took a deep breath. It all seemed rather extreme, but he had no better idea, other than his fuzzy-wuzzy notion of a making the world a better place. Surely, if this program were implemented, it would be better to be on the inside than the outside. The concept was rather intoxicating: Imagine the power this would give him over other people's lives! Everyone in the country would have an account with the government that would determine their quality of life. And every account would ultimately report up to him. He could peek in on friends and adversaries and know exactly what they were up to at any time. If they were slighting him in any way—*boom!*—he could strip them of their points. And if they were good—like those invited to his White House pool party—he'd give away points like candy!

"So what do you think of the program?" Bennie asked.

"Very impressive," Robbie replied. "I'll certainly consider it for my platform."

Nobody spoke for a moment as Bennie looked blankly at Robbie. "This is your platform."

"It's, um—what?" Robbie wasn't sure he'd heard correctly.

"This is how you'll run the country."

Robbie gulped. "No…" He looked around at the faces staring in his direction. "Or, I meant to say, yeah. Of course." He scratched his chin. "I see how this could work."

Marius stepped in front of Marty. "And how about you, Mr. McGarry? You sound skeptical."

Marty struggled to calm his heart. *These people are gangsters.* Would dissent from this lunacy require him to forgo Novocain at the dentist? Donate a vital organ to a comrade more deserving? Get him a ride in the trunk of a car?

He decided the best strategy was to live to fight another day.

"I'm true blue," he declared.

13. Life of the Party

Robbie and Marty emerged from the Willard Center with their limbs still attached, which Marty considered a victory.

"They seem nice," Robbie commented amiably as he clambered into the back of their waiting SUV.

Marty stopped at the door. "You're kidding, of course."

Robbie flinched as he watched Marty climb in and fasten his seat belt. "What?"

"They were nice like the Ayatollah Khomeini was nice," Marty replied. "Except they want to take our whole country hostage."

"What are you talking about?" Robbie asked.

"That America's Just Rewards program," Marty said as the vehicle pulled away from the curb on F Street. "In my humble view that was—how do I put it? *Insane.*"

Robbie guffawed. "Bennie's a genius."

"An evil one," Marty countered. "I was just relieved his creepy son Igor didn't spray me with chemical weapons when I asked a question."

"You're talking about Marius?"

"Marius, Igor… whatever. He was like Frankenstein's henchman. Do we really want data in the hands of people who want to run our lives? I think Marius might be a fucking bot."

"You're worried about nothing," Robbie smirked. "The big decisions won't be up to them. They'll be up to me."

Marty shook his head in disbelief. "So you think."

"So I know!" Robbie shot back.

Marty looked out the window, as the vehicle turned north on 15th Street toward the Hay-Adams hotel. The streets near the White House were starting to fill up with tourists eager to see what they didn't realize were the last vestiges of democracy in action. Pity they would see monuments to the past rather than the conference room of the Hands Up Foundation, which foretold the future.

Robbie turned back to Marty. "You know, Marty, this is why you don't get ahead. You're such a fucking know-it-all. It just pisses people off."

"I know," Marty replied with a sigh.

"Of course you do. You know everything," Robbie said sarcastically. "I thought maybe you'd grown up a bit."

"Nah," Marty said. "I'm clinging to my immaturity as long as I can."

Robbie scowled as he looked out the window. "I don't see any difference between America's Just Rewards and any other loyalty program."

"Right. It's just like Hotsy Totsy Hotels," Marty replied. "Except instead of getting free in-room Wi-Fi, America's Just Rewards lets you keep your kidneys."

Robbie scoffed. "Well, here's the deal, whether we like it or not," he said. "The road to the White House runs through Bennie Barbu." Robbie raised his chin, defiantly. "Once I get into office, I can do whatever the hell I want."

Marty laughed. "Don't count on it."

Robbie admonished him with a look. "I'll be the president, not Bennie."

Marty sighed. Whatever Robbie had been told during this whirlwind seduction in the capital had inflated his already significant sense of self-importance. He was on the threshold of great power. There was little chance he would step back now. "Why do you think they recruited you?"

"They told me very plainly," Robbie claimed. "With Dewey Fenwick out of the picture, they need someone to block Evita Manolo."

"Block her out or lead her in?" Marty asked.

"What do you mean?"

"They know she's too radical to get to the White House on her own," Marty said. "But you could clear the way for her to follow you in the door as your running mate. That puts her in prime position to become the president when they think the time is right."

"Bullshit," Robbie sniffed.

Marty replied. "Think about it: Why do they want you at the top of the ticket?"

Robbie folded his arms across his chest. "You seem to have all the answers. You tell me."

"You bring establishment respectability, like Dewey did," Marty said. "You have a great American name. Your family is famous for building things, not taking them down. You make a radical nutjob like Evita a whole lot less scary to middle America. You win the heartland, she wins the coast, and Bennie implements America's Just Rewards on everybody. It's a beautiful thing."

"Who said Evita's my running mate?" Robbie snapped. "I haven't decided that."

"I bet you Bennie has," Marty said. "And I'd put money on Evita."

Robbie's mouth fell open. He intended to speak but nothing came out.

"Bennie's a huge fan of hers," Marty continued. "He's pumped money into her congressional campaigns and her speaking tours. He gave her his jet to use as she barnstormed the country talking gibberish. Free this. Free that. Free everything. Don't worry; billionaires like Robbie Crowe will pay for it all. You might want to watch your wallet—and your back."

Robbie slumped uneasily in his seat. If what Marty said was even remotely true, Robbie needed extra security— someone to check his food, watch the doors, police the police who escort him around and make sure they did their job. And that meant only one man: his longtime crony Howard J. Doolin.

Robbie picked up his phone. "That does it."

"What?"

"I'm calling for backup." He punched in a call.

Marty slumped in his seat. "Oh no."

"Oh yes," Robbie said, punching the speaker button, and bringing up a man's voice.

"Dude!"

Robbie laughed. "Howie! Hey brother!"

Marty remembered Howard J. Doolin as Howie-Do-It, an incompetent boob who was unflinchingly loyal, a dependable mirror-mirror on the wall, ever ready to call Robbie the fairest of them all. Howie also happened to be a drug-addled low-life who formerly toiled in the basement of Crowe Power headquarters selling weed to the building crew and booking their football bets. Marty had no idea what Howie was up to now but was quite certain it was nothing legit. His core skills were spying on people, hacking into their computers, creating deep fake porn to embarrass ex-girlfriends, and assaulting anyone who got in Robbie's way. If Robbie were elected with Howie at his side, it was certain there would be more cocaine found in the West Wing.

Marty knew that didn't matter to Robbie. What counted to him was Howie's slavish devotion. Howie always said he'd take a bullet for Robbie. Perhaps Robbie thought that time had finally come.

"Wassup?" Howie asked.

"I've got a big assignment for you," Robbie said. He laid out the broad strokes of his sudden run for president, a description of the powerful people behind his candidacy, and the possibility that his supporters may have malevolent motives.

"Bro, I am so proud of you," Howie declared. "President. Man… That's the United States, right?"

"Yep," Robbie replied.

"I mean, woah! That's huge. So, um… you're thinkin' you do that full-time?"

"Well, yeah," Robbie said. "It's kinda required."

"That's cool. You know I'm there for you, dude," Howie declared. "I'll be your bodyguard, your stunt double, your taster, whatever. Just name it."

"Not sure about the stunt double, since we're not *exactly* twins," Robbie said. "But you get my point." Robbie told Howie to meet him in DC.

"You got it," Howie said. "Now… where is that exactly?"

"What?"

"You said, 'DC'."

"You're kidding," Robbie said. "*Washington*, DC?"

"Oh… right. Of course," Howie said. "I don't know what I'm thinkin'. *That* DC."

"Well, get moving," Robbie demanded. "I need you down here immediately. You'll find me at the Hay-Adams hotel."

Robbie clicked off the phone and turned to Marty triumphantly. "Now that's loyalty."

"That's a dangerous dumb ass," Marty noted.

"Yeah? Well, I know he'd do anything for me. Even the ultimate sacrifice." Robbie shook his head in disgust. "I sure as hell couldn't count on you."

Marty paused, thinking carefully how to frame what he wanted to say. "You know, Robbie, when I worked for you at Crowe Power, I made it a practice to avoid eye contact when you said something idiotic like that. Everyone on the management team did the same thing. Now that I've been away from it for a while, I don't think that served you well."

"Oh really," Robbie said. "And why not?"

"Everyone knew you couldn't handle disagreement, so they all looked away," Marty said. "You created a culture of bobblehead dolls, with your leadership team nodding at everything you said as if it made sense. But I know for a fact they weren't even listening. Sucking up isn't competence. It's just sucking up. You could use a little pushback now and then."

"From you? Ha," Robbie huffed. "You're not exactly my class."

Marty nodded. "Don't I know it."

The car pulled up to the Hay-Adams, and a uniformed bellman hustled out to open the door. As Robbie exited, Marty remained in his seat.

"Aren't you getting out?" Robbie asked.

"No," Marty said. "I'm staying over at the Marriott City Center."

Robbie looked disgusted. "Why there?"

Marty shrugged. "Points."

14. The Die is Cast

Ned entered the War Room that was buzzing with activity. Campaign workers oblivious to the impending candidate switcheroo plowed away on convention planning: checking delivery schedules for Let's Do Dewey! signs, coffee mugs, key chains and other merchandise; updating the website on Dewey's *"Big Thought of the Day,"* as if he had some that could be detected; and fine tuning talking points, FAQs, and media contact lists.

Ned approached Worth and Kristi, who were engaged in an animated conversation along the windows. He spoke urgently, but quietly, so only they could hear.

"Bennie signed off on Robbie as our candidate," Ned said. "But he also signed off on Dewey. Bennie says he's gotta go Tuesday."

"Go where?" Kristi asked.

"Wherever his soul is summoned," Ned said. "Bennie wants us to pull the plug."

"Oh lord," Kristi said, shaking her head. "You know Lady Janice won't approve until she gets her house in the Vineyard."

"I told Bennie that," Ned replied. "He said he'd address the situation, whatever that means."

"What do you think it means?" Worth asked.

"I don't want to know," Ned declared. "And neither do you."

Kristi shook her head. "Aw," she sighed. "Bless her heart."

They stared at their shoes in a moment of silence before Ned plowed ahead.

"All right. Enough about that. It's out of our hands," Ned declared. "We've got to get moving." He nodded toward the other side of the room. "Let's go to the whiteboard."

They walked to a corner away from the campaign drones. Ned picked up a blue marker from the marker tray and drew a horizontal line across the bottom. "Let's assume for a moment that Bennie persuades Lady Janice to sign off on Dewey's departure. That puts us here." Ned marked an X on the left side. "If he croaks Tuesday, we get a few days of mourning, visitation and all that crap. It's 'Dear old Dewey' time, blah, blah, blah. Sorrows and lamentations. Come Saturday," he said, marking an X on the right side of the line, "we're ready to switch it up and *par-tay*. We have a funeral gala— a kick ass band, dancing, the works. Dewey's in the rearview mirror and it's all Robbie all the time—*bang!*—right through Chicago."

Worth picked up his phone to check his calendar. "So if Lady Janice gets her way, we pull the plug on Dewey Tuesday." He looked up. "I guess I can do Tuesday."

"ETD?" Kristi asked.

Ned scratched his chin. "Departure time? Nine a.m."

Kristi called up her calendar. "You'll have to do it without me," she said. "I have a breakfast."

Worth offered, "How about nine-thirty? Otherwise, we could go Wednesday."

Ned shook his head. "No way, unless you want to take that up with Bennie."

Worth shuddered. "Never mind."

Kristi peered at her calendar through her reading glasses. "All right. Tuesday's a tight squeeze, but I'll make it work." She typed a calendar item into her phone with her thumbs. "Dewey… dunzo… nine-thirty… Tuesday. You want me to send around an invite?"

"Um… *no*," Ned said.

"Oh, duh," Kristi said, gently smacking her forehead. "I suppose we don't need a record of all this."

"No, we don't," Ned said. "But remember: once they take Dewey off the ventilator, it could take a while before his last gasp. You know what a stubborn old coot he is."

"He better check out by one-thirty," Worth said. "I'm playing squash at two."

Ned leaned over the board and marked an X above Tuesday on the timeline as Dinda walked over and joined the planning session.

"X for exit?" Dinda asked, catching her breath and crossing herself. "You're really doing this, aren't you?"

Ned nodded and snapped the cap shut on the marking pen. "God's will."

"Poor Dewey." Dinda picked up a red marker and drew a little heart over the X that denoted Tuesday. "Poor, poor Dewey. What does he die of?"

"We haven't decided," Worth said with a shrug.

"We could be honest," Dinda suggested.

That provoked a round of laughter, prompting Dinda to blush. "Sorry," she said. "I don't know what I was thinking."

"Come on team!" Kristi scoffed. "We can figure this out!! He was president of the United States, for crying out loud! We need something heroic. Better yet, something we can pin on Platt."

Worth considered her point. "What's a dread disease where Platt cut funding on research or vaccines? There's gotta be something."

Dinda, trying to squeeze the last bit of ink from her magic marker, repeatedly stabbed the board, creating a cloud of red dots. "Damn this pen..." She paused a moment and stared at the board. "Oh... my... *God!*" she exclaimed, pointing at the board. "There it is!"

"What?" Ned asked.

She circled the red dots. "Measles!"

Worth grimaced. "Measles?"

"Yes!" Ned said. "Of course! Platt slashed funding for vaccinations! Remember? He said, 'Measles, shmeasles'?"

"By God, you're right!" Worth exclaimed. "I love it!"

Ned hooked his arm with Dinda's and they joyously danced a little jig in front of the whiteboard. "If you were getting paid," Ned said, "I'd give you a big fat raise!"

15. Taking the House

Lady Janice arrived at the electronic gates to Bennie Barbu's estate in the historic Kalorama neighborhood in northwest Washington prepared to either receive her well-deserved consolation prize or break some knuckles if she didn't. Clearly, Bennie had plenty of money. For a man who didn't believe in borders, he sunk a lot of it into the stone fence around his mansion.

She didn't ask for much — what's a fifteen-million-dollar beach house in Martha's Vineyard to a guy like him? But it was surely the least he could do. After all she had done for the party, she was *owed*. Big time.

Who else could have put such a smiling face on Dewey's decline as he slid into the abyss other than the person who was most at his side? Who else would have faced the public and confidently declared Dewey was on top of his game when he couldn't even play? Who could have stepped into the job and helped run the White House as she did when it was obvious her husband could barely follow the spinning wheel on *Wheel of Fortune,* much less the swirling turns of international diplomacy? Yes, she was lauded in the media as the most influential First Lady since Eleanor Roosevelt, or possibly Edith Wilson, but what did that get her? Glory was nothing she could take to the bank, or to the beach. It was time to settle accounts while she still had leverage.

A house servant ushered Lady Janice into a red-brick courtyard between wings of the mansion and offered her a seat next to a bubbling fountain, where she awaited ol' moneybags. Much to her disappointment, she was greeted instead by Marius, who approached respectfully. *Bennie,* she seethed, *sent the junior varsity?*

"Lady Janice," Marius said with a nod and a smile. "So good of you to stop by."

Her majesty graciously allowed the top of her hand to be kissed. "Yes. Well," she huffed. "I was expecting to see your father."

"Oh, I'm sure he'll be around before long," Marius said pleasantly. He scraped a wrought iron chair across the bricks and set it close to her.

He sat down and leaned forward earnestly, almost as if he were interested in what she had to say. "What can I do for you today?"

Lady Janice took a deep breath. "I thought you knew."

Marius shrugged. "Just rumblings," he said, pushing her to explain it herself.

"Well, as Ned told Bennie, I would like a house." She raised her chin and regarded him over the tip of her nose.

Marius looked puzzled. "You already have a house," he said. "I'm quite sure you have two."

"Yes," she allowed, "but I was expecting a third house this year. You might have seen it: a lovely white mansion at 1600 Pennsylvania Avenue? Since that appears to be out of the question through no fault of my own, I think it's only fair that the committee compensate me with another house. You know… considering."

Marius nodded, sympathetically. "Considering what?"

"If it were up to me, Dewey would still be in the race," she said. "And I think he'd be a damn good bet to win, regardless of his condition. But the National Committee insisted he couldn't go on. So here we are."

"Right," Marius acknowledged, rubbing his chin.

"The committee owes me for my sacrifice," Lady Janice insisted, her voice rising. "Not to mention all I've done over the years to advance the party's cause. Would you like me to go down the list?"

Marius held up the palm of his hand and sat back. "No, no, Lady Janice. That won't be necessary. We're very much aware of your many contributions."

"Then I would think the party would show me some gratitude," she declared.

Marius took a deep breath to contain his anger. Did she have any idea what they had already done for her? "I completely understand," he said. "My father and I discussed it and we've agreed to let you keep the house in Beachville."

Lady Janice sputtered. "You… *what?*"

Marius slapped both knees and smiled magnanimously. "You can stay there as long as you like."

She guffawed. "*You're* letting *me* stay in my own house? What kind of crap is that?"

"It's not your house; it's ours," Marius said, innocently. "Check the title. Eleven Ocean Road is held by the Victory Trust. Victory Trust is owned by Progressive Black Action, which in turn is owned by the Hands Up Foundation, which of course, is owned by my father."

Lady Janice folded her arms across her chest. "You're saying Bennie owns my house."

Marius nodded. "Indeed. You live there under pop's good graces. And mine, too, since I am the trustee."

Lady Janice vigorously shook her head. "Dewey never said a word about that."

Marius winced. "He's probably not one to ask right now, is he?"

Lady Janice's mouth went dry and she reached with a shaky hand into her handbag for a pill. "I could use some water."

"So sorry. I should have offered this before." Marius reached behind him and smoothly pulled a glass of ice water from a silver tray. He handed it over to Lady Janice, who popped the pill and took a slug.

Sensing her discomfort, Marius offered another olive branch. "Would it help if we let you keep your house in Bethesda, too?"

"*Let* me?" she blurted. "Are you saying…?"

"Yes. We own that property as well, through a different series of trusts and non-profits. The Equity Now Foundation. The People's Liberation Movement. I could tell you more, but you don't really need to know," Marius said, almost apologetically. "Out of our deep appreciation for your service, we're happy to let you have it as long as you wish."

Lady Janice was reeling. How did Dewey allow her to become a dependent of the party bosses? She felt like saying, "Never mind," and slinking back to her car. But settling for living in homes she already believed she owned was not the bargain she came for. As the pill kicked in, and her anxieties eased, she recalled she was holding one last ace: the near corpse of Dewey J. Fenwick. He was still alive, and she could theoretically keep him that way forever.

A door squeaked open behind Lady Janice and Bennie shuffled out, using a cane for balance. "Good morning," he called cheerily. He took a chair next to his old friend Lady Janice and patted her knee. "Hope you're doing all right," he said.

"Frankly, Bennie, I've been better," she sniffed.

"I can imagine," Bennie said. "I'm sure Dewey's illness is weighing heavily on you."

"It's not just that."

Marius chimed in. "I've been explaining to Lady Janice the housing situation. She expressed an interest in keeping both houses that we own, which I agreed was fair."

"Good," Bennie said. "Then we're settled."

Lady Janice bristled at the Barbus' condescension. Preening over having the upper hand was *her* play. She was a First Lady, a Vogue cover girl, the former chair of the former Kennedy Center for the former Performing Arts, and "Dewey Fenwick's Best Asset," according to *The New York Times* Magazine. Now they wanted to trundle her off to the exits without so much as a parting gift. *Like hell!*

"Not quite," she declared. "I want another house. Martha's Vineyard. On the beach."

Bennie smiled. "Do you have one in mind?"

"Oh yes," she said. "It's a lovely home on the bay. Needs some work, of course, but it's got the right bones. Dewey and I dreamed for years of owning it. Now it's on the market and I would like to have it."

He patted her knee. "Then I certainly hope you get it."

Lady Janice fixed him with a glare. "I believe you should pay for it."

Bennie squinted. "Well, as you know, Janice—"

"*Lady* Janice," she corrected him.

Bennie smarted but let it go. "The committee is rather strapped. With all due respect, we are spending any available funds we have on the next president, not the last one," he said. "We are grateful, of course, for Dewey's service, and for yours, but, frankly, I'm not investing in Fenwick futures. I'm short on Dewey, long on Robbie. We have to move on if we're going to stop this Platt menace and implement our system."

Lady Janice's annoyance turned to simmering rage. She dug deep into her Beachville strip mall roots, recalling her hair bender days, and how she responded to a rich woman who refused to pay for a cut and color that took all afternoon. The old bag never got out of the parking lot after Janice put a knife in all the tires on her Mercedes.

"You're not moving anywhere as long as Dewey's lying in a hospital bed," Lady Janice declared hotly. "You want me to pull the plug? Pay me. You want me to vouch for Robbie Crowe's so-called friendship with my husband? I want my commission." She looked at Bennie, then Marius, then back again to Bennie. "And let me be clear in case there's any confusion by either of you: Dewey's departure is delayed until I'm satisfied. That ventilator stays on until I say it's turned off." She regarded the polish on her fingernails as she rolled her tongue around in her cheek. "And at the moment, I haven't decided when that will be."

Bennie rested his wrists on the crook of his cane. "Good to know where you stand, my dear," he said. His voice turned cold. "Now let me be clear so that there is no confusion on your side, either. Dewey is ticketed for departure on Tuesday, whether you pull the plug or not. If you don't wish to accompany him on his final journey, I suggest you drop this demand now."

"Are you threatening me?" she bristled.

"Yes," Bennie replied.

She shook her head. "You know, I could tell stories…"

Bennie regarded her with an icy stare. "Not for long."

He really would *kill* her? Lady Janice looked to Marius for support, but he was scratching his beard and looking up into the trees at a noisy bird. *Was that a blue jay?*

"I… I don't know what to say," Lady Janice said.

"Try 'thank you,'" Bennie suggested. "You've been amply compensated for your services, Janice—"

"*Lady* Janice," she corrected again.

That was too much for Bennie. "No, no, no. We're going to cut that bullshit right now," he said. "You're not titled in this country or any other. As far as I'm concerned, you're not exactly a lady either. You're Janice, hair bender from the beach. You've had a remarkable ride well past your station, but you need to see the reality that is staring you in the face. It's the end of the line."

She fought back tears but remained steady. "Not until the convention."

Marius studied his father and braced for what he might say. Should he start the car and open the trunk? Much to his surprise, Bennie did not blow up or call to have her rolled up in a carpet and taken to a landfill.

Bennie scratched the stubble under his chin and said, "I tell you what," he said. "In the interest of keeping peace in the family, we'll take care of it. The house will be yours."

She brightened. "It will?"

Bennie turned to Marius. "Do whatever it takes," he said. "I know Dewey would want her to be happy."

Lady Janice beamed, and hugged Bennie. "Thank you."

His smile vanished as she reentered the house to leave. He held up his hand to Marius until he heard a door slam and was certain she was gone.

As Bennie dropped his hand, Marius said, "I can't believe you're going to buy that witch a house."

"We'll buy it for her," he said. "What happens after that, who can say?"

Ah, Marius thought as he broke into a grin, for Bennie clearly had a plan. *That's my pop!*

16. Making History

Ned stared blankly at his computer screen, mulling ways for the comatose Dewey Fenwick to magically hand the baton to Robbie Crowe before checking out of Agnew Memorial and into a cemetery. A statement issued by the campaign wouldn't do; that could be dismissed as a fake without Dewey's voice. An AI video would be called out as a campaign invention. And Dewey was surely in no position to speak for himself.

A letter from the former president might make sense, Ned thought. After all, Ned still held the autopen he had used to put Dewey's signature on dozens of executive orders, some of which Dewey was aware of at the time. Still, it would require a willing media stooge to vouch for a letter's authenticity at this stage. Perhaps a well-known print reporter or TV host could be called to the hospital room for an exclusive private audience along the lines of Boof and Skeeter.

Ned called up his media contact list and began scrolling through names. In campaign circles, Ned was known as the Maestro of Media, a message orchestrator who knew when to blow horns, beat drums, or insist on more cowbell. This play, Ned decided, required heartstrings. Who best to pluck them?

Dinda banged through the door, disrupting his focus. "Ned," she said breathlessly.

"What?" he barked.

"I just got a call from the Amalgamated Press. They want a response to Platt awarding the Presidential Medal of Freedom to Aunt Jemima."

Ned laughed. "No way," he said. "That's gotta be a gag."

Dinda sighed and stuck her phone in his face. He snatched it away and watched a video of Platt in the Oval Office announcing his latest list of awardees. Aunt Jemima, iconic mascot for a cancelled brand of pancake mix and syrup, was the first medal Platt awarded to a fictional character.

"Aunt Jemima has a noble history, first as a mammy from the old South wearing a very becoming doo rag, and later as a modern woman with a very pretty hairdo," Platt declared.

"Today, I am restoring her rightful place in our country and to America's breakfast tables. She was a great symbol in the fight for pancake equality, making it just as easy to whip up instant flapjacks as it was to make scrambled eggs. That was before she was unjustly cancelled by the woke mob. To me, she was not only an American hero, she was a friend."

Ned gave the phone back to Dinda. "You have to hand it to him," he said. "He's got a sense of humor."

Dinda flushed red. "You think this is *funny?* It's an outrage!" She pointed toward the hallway. "Our switchboard is lighting up like a burning cross. We have to respond. What do you want me to tell the Amalgamated Press?"

Ned leaned back in his chair, clasping his hands behind his head. "Tell 'em it's a dog whistle."

"To whom?"

"Usual suspects," Ned said.

Dinda sagged. "White supremacists?"

"They're everywhere," Ned replied. "Think I just saw one in the hall."

"That's so *boring,*" she complained. "Can't we come up with something new?"

Ned sat up and spoke sharply. "When in doubt, go with what's tried and true. Platt blows his dog whistle; we blow ours. The difference is we have way more dogs in our kennel than he has in his. Toss our watchdogs a little red meat cut from Platt's shanks. They'll bark like mad."

Dinda pouted as she walked away, punching up the number to the Amalgamated Press to deliver the campaign's message of the moment. Within an hour, commentators across the broadcast, cable, podcast, and internet spectrum were dutifully calling Platt's award to Aunt Jemima a sop to white supremacists and explaining the deeper meaning of Platt's villainy.

It was, they claimed, a needlessly provocative decision that provided more evidence the evil Platt wanted to roll back the clock to the 1850s, strip Black people of their voting rights, put them in chains, brand them with his initials, stick them in bowels of galley ships and make them row their way to Africa. This was an appeal to the Ku Klux Klan, to extreme right-wingers, and a signal to domestic terrorists to come out of their hidey holes. America was less safe today because of this needless tribute to Aunt Jemima, a stereotypical symbol of a repressive era. Our sacred democracy was becoming a fascist dictatorship run by a diminishing population of pale males like Platt.

Ned walked down to the production studio to see the media chorus in full voice. There, on a bank of screens, the talking heads were working themselves into a frenzy, predicting—if not egging on—demonstrations in the streets, boycotts, and vandalism of any diner that dared to display an image of Aunt Jemima.

Binkie Smithers on the talk show *The Coven* insisted it was only a matter of time before the dictator Platt was throwing people in jail for refusing to eat Aunt Jemima pancakes. Binkie urged her followers to go to the Piggly Wiggly and buy Log Cabin syrup in protest. That suggestion, in turn, caused a roaring backlash on her set from panelists claiming it was immoral to support *any* product depicting log cabins, a disturbing symbol of settler colonialism. "Piggly Wiggly?" scoffed commentator Yappy Hoffman, an animal rights activist. "No thinking person should shop at a store that makes pigs wiggle against their will. That's not who we are."

Token moderate Hoot Biddle told guests on *Consensus* that he liked Aunt Jemima syrup, triggering shrieks of protest. Host Jinxie Jones ordered him off the set, stripped him of his ID badge on the way out, and announced he would not get it back for two weeks since he was now on probation. Boof and Skeeter, meanwhile, worked themselves into tears. Boof declared, "As God is my witness, I'll never eat instant pancakes again."

In this escalating contest to show who was most offended by Platt's latest outrage, the bow-tied commentator Finn Tingleberry of the famously dull FFS show *Potomac Perspectives* stood apart, distinguished by his quiet dignity. "I don't know how much more of this assault on decency our great nation can endure," Finn intoned somberly. "All of the progress we have made in civil rights has been torn asunder by this aspiring dictator. Today, it's a fictional character. Tomorrow, who will he honor? Pepé Le Pew? This, in a word, stinks. Such a thing would never happen under a President Fenwick, a man of decency, conscience, and principle."

"And a pulse," Ned said. "I've got to call Finn."

"Why?" she asked.

"Dewey's going to write a letter to the American people."

"He can't move," Dinda replied.

Ned dramatically rubbed his temples. "I'm channeling his thoughts."

"He's not thinking anything," Dinda said.

Ned grinned. "Then it should be pretty easy. Get me a draft by four o'clock. Say something like, 'I want my devoted friend Robbie Crowe to carry our banner forward to victory.' We'll run it through the autopen for his signature. And I'll bring in Finn Tingleberry for the scoop."

Ned left the studio and headed back to the War Room. He returned to his desk, stuck AirPods in his ears, and phoned Finn, who saw the ID on his phone.

"Hello, Ned," Finn said warmly. "How nice to hear from you."

"I just saw your commentary on FFS and I wanted to tell you I thought it was magnificent," Ned said. "A perfect response to Platt's cynicism."

Finn choked up. "Thank you, my friend," he said softly. "It came from the heart."

"I know it did." Ned's voice dropped. "Listen, Finn. I've got some very difficult news to share with the nation. Given the sensitivity, I wanted to bring it to you first." He explained that despite the best efforts of doctors at Agnew Memorial, what seemed like a routine hospital visit for the former president had turned grave. "Sadly, it's possible he might not make it. Selfless man that he is, he's not thinking of himself. He's thinking about our country. Naturally he wanted to offer his thoughts on the situation to you."

Finn trembled. "I'm devastated to hear this. But... I am, of course, deeply honored he would think of me at such a time."

"Your integrity precedes you, Finn," Ned said. "He's been sleeping most of the time, but he did wake up briefly to catch your commentary."

"He did?" Finn asked. "What did he say?"

"He said, 'We need more people like Finn Tingleberry."

"Really?"

"Word for word."

Finn's voice quaked. "You know me, Ned. I've just tried to be fair."

"And you are," Ned said. "Eminently so."

Ned advised Finn that the campaign would issue a press release later in the day about Dewey's condition, but Finn would be afforded an exclusive visit with Dewey in his private room. Ned added that he would not soon forget Finn's Emmy-winning interview conducted with Dewey when he announced his candidacy earlier in the year. Finn had expertly edited Dewey's meandering gibberish into coherent prose, which took four hours of slicing, dicing, and splicing, along with a dash of AI.

"That delicate touch is needed once more," Ned said.

"I will treat it with the utmost care," Finn assured him.

Ned hung up and began typing out the advisory.

FOR IMMEDIATE RELEASE
President Fenwick Hospitalized
In Critical Condition
WASHINGTON, DC—Former president Dewey Fenwick, his party's leading candidate for the presidential nomination, is listed in critical condition at Spiro T. Agnew Memorial Hospital today after contracting measles. Family members and close associates have been called to his bedside.

"This situation was completely avoidable," said Worth Talmadge, chair of the National Committee. "If not for President Platt's heartless cuts to measles research, Dewey Fenwick would be on the campaign trail today, meeting with the American public."

In keeping with the campaign's unswerving devotion to transparency, updates on President Fenwick's condition will be released the moment they become available.

Ned sent the draft to Worth for approval, then grabbed his satchel as Dinda approached.

"Where are you going?" she asked.

"Hospital." He looked at his watch. "Make sure Worth signs off on this, then get it out on the wires. And call Rent-a-Vigil. I want a hundred people outside holding candles and signs within the hour."

"They charge double for short notice," Dinda advised.

"Pay triple. I don't care. We need a scene out there," he said. "Robbie is on his way to meet Evita right now. Once the media set up, pull Robbie out of that meeting and have him ride over to Agnew Memorial. I want him coming out the hospital with Lady Janice to meet the press."

Dinda bit her lip. "You want them to hold hands?"

Ned frowned. "He's a friend—not a boyfriend," he said. "She can hold his arm for steadiness. Let's show the world that Robbie's a rock, a steady leader we can trust."

Dinda winced. "Can we?"

Ned grinned. "He'll have to do."

17. The Cadaver-in-Chief

Ned slipped into the hospital through an employee entrance and made his way to Dewey's private suite on the top floor, where guards were stationed next to the door. He found the former president lying peacefully in his hospital bed, his chest rising and falling in rhythm with the ventilator pumping air in and out of his lungs. Ned tugged the hospital gown up and over the spot in Dewey's neck where the breathing tube was attached to his trachea.

Dinda joined him bedside. "Do you think Finn will notice he's hooked up to a ventilator?"

"Not unless I pull out the hose and slap him it," Ned replied.

Dinda reached into her satchel. "Do you want to see the letter?"

"Read it to me," Ned said.

Dinda laid the letter on a tray table, took out a pen to make Ned's edits, and began reading. "'My Fellow Americans... '"

"No, no. Stop right there," Ned commanded. "You can't say 'fellow'. That suggests he's writing only to men. Remember our base. We need some inclusive gibberish in there."

"Like what?"

"To My Fellow, My Female, and My Non-Gender Specific Americans," Ned said.

"Wordy, but okay," Dinda said as she made a note. She continued, "'As my journey on this earthly plain ends next Tuesday—'"

"Oh, *hell* no!" Ned snapped. "You can't say when he's going to croak, Dinda. How would he know?"

Dinda protested, "I didn't say what time."

Ned shook his head. "Take it out."

Dinda sighed and made the notation, "'As my journey on this earthly plain nears an end, it appears I can no longer continue my quest to again become your president. Though I am confident I would still be up for the job, our constitution forbids anyone from taking office who is technically deceased.'"

"Strike that last sentence," Ned said. "It's a stretch."

Dinda sagged. "This whole thing is a stretch."

Ned brushed her off. "Just keep going."

Dinda returned to the letter. "'I want to express my hope that you support L. Robertson Crowe III as my replacement,'" she continued. "'My dear friend Robbie is certainly no worse than Roland Platt. He will make a fine nominee and an outstanding president of the United States of America. I know I can count on him to carry our agenda forward—"

Ned shook his head. "Hold up."

"What?"

"Take out the 'no worse than Roland Platt' part.'"

"Why?"

"I'm not so sure he is, for one thing."

"Oh, so now we're being honest?" she grumbled. "When did that start?" She drew a line through the phrase and continued reading. "Finishing up here. 'God bless each and every one of you. And God bless America.'" She paused for the dramatic close. "'So long, sports fans.'"

"Sports fans?" Ned chuckled. "What the hell?"

Dinda smiled. "He always said that instead of goodbye. I thought it was cute."

"It's corny."

"*He* was corny. It was part of his charm."

"He had charm?" Ned sighed. "All right. I guess I can live with it."

Dinda smiled and left the room to make the changes and Ned walked to the window, discreetly parting the blinds. Just beyond the hospital's port cochere, a battery of TV cameras was setting up to record comings and goings and await announcements. A half dozen police cars were on hand to keep order as Dewey's Rent-A-Vigil devotees began to assemble with candles and signs proclaiming "Best President Ever!", "We love you, Dewey! Oh yes, we Dew!", and "Dew Get Well!"

Ned shook his head. "Sorry, sports fans," he said to himself. "Game's about over."

He watched a black car pull up, prompting a blaze of klieg lights and camera flashes as police cordoned off a path for the car's occupants. A rear door opened, and Dr. Feeley emerged, who then helped Lady Janice out of the car. She nodded somberly to the assembly, and grasped Feeley's hand as they made their way into the hospital.

"What the livin' fuck..." Ned growled. He turned to find Dinda had returned with the reprinted letter, which she laid on the tray table next to

Dewey's bed for the signature. "Didn't anyone tell Lady Janice she's not supposed to hold hands with Feeley in public?"

Dinda seethed. "You think she listens to me? I told her twice."

Lady Janice arrived in Dewey's suite a moment later. She walked slowly into the room, took a deep breath, and approached her husband's bedside. After a silent something—a prayer, perhaps, or a wish for that new house— she gripped the rail on the side of the bed, bent over and kissed Dewey's forehead. Then she turned and addressed Ned.

"I don't see any measles."

Ned winced. "Shit. I knew we forgot something."

She shook her head in disgust. "You fucking people..." She reached into her purse and rummaged around, finding a lip pencil and blush. "I'll do it myself." She turned to Dr. Feeley. "Franklin, dear, find me a photo of measles on your phone."

Feeley did a quick search and held up his phone with images of faces with measles. "Here you go, pet."

Lady Janice put on her reading glasses to study the photos, then leaned over to brush a pinkish rash on Dewey's cheeks and forehead. She topped that with a constellation of reddish spots that Ned thought vaguely resembled Virgo, Dewey's astrological sign. She worked efficiently and fast, displaying the cosmetic wizardry that made her the go-to face beater at Yvonne's House de Beauté in the Sandy-Dandy strip mall in Beachville.

She stood back and turned to Feeley. "What do you think?"

Feeley nodded approvingly. "Pretty convincing, I'd say."

Ned concurred. "If Dewey saw what we were doing to him, his cause of death would be acute embarrassment. But, it's the best we can do."

A Secret Service agent entered the room. "Mr. Finn Tingleberry is here to see President Fenwick. Is it okay if I let him in?"

Ned cleared his throat. "Yes, of course. Please do."

Dinda nodded toward the letter on the tray table and tugged on Ned's sleeve. "You didn't sign the letter for Dewey."

Ned's eyes went wide. "Where's the auto pen?"

Dinda shrugged. "I thought you had it."

"I told you to bring it," Ned claimed.

Dinda shook her head. "No, you *didn't*."

It was too late. Finn entered the private suite looking every bit as grave as Dewey's outlook, choking up at the sight of the fallen leader's helpless condition. Careful not to disturb the patient, Ned quietly introduced Finn to all but his old friend Lady Janice, with whom he was long acquainted. He offered a limp bear hug.

After a moment of awkward silence, Finn sucked in his breath and asked the big question. "Is he going to make it?"

Ned shook his head. "It doesn't look that way." He nodded toward the bed, and the group shuffled over. "Dr. Feeley, perhaps you can explain his condition."

Feeley glared at Ned for putting him on the spot, then turned toward Finn. "The president contracted measles several weeks ago. It appeared to be a mild case, but serious complications set in."

As Feeley droned on, offering an improvised dissertation on the history of measles from the Middle Ages, a large spider descended a silken thread from the light fixture and crawled across Dewey's face, coming to a stop just west of his nose. It paused there, as if it were trying to figure out whether Dewey's nostrils were a suitable place to weave a web. Certainly, there was enough hair in there to provide a head start.

"How long do you think he has to live?" Finn asked.

Dinda, Janice, and Feeley answered in unison, "Tuesday."

Ned rolled his eyes. "That's just a guess, of course. Nobody but God can say for sure."

"Of course," Finn agreed. He scanned the faces of Dewey's grieving loved ones. "I'm so sorry for all of you. And especially for our country. We were counting on him to stop the Platt menace."

The group returned its mournful gaze to the patient, watching the spider raise its front legs, before deciding to stay put. Ned certainly couldn't slap it, but neither could he let it park on Dewey's defenseless cheek, or lay eggs in his nose. As he reached into his pocket for a tissue, Finn reached out to brush off the intruder. The spider disappeared, but the measles smeared, turning Finn's fingertips red.

"Oh, my goodness," Finn exclaimed as backed away from the bed, staring at his stained fingers. "It's... it's... "

"Contagious!" Ned cried.

"Oh no!" Finn yelped.

Ned elbowed Dr. Feeley, who reached into his bottomless bag of bullshit for a rhetorical tourniquet before their credibility bled all over the floor.

"That's quite common for certain strains," Feeley claimed.

"What strain does he have?" Finn asked anxiously.

Feeley cleared his throat. "Why they're, um… German measles."

Finn was baffled. "I had German measles as a child. It lasted four days. Didn't you say he's had it for several weeks?"

"I did say that, but, um…" Feeley babbled, before leading Finn on a magical medical tour. "These are *East* German measles, created in a lab by mad scientists behind the Iron Curtain following World War II. It was all part of a biological weapons program developed by some of Hitler's holdovers and—"

"Hitler?" Finn said, alarmed. "I should have known. I bet Platt had something to do with it."

Ned shrugged. "He was just a baby then but yeah. Probably. He was evil as a baby, too."

Finn kept his infected hand aloft. "And these measles spread by touch?"

Feeley nodded. "Guess so."

"My God in heaven!" Finn said. "My wife is pregnant. This could be catastrophic."

Ned saw an opportunity. "Finn, you should scrub your hands right away."

"May I use the bathroom?" Finn asked.

"Of course," Ned replied.

Dinda rushed Finn over to the bathroom to stop the deadly makeup from spreading. Ned slipped around the bed, pulled a pen from his pocket and signed Dewey's name to the letter.

A shaken Finn emerged from the bathroom, trembling over his exposure to the Maybelline malady.

"The president's last request," Ned said, "was that you read this."

Finn took the letter and scanned it. "Robbie Crowe for president?"

Ned nodded somberly. "It's his dying wish."

Finn held up the letter. "When did he write it?"

"He dictated it to me this morning and signed it just before you came in," Ned said. "Last thing he said to me was, 'Our democracy cannot survive another four years of Roland Platt. Tell Finn that Robbie is our only hope.' You're holding history in your hands there, Finn. This letter might be his last official act."

"Wow. This is historic," Finn said. He paused, considering his next request. "I don't want to be untoward, so please stop me if you think I'm out of line. But… this is such an important occasion. Is it possible to get a photo with him?"

Ned looked at Janice, who shrugged indifferently, then back to Finn. "I don't see why not," he said.

Finn handed Ned his phone and walked around the bed, while Dinda grabbed the controls and pushed a button to tilt the bed so that Dewey appeared to sit up. As the bed reached its apex, Dewey's eyelids drooped open, and his vacant eyes stared into space.

Lady Janice shrieked at her husband's zombie visage. "*Ahh!!*"

Feeley, horrified, wrapped an arm around her and guided her away. "Don't look, darling," he said.

Ned ignored their panic. He held up his camera and trained it on Dewey and Finn. "Say, 'cheese,'" he told Finn.

Finn wrapped his arm around Dewey's shoulders and Ned snapped away. "Work with me now," he said, taking shots in horizontal, vertical and portrait mode as Finn worked through different poses.

"Looking good!" Ned claimed. He lowered the phone and flipped through the shots of a proud Finn, oblivious to the blank expression on Dewey's face. "Oh, we've got some keepers here," Ned said. "You'll treasure these beauties."

Dinda pressed the control button to return the bed to its previous lie-flat position, which closed Dewey's eyes, perhaps for the last time.

Finn looked at the photos, his eyes welling with tears. "That's the Dewey I know. Always rising to the occasion." he said, his voice choking. He paused to regain his composure. "Can I talk about this letter on FFS?"

"Whatever you think is best, Finn," he said. "Dewey was counting on you to use your best judgment."

"I'll pop up something tomorrow," Finn promised.

"How about five o'clock today?" Ned asked. When Finn looked surprised, Ned clasped him by the shoulder and looked him in the eye. "It's what Dewey wanted."

Finn thought of his Dewey duty. "Tell him he can count on me."

Ned choked up. "I will. As soon as he wakes up."

18. Evita Meet and Greet

Robbie and Evita Manolo met behind closed doors in her office across from the Capitol while Marty strolled around her waiting room, perusing the photographs, awards, certificates, and magazine covers that served as her evolving biography.

No doubt about it: Evita was glamorous and charismatic figure, a trendy fashionista who's smiling visage graced the covers of every magazine from *Haute Stuff* ("What to Wear to the Revolution") to *Nibbles & Noshes* ("Bolivian Jungle Picnic? Evita's Recipe for Silpancho!") to *Suburban Woman* ("A Pink Pussy Hat that Doesn't Make You Look Like a Weirdo"). Young leftist women with pin-cushion faces found her empowering. Older conservative men found her alluring and believed that, given the chance, they could bring her around to capitalism through some dazzling sexual techniques.

Framed photos on the wall featured her smiling broadly as she posed with some of her favorite dictators, ayatollahs, race hustlers, and death row inmates, as well as the celebrities, journalists, and Hollywood stars who adored them. One fading color shot showed a young Evita working behind the twirling weenie warmer at her first job at a convenience store. The oft-told story was that she had been on the job three days when she called for a strike to protest working conditions. Three people boldly walked out and reaped their reward: a 20 percent cut in hours and the firing of Evita's friend, Todd, the stock boy. Still, it was deemed a success because they bravely stuck it to "The Man," an assistant manager named Wendell.

Marty noted that it surely helped Evita's star power that she didn't display the grim sourpuss visage of old-time commies. She presented a fresh and vibrant image, a walking, talking rebrand of Marxism that worked for the times. She was young, glib, and beautiful, with sparkling eyes, a brilliant smile, impressive boobage, and a stylish wardrobe that accentuated her best assets. Marty was no fan, given her radical politics, but he understood her seductive allure. Nine out of ten lonely peasants working a long day on the collective farm would surely fantasize about coming home to her rather than a goat.

Marty sat down on a sofa and checked his phone for news. Dewey's health dominated the headlines, pushing Platt to the sidelines for once. The president's post on social media that he was holding a "Christmas in July Sale" on the White House lawn to sell many of the mansion's historic furnishings and fixtures didn't even make the top ten stories of the day. That prompted Platt to issue a second post on social media claiming Dewey was faking illness to take attention away from his garage sale. He announced he was adding Dewey's presidential portrait to the lawn, too.

Marty heard the door creak open and turned to see Robbie emerging from Evita's lair with his face flushed and his gait wobbling. Marty had seen this look before and knew exactly what it meant: Robbie was in love. Despite cautions in the car on the way over, Robbie's brain was once again overruled by his more dominant organ, prompting yet another reckless judgment.

"Let's bounce," Robbie announced.

They headed out in silence and said nothing until their car pulled up to a stoplight at 6th Street. Finally, Robbie turned to Marty. "What?"

"*What* what?" Marty replied with irritation.

Robbie pressed. "You're judging me. I can feel it. So... out with it. *What?*"

Marty sighed. "You know what," he said. "I don't have to say it."

"Yes, as a matter of fact, you do," Robbie insisted.

Marty debated briefly whether to respond, which was bound to trigger an argument. "Did you get it on in there?"

Robbie chortled. "Oh, my God! You are such a pathetic loser!" He shook his head and looked out the window away from Marty. "No."

"You didn't?"

Robbie turned back. "Of course not!" he snapped. "In the office?"

"Wouldn't be your first time."

Robbie winced. "Well, there is that."

The car lurched away from the light and continued up Pennsylvania Avenue. "This was nothing more than getting acquainted. That's all." Robbie shrugged. "You've gotta admit though: she's got it *all* going on."

Marty sighed. "Not my type, but okay."

"Why not?"

"Sorry, Robbie. The commie thing is a non-starter for me."

Robbie shook his head. "If this were a couple of years ago, I would have agreed. But she gives it a certain aura, you know? When she talks about it—so easily, so confidently—it all kind of makes sense."

"I can imagine," Marty replied. "What did she say?"

Robbie grimaced. "I don't really know. I was focused on her tits."

"Okay. *That* makes sense," Marty said. "Did you ask her to join you on the ticket?"

"No. It just—" Robbie sighed. "It felt a little sudden. 'Hi, I'm Robbie. Want to be my vice president?' It was like asking a first date to bed as soon as you meet. Not that I've never done that, but I'm not even sure I want her on the ticket. We need to kind of feel each other out."

"I'm sure you'll get to that."

Robbie rubbed his chin. "We're having drinks later on."

"Of course you are," Marty said. "And where might that be?"

"Well, obviously, it can't be out in public," Robbie said. "If we're going to set tongues wagging, I prefer the first one is mine."

"So let me guess…"

"We're meeting in my suite."

Marty rolled his eyes. "Does it bother you that you might be falling into a trap?"

Robbie bristled. "You keep suggesting there's some sort of nefarious plot afoot. How bad can it be if I become the most powerful person in the world?"

"The trap is you *think* you're becoming the most powerful person in the world."

They rode in silence to the hospital, where the road was lined with TV trucks. Police directed traffic and held back crowds so that ambulances for more pedestrian patients could get through. As Robbie and Marty waited in line, safely concealed behind tinted windows, Marty held up his phone and turned up the volume.

"News is breaking," he said.

Finn Tingleberry was on the set of *Hot Leads* where he sat with the host, Myra Quisling, who delivered the news. "FFS has learned that former President Dewey Fenwick is near death in a Washington hospital as he battles an aggressive strain of measles. Fenwick was expected to be coronated as his party's nominee for president just sixteen days from now but he is dropping out of the race. He has requested that noted New York businessman and philanthropist Robbie Crowe take his place atop the ticket."

Myra couldn't go on. She dabbed her eyes with a handkerchief. "Poor guy. Maybe the last president in this country to exemplify decency and honor. Finn Tingleberry, you visited Dewey Fenwick in the hospital today. What can you tell us?"

"It was quite emotional, as you can imagine," Finn said as he struggled to avoid a breakdown. "It's a very difficult time for his family and his supporters."

"Of course," Myra said. "Our prayers go out to the former First Lady, Janice Fenwick. How is she holding up?"

"She's devastated, of course," Finn said. "As we all are."

Myra shook her head. "Everyone but Platt, who must be relieved that this rugged fighter at the pinnacle of his political life is dropping out of the race."

"No doubt," Finn said. "Dewey Fenwick is eighty-seven, but until just a few days ago, he was a remarkably vigorous eighty-seven. From what I hear, he was playing tennis. Riding his bike. Running on the beach. To see him cruelly cut down because Roland Platt wouldn't fund measles research is an unconscionable sin. Some might even call it murder."

"So… Robbie Crowe," Myra mused. "Bit of a surprise there."

"An astute call, I believe. Based on what I've learned, it shows Dewey Fenwick's sound judgment right up to the end," Finn claimed. "Crowe is a revered name in American history. And Robbie has experience leading a vast enterprise. Those who have followed his career know him as a man of impressive vision—always looking out for the greater good. And from everything I've heard, he's a man much like Dewey Fenwick himself: humble, decent, someone who knows he's not perfect. He might even make a few mistakes from time to time—like all of us do—but he will give you every ounce of effort, twenty-four seven."

Robbie sank back into his seat. "That's fucking beautiful!" He looked at Marty. "I don't know why you're so down on these campaign people. They know exactly what they're doing."

Marty nodded. "That's what I'm afraid of."

The car moved up in line at the checkpoint, the driver flashed his credentials, and their car was directed to a VIP entrance at the back of the hospital. Security personnel hustled over to escort them to the elevator, and they were whisked to the top floor to find the brain trust at work.

Lady Janice was busily restoring Dewey's measles with lip pencil. Feeley was watching a rerun of *ER* on TV in search of more medical tips. Ned and Dinda were typing on their phones. Nobody bothered looking up when Robbie and Marty entered, until Robbie cleared his throat.

Lady Janice wheeled around. *Woah!* This is unexpected! *Robbie's actually kind of cute in a dorky kind of way...* It suddenly occurred to her that maybe she should think about another bid for First Lady. She could make history as the first First Lady for two presidents! A double-header!

She approached Robbie with her hands out as Marty peeled off to check his email.

"You must be Robbie," she said.

"That's what they tell me," Robbie said with a grin.

"Well, they tell me you're my longtime friend," she said, playfully. "And all I can say is: where have you been all my life?"

"How well do we know each other?" Robbie asked as he took her hands.

She gave her hair a Beachville twirl and licked her lower lip. "Not well enough."

Robbie chuckled uneasily and dropped her hands. *She's flirting with me? In front of her dying husband?* "It's an honor to meet you —" *What do you call a former First Lady?* "Your... ladyship."

She guffawed. "What do you think I am? A fuckin' boat?"

"No... I just —"

"Forget it," she said with a laugh as she slipped her arms around his waist. "We'll keep it simple. Call me Lady Janice."

"Right. Well... Lady Janice, I'm just sorry to meet you under these circumstances."

She shrugged and glanced over at Dewey, still sucking helplessly on a gurgling tube. "What are you gonna do, right?"

He carefully pulled her arms away from his waist. "I mean, to lose a spouse like this... I wouldn't wish it on anybody."

She stopped him. "Forget it," she said, gazing into his eyes. "We've all gotta go sometime." She chuckled. "He's just gotta go Tuesday."

Feeley, sensing a romantic rival, loudly pushed his chair back and walked over. "Lady Janice, darling. Maybe you should take it easy. You're overwrought."

She shoved him away. "You think I'm fat?"

"Overwrought, not overweight."

She pointed to a chair. "Take a timeout. I've got to talk to my old friend Robbie." As Feeley slunk away, she turned back to Robbie. "Truth is, I feel relieved. It's been six years of watching him slide toward the cliff. It's like, enough already, you know? I'm ready for some me-time." She turned to Robbie. "Me could include you."

Marty waltzed over, holding up his phone. "Platt just announced he's made a trade deal with Mexico. They get El Paso; we get Cancun and a resort town to be named later."

"Hope it's Cabo," Lady Janice purred. She batted her eyes at Robbie. "I *love* Cabo."

Ned joined the conversation. "I don't love the competition for news." He called over to Dinda. "Alert the media they can expect an update on Dewey in fifteen minutes. Then we'll go out and talk to them. Lady Janice, are you okay holding hands with Robbie as you go out the door?"

She hugged Robbie's arm. "I can do better than that."

Ned winced. "Remember: he's Dewey's friend, too."

She rolled her eyes. "They don't want me to have any fun," she pouted. Then she turned back to Ned. "Perhaps you haven't noticed, but Dewey couldn't care less. Look at him. Even now, he could give a shit what I do."

"He's brain dead," Ned said.

"Oh, give me a break," she spat. "If it wasn't that, it would be something else. He's always got an excuse."

She grabbed her purse and headed into the bathroom to refresh her makeup. "Maybe I should put on some measles, too. Just to freak everybody out."

Marty approached Robbie. "Looks like you found a friend."

"What's her deal?" Robbie asked. "She's practically humping my leg."

Ned joined in. "Grief does strange things to people."

"I don't think that's grief," Robbie replied.

Ned nodded. "What can I say? She *really* wants to go back to the White House. You know what they say about power. It's the greatest aphrodisiac."

"Dewey's lying ten feet away," Robbie said.

Ned shrugged. "If he weren't lying there, he'd be lying some place else. TV. Radio. A bar." He sighed. "She asked that he be cremated."

Robbie shrugged. "I get that."

"Today," Ned said.

"Oh." Robbie shook his head. "Isn't it customary to wait until the person's dead?"

"Pretty much."

Robbie whistled softly. "Tough crowd."

"Their marriage was… um, difficult." Ned handed Robbie a sheet of paper with talking points on them. "It will help if you two can find a way to work together. Better still if you can keep her on script."

19. Family Ties

Lady Janice hugged Robbie's arm a little too tightly as campaign leaders emerged from the hospital to a strobe of flashing lights from the gathering media mob. Robbie wanted to pry her hands away but didn't know how with such a large audience watching him.

Ned stepped in front of a marble statue of the hospital namesake, former Vice President Spiro T. Agnew, who had resigned from office in disgrace for accepting bribes and kickbacks. The statue showed him in happier times, smiling and waving, with a slot in his suit pocket for admirers to deposit dollar bills, possibly for charity.

"Good afternoon," Ned said somberly into an array of microphones. "I'm Ned Witherspoon, the former deputy chief of staff for President Dewey Fenwick. I'm sorry to report that the president's condition has deteriorated significantly over the past few hours. While he is resting comfortably, his prognosis is poor, and doctors tell us his chances of a full recovery are remote." He paused to catch his voice. "This is a very difficult time for all Americans, but especially for the Fenwick family, so we will keep our comments brief. The former First Lady, Janice Fenwick, would like to say a few words."

Lady Janice glanced at the notes Ned had given her, took a deep breath and proceeded to demonstrate she still possessed formidable skills as a performer. "Thank you, Ned," she said softly. She turned her chin up to face the bank of cameras and microphones. "I want to express my deep gratitude for the outpouring of support we have received from the people keeping vigil here at Agnew Memorial as well as millions of Americans across our land. Your thoughts and prayers are helping us through a very difficult period."

Lights flashed. Cameras clicked. "Speaking on behalf of Dewey, our son Hilton, who is with us in spirit from the clinic in Minnesota, and myself, I also want to thank our dear friends in the news media, who have been so supportive of Dewey and our family over the years."

A murmur of approval and a smattering of applause rose from the assembly before Lady Janice continued.

"Dewey began his latest campaign for president with one mission in mind: to bring kindness back to our government and rescue it from the clutches of Roland Platt, who has taken a wrecking ball to our great institutions." She paused for that to sink in.

"While Dewey's part in this campaign must now come to an end, we should all be comfortable knowing his dear friend, Robbie Crowe, has selflessly agreed to carry on in his stead. Dewey and Robbie share many common bonds, especially a belief that saving our democracy is the most important priority for our nation. I hope you will honor Dewey's commitment by doing all you can to support Robbie as our party's nominee."

A reporter shouted, "Why not Evita Manolo? She was second in the primaries."

Another yelled, "And what about Hiram Fry?"

Ned stepped in. "Let me remind you: voters selected Dewey Fenwick. As the presumptive nominee, it's important to respect his wishes." He made a fist with his left hand and pointed to four fingers, which he raised one at a time. "W…W…D…D. What Would Dewey Do? That's our guiding philosophy."

Several reporters repeated Ned's formulation on their own hands, then nodded in agreement. *Makes sense!*

As Lady Janice began to turn away, the press shouted out questions all at once, creating a cacophony where only the loudest and most insistent voices could be heard.

"Mrs. Fenwick! *MRS. FENWICK!*" one reporter yelled above the others. "Is there a chance your husband will appear at the convention next month? The betting line in Las Vegas is ten-to-one against."

Ned stepped in and glared at the reporter. "That's a *completely* inappropriate and deeply insensitive question." He shook his head in despair. "This is not about betting, or making money, or Vegas odds." Ned pointed indignantly to a window on the hospital's top floor. "There's a great man upstairs fighting for his life. After all he has given to our country, we owe him more respect than talking about making money on his survival."

The reporter ignored Ned's admonishment and shouted a follow-up. "Dr. Feeley! The over/under says Dewey will be dead by Thursday. What say you?"

Feeley's head moved to and fro as he pondered the question. "You might want to take the under."

A hubbub ensued among the crowd, prompting Ned to huddle briefly with Lady Janice, Robbie, Feeley and Marty. "What the fuck, Feeley? Do you ever think before you speak?" After a moment of animated discussion, Ned turned back and told the reporter, "There's simply no way of knowing if or when the former president might pass," he said. "It's in God's hands."

A reporter from the renegade Freedom News said, "We're told by staff here at the hospital that President Fenwick has been in a coma for three days. If that's true, how did he manage to endorse Robbie Crowe?"

Lady Janice fixed the heretic with a withering stare. "If you know my husband, you know he is a man of enormous will. Believe me, when he wants something done, he lets you know he wants it with every fiber of his being. We got the message loud and clear."

Farrah Fong, a reporter who had demonstrated unflagging loyalty to the party for years, stood near tears at the front of the throng. "Mrs. Fenwick!"

Lady Janice acknowledged her with a nod. "Yes, darling."

"Even if—God forbid—your husband dies, why couldn't he run again?" Farrah asked. "Many Americans have told us they would prefer a dead Dewey to a live Platt. Couldn't your husband still govern with the assistance of his aides?" There were nods of near universal agreement among the assembled media, but Lady Janice held up her hands, signaling a halt to such speculation.

"Thank you for suggesting that. I think your question shows how much faith we all have in Dewey's incredible strength, in this life and beyond," she said. "But resuming the presidency as a deceased person is not something Dewey wanted for his family or his team. Moving a casket across the country from a van to a plane to a hotel to the White House… Interviews conducted through a Ouija Board…" She dismissed the idea with a wave of her hand. "Logistically, it just wouldn't work."

Ned pushed to the fore, lest this messaging move any further off track. "That's why he made the decision to throw his support to his lifelong friend, Robbie Crowe." He turned to Robbie. "Robbie, would you care to say a few words?"

Robbie nodded somberly and stepped up to the microphones. "Yes, of course, Ned. Thank you," he said. "And, of course, my deepest thanks and appreciation to Lady Janice, and her son, Hilton. We pray that a thirteenth trip to rehab will prove lucky for Hilty."

Robbie looked at his script from Ned. "I am deeply humbled that my dear friend Dewey would select me to carry his great legacy forward. In a conversation at his bedside a short while ago, he showed me what strength is all about. His voice was so soft I could barely hear, but he mustered all his energy to say, 'I haven't got a complaint in the world, Robbie. I'm not afraid. But I do fear for our great nation under Roland Platt. Someday this fall when the campaign's up against it, and the breaks are beating the boys, ask 'em to go out there with all they've got and win just one for ol' Dewey.'" It suddenly occurred to Robbie that he had plagiarized the script for Ronald Reagan in *Knute Rockne, All American*. He looked over at Ned, who nodded toward the text. *Keep going!*

Robbie looked down and read the last line. "Now dab your eyes with a tissue."

Robbie, panicked, realized the last line was a stage direction not to be read. He looked back at Ned, who nodded toward the obedient reporters dutifully wiping away their tears for Dewey and democracy, too. Robbie fished in his pocket and found a monogrammed handkerchief to pat his dry eyes even drier.

Ned touched his shoulder and whispered in Robbie's ear. "My fault. I should have put that dab your eyes bit in parentheses." Then he leaned into the microphone. "Thank you all for coming."

Police formed a cordon to allow Janice, Feeley, and Robbie to reach a black SUV, where all of them climbed into the back seat, leaving Marty to find his own ride. As they pulled away from the hospital, Lady Janice gripped Feeley's hand on her right and reached out to Robbie's thigh with her left. Slowly, she moved her hand up his leg, then down, then up again, stroking it firmly. "You feeling better?" she asked.

Robbie shrugged. "I'm feeling fine."

Feeley took note. "Janice!" Feeley barked as he nodded toward Robbie. "Seriously?"

"Don't be a dope," she rebuked him. "I'm grieving."

"Dewey's not even dead yet," Feeley griped.

"I'm *practicing* for when he is, you blithering idiot. What do you not get?"

Feeley steamed, "How can you—"

Janice cut him off and leaned forward to the driver. "Enough is enough! Fredo? Stop the car!"

Fredo cocked his head. "You want... what?"

"I said, stop the fucking car."

"I'm sorry, Mrs. Fenwick. Stop where?" Fredo asked.

"I don't give a damn. Anywhere," she snapped. "Right here is fine."

Fredo pulled the car to the curb in front of a Quik-Tik, where a half dozen winos were hanging out near the door, stumbling around swigging from bottles in paper bags, and smoking weed.

"Get out!" Lady Janice commanded.

"Here?" Feeley cried. "How am I supposed to get home?"

"Not my problem," she said.

"But Jan—"

"Don't 'but' me! I think you've butted me enough for one week. Get out."

Feeley opened the door and stepped to the curb next to a bus stop, and Lady Janice turned to Robbie. She hugged his arm and looked into his eyes. "Where were we?"

Robbie shifted in his seat and carefully removed Janice's hand from his leg. "I don't know where we were, exactly, but I know where I'm going." He reached out to Fredo's headrest. "Take me to the hotel."

Lady Janice ignored the instruction. "What do you say we get a drink?"

"I'm meeting Evita."

Lady Janice recoiled and folded her arms across her chest. "That slut?" she scoffed. "What does she want?"

"I don't know. Guess I'll find out soon."

"My husband isn't even dead yet, and she's already making her move?" Lady Janice shook her head. "That's disgusting."

"You just said—"

"Never mind what I said," Lady Janice replied. "Look, if you can't be man enough to stand up to her, I'm not sure you can do the job as president. I've been around these people long enough to know they'll push you around at every opportunity if you let them."

"Well," Robbie said, "I have no intention of—"

"Did you hear what I just said? You have to stand up for yourself."

"I did, but—"

"Stop it." She patted his leg. "After you talk to Evita, you come see Lady Janice." She apprised his visage from one angle, then another. "You know, I could do something with that hair."

"What are you talking about?"

She wiggled her fingers over his eyes as she looked up at his 'do. "It's like the colors are all fighting each other, but nobody's winning. And the cut? It's from the nineties or something. Who still does that?"

Robbie bristled. "I have a guy who comes to my office."

"Next time, don't answer the door," she said. "Call me. I'll straighten you out, if Evita doesn't do it first."

20. Robbie the Rich

In the warm glow of his suite, Robbie sat in one corner of the sofa, gazing across the cushions at the lovely Evita Manolo, slouched languidly in the opposite corner, her high heels kicked off under the coffee table. Evita's political sympathies were proletarian, but Robbie was finding her tastes in wine decidedly bourgeoisie.

They were well into their second bottle of a vintage 2009 Château Margaux and nibbling their way through a charcuterie board of cheeses, Spanish almonds and olives, as the socialist diva offered her perspective on what it's like to be oppressed based on horrific experience.

"When I turned sixteen, my parents cut off my allowance. Just like that," she said, snapping her fingers. "There I was, tenth grade, having to go out and get a part-time job while I was going to school if I wanted to have any spending money."

Robbie studied her lovely brown eyes, her perfect red lipstick, and the plunge of her decolletage. He couldn't quite track what she was talking about, but he empathized immediately. "That's awful! What did you do?"

"I got at a job at a Quik-Tik convenience store? Like, right down the block?" she said. "It was the worst freaking job in the *world!* I had to keep an eye on the hot dogs twirling around on one of those hamster wheels, you know? If the wieners got too shrunken and wrinkly, I had to take them off and grind them up."

Robbie crossed his legs. "Ouch."

"Sometimes, a good one would fall on the floor, and the boss wouldn't let me throw it out, 'cause he was a greedy capitalist pig. So, I had to wash it off and put the weenie back in the thingy."

Robbie was drifting off in a daydream. "Ah. The weenie and the thingy. Tale as old as time."

"No kidding," Evita said. She swirled the wine in her glass and held it up against the light, admiring its legs almost much as Robbie was admiring hers. "And then there were those mustard and ketchup packets. Oh my *God!* People were always dropping them on the floor and stepping on them, like, every hour, and they squirted all over! Guess who had to clean them up?"

"Not you?" Robbie exclaimed.

Her eyes widened as she nodded vigorously. "Can you imagine?"

Robbie shook his head. "Unreal!" *Can we get down to business?*

She leaned over and patted his knee, underscoring that she wanted him to pay attention to this tale of woe, and focus on her eyes rather than her breasts. "I was just a kid, you know?" she said. "I'd have to clean up all this totally disgusting splooey."

"Splooey, huh. Is that a word?"

"Pretty sure," Evita said. "And I'd have to grab a mop, and get the bucket, and fill it with soapy water and put on these horrible rubber gloves. I could have used waders." She shook her head and ran a hand through her lustrous long dark hair. "That's the white male patriarchy for you."

"Was there a patriarchy in the store?"

"Oh yeah. It was basically just this guy named Wendell, but still... I took all that abuse for nothing! Just so I could have money to buy ripped jeans, and take all the Twinkies and Ho Hos I could steal. How was I supposed to feed a family of four?"

"I can't believe you had a family of four in the tenth grade."

"Well, no. I didn't. But some people do who make that kind of money. And theoretically, that could have been me. I mean, if I had children and stuff."

Robbie shook his head, despairing over something he was supposed to be sad about. What that was, he couldn't be sure. "It's not fair," he allowed.

"Not at all!" She reached over for the bottle and poured the last of the wine into his glass, then hers. She paused, baffled. "That's our second bottle, right?"

That was about as high as Robbie could count at that point. "Yeah."

She shook her head. "These bottles must be smaller than normal."

Robbie shrugged. "Gotta be."

"Corporate greed," she muttered. "They're trying to screw us."

Robbie brightened. *Finally, a good idea...*

"Do you have more?" she asked.

"I practically have a wine cellar up here." He got up slowly and shuffled over to the bar. *This chick's got a hollow leg.* He pulled out a bottle of red wine with a script on the label that he couldn't read in the dim light but thought it looked kind of French. He grabbed the corkscrew, returned to the sofa, sat down and poured wine into her glass as she sank deep into the pillows and looked out the window.

"Do you see the waxing gibbous?" she asked, stretching out her legs.

Robbie blushed. "Maybe if you moved your knee."

"What?" Evita said.

Robbie snapped out of his trance. "Sorry. I'm not sure what a waxing whatever is. I thought maybe it was slang."

She shrugged. "Gibbous. It's something about the moon—a phase or something." She drained her glass and set it on the table for him to fill again. "I think of going there sometimes to, you know, start a system from scratch, one that works for everyone. They call it a universal basic income. Let's spread it across the universe."

Robbie was feeling woozy. "That's a lot of territory. How would you pay for something like that?"

She patted his knee. "Guys like you have to give a bit more. 'Fair share,' and all that. Sometimes people can't work. They've got babies, or they're taking care of their parents, or they want to do drugs all day. Maybe they just don't feel like it."

There was something beguiling about her pitch, Robbie thought. She was unapologetically direct in saying she wanted to take his wealth and give it to others. Maybe, as he gazed at her through his red wine goggles, he deserved to have another slice taken off the top.

"This may sound hard to believe but there are times when even I don't feel like working," Robbie admitted. "But I push myself through. You don't get to where I am just by being born."

Evita looked dubious. "It didn't hurt."

Robbie grabbed a few almonds and tossed them into his mouth. "No, but still," he said. "The only thing I don't get is: suppose *nobody* wants to work, who's gonna do all those crummy jobs?"

Evita sat up excitedly. "Migrants! That's what they're for! There are lots of people out there who would be happy to do those shitty little jobs! They make, like, a dollar a day working in mines in East Donkeydoo or Outer Baloney. They'd love to come here and make money. So it's like I said in a speech: let 'em come! Open the borders and wave 'em in, like we did under Dewey Fenwick. *Bienvenido, muchachos!* Then crank up the minimum wage so they can feed their families. Make it fifty bucks an hour!

A hundred! I don't care! It's not my money!" She smiled and twirled her hair.

Robbie stretched an arm across the top of the sofa, his fingers nearly reaching hers, but not quite. How much of this gibberish was he supposed to endure? He'd be damned if he'd ask her to be his VP without conducting a full background check.

"How did your family make its money?" she asked. "I heard your ancestors were like, robber barons or something."

Robbie recounted the Homer Crowe story, sanitized for his protection. One of America's early industrialists in the go-go years of the early twentieth century, Robbie's great-grandfather Homer was celebrated for his ingenuity in creating power plants that illuminated America. He expanded Crowe Power into a global juggernaut and became a symbol of the nation's growing might. Homer began leveraging his fame into a weekly national radio show, where he expounded on various social topics that were far outside his expertise, but well within the range of popular crackpot opinion. Robbie's version for Evita left out the part about Homer's xenophobia, and focused instead on his presidential campaign of 1932, featuring a whistlestop tour across the nation, resulting in boisterous rallies, a trail of impregnated women, and electoral failure. America wasn't quite ready for his proposal to track subversive activity through surveillance, maintain files on every citizen, barge in on homes unannounced to evaluate their cleanliness, and demand healthy behaviors. But, based on Bennie's proposal, it was ready now.

"Homer was ahead of his time," Robbie said wistfully. "He would have loved America's Just Rewards."

Evita giggled. "Oh my God! *I* love it, too! Don't you?"

"I guess so," he conceded.

Robbie was feeling woozy from the wine, and decided he'd reached his limit, especially if he were to perform sexually at the level expected of a man of his not-yet-rising stature. He reached for the silver bowl of French chocolates sitting on the coffee table and offered it to her. She shook her head. "I'm in the mood for a gummy."

"I don't... Hmm." Robbie looked around for gummy candy. "I don't think I have any."

"No worries. I do," she said. She pulled her massive purse onto her lap, rummaged around, and pulled out a colorful bag of candy. "Try a couple. They're yummy."

Robbie took two green gummies from her palm, popped one in his mouth, and chewed. "Not very sweet," he said. "What flavor is this?"

Evita looked at the package. "Sod."

"Ah," Robbie replied, putting the second one on his tongue. "No wonder they remind me of playing baseball."

"I think of a farm," she said. "Sheep would like them." She laughed. "But then they'd get really stoned."

Robbie's eyes widened. "Stoned?"

Evita shrugged. "Well, yeah. These are cannabis. That's why I only gave you two."

Robbie panicked. *Shit!* He hadn't ingested pot for years. He had no idea how this would affect him.

"I thought you knew," Evita said. "You seem so hip—I mean, for your age and all."

Robbie nodded. "Well, yeah. I'm totally down with it." He wondered how long it would take for the THC to kick in. "I'm sure this will be fun. Although I probably wouldn't have had so much wine."

Something in the suite caught Evita's eye. "Oh my *God!*" she giggled.

"What?" Robbie asked.

"You've got a Magic 8-Ball!" She popped off the couch, retrieved the toy from the credenza and brought it back. She smiled and shook it up. "I totally *love* these things," she said. "I ask it questions all the time—especially about economics. I always get a good answer. That's how I found out capitalism was bad. The ball told me!"

Robbie licked his lips and reached for a bottle of water on the table. He took a gulp and leaned back on the sofa, feeling lightheaded. Then he looked over at Evita, who was becoming more beautiful by the minute. She blathered on a while as he stared, considering her brown eyes and the contours of her body and her waxing gibbous. "You know what you are?"

She laughed. "I'm afraid to ask."

"You are fucking *awesome.*"

She smiled sweetly. "Why… thank you."

"I mean it."

"So nice of you to say," she said.

He cocked his head. "You know what you should do?"

She laughed. "No. But I think you're going to tell me."

He pointed his little finger her way. "You should be my vice president."

She clapped her hands together. "You mean it?"

"Absolutely," he said. "You're awesome. Did I mention that?"

"About two seconds ago."

"Right, right," he said, pushing his hair back. "And you know what? I am awesome, too." He giggled. "Now, you take the two of us together? Double-fucking awesome." He reached over to high five Evita but missed her hand.

She said giddily, "Let's ask the eight ball!" She picked up the Magic 8-Ball and shook it lightly. "Should I be Robbie's running mate for president?" She turned it over and looked at the answer. "Check it out!"

YES, IN DUE TIME

"The time is now!" he declared.

Giddy, she reached over to fist bump Robbie, and connected on her first try. "I accept!"

Robbie, buzzed like he hadn't been in years, smiled through his crooked Picasso face. This called for a celebration! He looked for his wine glass, which took a moment to locate, since it was spinning around like it was on a turntable. At last, he secured it and raised it to his running mate. "To Crowe-Manolo. A winning fucking ticket if I ever heard one."

"Oh yeah!" Evita cheered.

They clinked glasses. Robbie sipped. "Crowe-Manolo… I love the way that sounds."

"Me, too," she cooed.

"Crrrr-owe-Man-ooo-looo," Robbie mumbled. "Crowe-o-Crowe-Man-oh-oh-oh-lo…".

He picked up the eight ball and silently asked whether Evita would go to bed with him.

NO, DEFINITELY NOT

That was the last thing he remembered.

21. Love and Loss

Robbie woke Tuesday morning on the sofa to find that Evita was gone, and that was not all. As he hobbled around the suite, he found the money clip that had been tucked away in his pants pocket was emptied of cash. Chocolates were strewn on the coffee table, but the silver bowl was gone. Both monogrammed robes from the closet had disappeared. His Piaget watch could not be found, but a scribbled note was.

Crowe/Manolo!!!
Rob from the rich (like you!) + give to the poor (like me!)
Let's do this!
—Evita

Well, Robbie reasoned, stealing from billionaires wasn't just a theory with Evita. It was an actionable strategy. She told him exactly what she wanted to do and she did it. Gotta give her credit for that, he mused. But, damn! All that time and money and his only souvenirs were a chocolate mess and a headache? And, oh yes… a running mate whom he had still not vetted to his satisfaction.

He walked to the windows and noted the White House and the rest of Washington were shrouded in a dull orange haze. The scene resembled a post-apocalyptic movie after aliens arrived and sucked the brains out of the populace. While that might help his election chances, he couldn't help wondering what was going on.

He found the TV remote control, which Evita thankfully did not steal, and flopped back on the sofa, idly flipping through channels for news as his mind drifted back to the night before. Even in his own orange fog, one thing had become very clear: he was more obsessed with the lovely Latina today than he was yesterday. All his life, he was beset by anxieties and doubts about his station in life, yet she had come from far more ordinary circumstances and possessed the most amazing confidence he had ever seen. And it had no relation to whether she was making any sense. Her apparent conviction behind anything she said could make the most stupid idea sound perfectly reasonable. And she had plenty of stupid ideas. Go ahead and knock someone out! Steal their stuff! It's social justice!

Robbie lost interest in the television and began to piece together his recollections of the evening. He recalled Evita's animation, her entrancing eyes, and her pendulous boobs casting a hypnotic spell. What he couldn't remember was closer to home: *who was he?*

The bedrock assumptions he held about his life were suddenly on shaky ground. Maybe family fortunes like his really were made on the backs of underpaid teenagers working the counter at Quik-Tiks slinging wrinkled weenies and swabbing splooey on the floor. Was that fair? Was it just? Not in the hellhole world that Evita described, cleaving neatly between the oppressed, like her, and the oppressors, like Wendell at Quik-Tik and him.

Who was he, after all, to command such wealth? What had he done to deserve it, other than to be born in the shade of a lush family tree? He hated to admit it, and never would to anyone outside the company, but he knew that the oft-told Homer Crowe story of innate genius and moral purity was a fantasy concocted by legendary PR wizard H.K. Blarney at the Crowe Power Company back in the 1920s. Yes, Homer was rightly credited for bringing light and power to lift lives throughout the world, but at what cost? Robbie knew enough of the backstory to feel a stinging sense of guilt over ill-gotten gains. There were governments in South America and the Middle East that Homer helped topple so he could grab their electricity contracts. There were labor strikes in the 1930s that left a sizable death toll from his company goons. A long trail of Homer's children and grandchildren were never acknowledged, mistresses were bought off for their silence, and politicians paid off by the score. Maybe there was something to Evita's claims about a white patriarchy.

If Robbie came clean, and confessed his family sins to Evita, would that be enough to get her to love him? And if he didn't confess, was that wrong? Robbie felt himself in a moral quandary. It wasn't until the he fumbled his way into the FFS Headline News channel that he was reminded what bridged the divide between him and Evita and everyone else in the party: Roland I. Platt, Menace to Society. Correspondent Taneesha McQueen reported that the orange haze enveloping half the country was coming from wildfires blazing in Quebec and Ontario, and that Platt had responded with a typically churlish screed. A scrolling text at the bottom said:

PLATT ORDERS WINDMILLS TO
BLOW SMOKE BACK TO CANADA

President Platt was on the North Lawn of the orange White House, alongside his press secretary who was wearing a gas mask. "I want all our country's windmills turned north," he declared. "If the wind ever blows again, they can blow all that shit back north of the border. They sure as hell aren't creating any reliable electricity. Maybe we can make them useful for once."

Platt went on to blame the raging wildfires on Canada's inept forest mismanagement. He suggested the fires were deliberately set to retaliate for his blockade of Nova Scotia over salmon tariffs.

McQueen reported, "A spokesperson for Robbie Crowe, Dewey Fenwick's hand-picked replacement as nominee for president, condemned the plan, saying it was an unnecessary provocation of our kindly northern neighbor, and threatened vital imports of hockey pucks as the nation heads toward autumn."

"'This is no way to treat our docile friends to the north,' Crowe said in a statement. 'This is one more reason why Dewey Fenwick and I have felt so strongly that we need to evict Platt from the White House this November.'"

I have? Robbie wondered. He'd never seen the statement attributed to him, but he liked the sound of it. Muscular. Certain. Commanding, even. His reverie was interrupted by the phone vibrating in his pocket. He pulled it out to see it was pain in the ass Marty, bugging him yet again.

"What?" Robbie spat.

"I'm downstairs," Marty said. "Are you coming?"

"Where?"

"Hospital. Don't you want to say goodbye to your dear friend, Dewey?"

Robbie yawned. "Damn. Is that today?"

"Yes."

"Fine. *Fine!*" Robbie said with disgust. True, it wasn't a great day for Dewey, but the demands on him were worse. He had to live through so much aggravation! "I'll be down in a second."

22. Know When to Fold 'Em

Dewey's inner circle gathered quietly in his hospital room to escort him out through the earthly portal—and to make sure he left on time. If they were going to jumpstart the Robbie Crowe bandwagon, they needed a charge from Dewey's dying battery, preferably by noon. Worth, Kristi, Ned, and Dinda stood around the bed looking at the prostrate former president, a diminished shell of the robust man he once was.

"I'm calling the doctor," Ned said impatiently as he looked up at the clock. "We need to get this show on the road."

Kristi looked incredulous. "You can't do that."

Ned looked her off. "Why not?"

"It's not your place, dearie!" Kristi glared at him and shook her head. "Aren't we missing somebody?"

Ned glanced around and shrugged. "Who?"

"Um… *Wifey-poo?*" Kristi suggested.

Ned rolled his eyes. "Lady Janice? Oh, please. How long are we supposed to wait? We said nine-thirty. It's nine-forty already."

Kristi was appalled. "Ten freakin' minutes, sir! I'm glad it's not me on this bed."

Ned felt a heavy pressure in the back of his neck. If they didn't get the Crowe campaign going, Platt might build a lead they couldn't overcome. "If she's not here in sixty seconds, I say we pull the plug."

"You'll do no such thing!" Kristi snapped.

"No?" Ned sputtered. "I just might trip over the cord."

"Stop it, Ned!" Kristi appealed for help. "Worth, darlin', can you—"

Worth nodded toward the corridor. "Forget it," he said out of the corner of his mouth. "Here comes Dewey's Beachville baby now."

Lady Janice and Dr. Feeley entered the suite looking haggard. "Morning," she muttered. She looked around at the somber faces. "Some day, huh?"

Kristi moved in to give Lady Janice a hug. "I'm so sorry it's come to this."

"Yeah, well." Lady Janice sighed. She nodded toward the bed. "How's he doin'?"

"Same." Kristi extended a hand and led her to the bedside. "He looks like he's at peace."

"Good," Lady Janice replied. "Maybe I'll finally get some, too." She stood at the bedrail, patted Dewey's hand, and closed her eyes. Feeley walked over to put his arm around her as Dr. Nabob entered the room. Lady Janice turned, crossed herself, and looked at the doctor. "I guess it's time."

Nabob nodded solemnly, moved around the bed, and turned off the ventilator. The lights on the machine blinked off, Dewey's breathing diminished, and the final leg on his journey began.

"That's it?" Lady Janice asked.

Nabob nodded.

"How long before he… you know," Lady Janice asked.

Nabob replied, "Expires? It could be minutes. It could be hours. You never know." He looked at the dark facial expressions in the group. "I'll leave you alone with him."

"Thank you doctor," Lady Janice said. She watched him leave then turned to the others as the door closed. "What the fuck are we supposed to do now?"

They stood for a moment in awkward silence, rocking on their feet, fidgeting with their hands, pulling out phones to check for emails, staring at the ceiling.

Dinda said, "I think we should honor him by remembering our best times with him."

Lady Janice nodded thoughtfully. "You know what my best times were with him?"

The others shot glances around the bed. *Is this something we want to hear?*

"Was clothing involved?" Worth asked.

"Sometimes," Lady Janice said. "We loved to play cards in the summer with our friends out at the beach house." She smiled at the memory. "We'd have the doors open to the porch. The breeze would come drifting off the ocean. We'd play some funky old rock and roll on the sound system. Drink beer. Washington seemed a million miles away."

Dinda smiled. "Nice."

Lady Janice blinked, as if an idea had suddenly come to her. "You know, I've got cards in my purse." She looked around. "Why not?"

Ned shrugged. "I'm up for a game." He looked around the bed. "Anyone else?"

There were nods from Kristi, Worth and Dinda.

"Franklin," Lady Janice said. "Get me my bag."

Feeley dutifully fetched her purse and handed it over. Lady Janice dug through her bag and found her cards. She unrolled the rubber band holding them together and began shuffling. "Dewey's favorite game at the beach house was Indian Poker," she said.

That shocked Dinda's sensibilities. "*Indian* poker? With all due respect, Mrs. Fenwick, I don't think we can say that," Dinda insisted. In a whisper, she added, "Dr. Nabob is Indian."

"Different kind of Indian, honey," Lady Janice said with a shrug. "We're talkin' feathers, not dots."

"Um… I don't think you can't say that, either," Dinda said.

"Say what?" Lady Janice snapped.

"What you just said."

"I can't say 'dots'? Why the hell not?" Lady Janice asked sharply.

"Again, with nothing but respect: Some people find it offensive," Dinda replied.

"Find what offensive?" Ned asked.

Dinda said, "The 'feathers/dots' thing. You can say it's Indigenous peoples of the Western Hemisphere, which refers to the feathers. Or you can say persons who originated from the subcontinent of India—you know, with the little dots on their forehead."

"Good Lord, Dinda," Ned said. "How do you even get out of bed in the morning worrying about shit like that?"

"How about this," Lady Janice offered. "We'll call the game by its other name, all right?"

"What's that?"

"Blind-man's bluff," she said.

Dinda, exasperated, said, "I'm sorry, but *no!* We can't say that, either."

"It's a fucking card game. What are we supposed to call it?" Lady Janice snapped. "How about 'a visually impaired person's deception'? You feel better, cupcake?"

"Not at all!" Dinda said. "What if a blind person came stumbling in and heard we're playing something that he knows is actually blind-man's bluff?"

"Great point," Ned said sarcastically. "And what if monkeys fly out of my butt when we're playing Monkey See, Monkey Do? Who gives a shit."

"I'm just sayin'." Dinda said. "We're the caring party. We should be more culturally aware."

"Whatever," Worth muttered. "Could somebody please deal?"

Lady Janice finished shuffling and placed the deck on Dewey's belly. "Who wants to cut?"

Kristi reached in. "I will." She took off half the deck, put the bottom half on the top, and tapped it with a knuckle.

Lady Janice picked up the cards. "Everyone know how to play?"

She explained that each player is dealt one card, which they hold face out on their forehead, so that every player sees it except themselves. Bets are made, with the highest card winning the round.

"We need chips," Ned said.

Feeley looked around the room. "These can be our chips." He pulled cotton balls from a drawer and distributed them, along with surgical masks, rubber gloves, Band-Aids, syringes, thermometers and facial tissue. Every item, he explained, was worth ten dollars, which would be paid to the winner via Venmo or PayPal.

Lady Janice passed a card to every player and demanded they all ante up. Ned held up a nine of clubs, Kristi a three of hearts, Worth a king of clubs, Feeley a two of hearts, Janice a queen of diamonds, and Dinda an ace of spades.

"Ned," Lady Janice said, "your bid."

Ned dropped a cotton ball onto Dewey's midsection. "Ten bucks," he said.

Kristi tossed in a couple of syringes. "See you and raise you," she said.

Worth added two surgical masks. "I'm in."

Feeley laid down three thermometers. "Raise you ten."

Dinda considered the bet, which was far more than she could afford. "Fold," she whimpered.

"Already?" Ned asked.

"You know I don't make any money," she said.

"Stay in," he commanded. He took a handful of cotton balls from his reserve and put them in Dinda's pile of surgical masks. "I'll stake you."

Dinda added three cotton balls to the pot.

Janice tossed in three Band-Aids. "Call."

Everyone pulled their cards down and looked at them. "An ace of spades!" Dinda yelped. "I can't believe it!"

"See?" Ned said. "I told you you'd get paid."

Around and around they went for four more hands before Lady Janice said, "This just doesn't feel right without beer. Can we get something to drink in here?"

"I don't think this hospital has a bar," Worth said.

"And Congress wants more money for health care?" Lady Janice snapped. "Put some booze in hospitals and the bill would sail through."

"Marty's on his way over with Robbie," Kristi said. "I'll text him to see if he can pick up a twelve-pack."

The play resumed for five more rounds, with much hilarity, despair, laughter, and accusations of cheating. By the time Marty arrived with twelve cans of Bud Light and a bag of Doritos, Dinda was up six cotton balls, five surgical masks, three Band-Aids, and seven thermometers. As Marty passed out cans of beer to the delight of the players, Dinda stole the deal and distributed cards.

Ned noticed a moment too late. "You are a fucking card shark," he accused her. "Where'd you learn that?"

"Summertime in northern Michigan," she said proudly.

"Really," Ned said. "You learn any other neat tricks up there?"

"Of course," she said with a sly smile. "I went to band camp."

Lady Janice offered Robbie a chance to play but he politely declined, preferring to search his email and text messages for a missive from Evita. Marty watched the card game from the armchair and considered how the passing of great leaders had changed. Sure, Cassius, Brutus and other Roman senators stabbed Julius Caesar on the Senate floor, but at least they cared. Nobody gave a shit about Dewey, whose not-quite-dead body served as a card table.

Marty watched Lady Janice gleefully win a round and sweep a mound of cotton balls off Dewey's chest and into her pile, and thought something was amiss. He rose from his chair and walked to the bedside. "Excuse me for interrupting," he said as he approached. "But he doesn't appear to be breathing."

"Who?" Lady Janice asked absently, as she dealt the next round of cards.

"Your husband," Marty said.

"Really?" Lady Janice asked idly as she slapped an ace of hearts on her forehead. "How can you tell?"

"His chest isn't moving at all," Marty said.

Feeley, holding a two of clubs over his eyebrows with his left hand, reached over with his right hand and felt Dewey's wrist. "By golly, you may have something there," Feeley said. "He's cold."

"How cold is he?" Worth asked, holding a three of hearts.

"Colder than the beer," he groused. "I think he's been gone a while."

"What the hell, man!" Ned said, dropping his card. "Would have been nice if somebody said something."

"Now that I think of it," Feeley said, "I might have heard a last gasp about three rounds ago."

"You didn't think to tell us, *doctor?*" Worth said heatedly.

"It wasn't exactly an emergency," Feeley explained indignantly. "I was collecting my chips. What was I supposed to do? Leave the pot just sitting there? You bastards would have taken it."

Lady Janice asked hotly, "Are we gonna play or aren't we?"

Dinda looked very sad as she put her card on Dewey's chest. "I think the game is over."

Lady Janice dropped her card and saw it was a king that would have easily won the pot. "Damn it, Dewey!" she cursed. "Your timing, as usual, is impeccable!"

"All right. Count your chips, everyone," Ned commanded. "We need to clean up this mess before a nurse pops in."

Marty hurriedly gathered empties and put them in a bag, while Ned plunked the Doritos in a sterile disposal container, and Lady Janice brushed orange crumbs off her husband. Feeley sauntered out of the room to alert the medical staff that a bed was opening up.

Nabob led a team of doctors and nurses into the room, where they checked for vital signs in his wrist, his neck, and his forehead. "He's gone." Nabob looked at his watch. "Eleven-fifty-nine."

Ned nodded, impressed. "One thing you could say about Dewey: He was always on time."

Lady Janice sighed and choked out a few tears of relief. Kristi moved in to hug her, as did Feeley, who hugged her from behind, creating a comforting human sandwich.

Worth sidled up to Robbie. "The king is dead," he whispered. "Long live the king."

Robbie took a deep breath. "What do you think?" he asked. "Am I the king of spades or king of clubs?"

"King of hearts, my friend." Worth clapped him on the back. "It's all about love."

23. Mourning Has Broken

DEWEY FENWICK DEAD AT 87
Forty-eighth President Won Most Popular Votes in History;
Party Turns to Robbie Crowe

By Tom Blankenship
Amalgamated Press
Washington Bureau Chief

WASHINGTON, DC, July 18—Dewey Horatio Fenwick, who rose from small town obscurity to become the most prolific vote generator in US history, died today following an acute attack of measles. He was surrounded by family and friends at Agnew Memorial Hospital, his campaign announced.

"Sadly, his effort to retake the White House is officially over," said Ned Witherspoon, Executive Director of the National Committee. "His family decided the rigors of a campaign would take too great a toll on him, especially in his deceased condition."

Fenwick's passing comes as a blow to the party, which was counting on another large turnout from dead people and family pets to unseat President Roland Platt and save democracy.

"Dewey Fenwick's incredible ability to connect with people who were unable to go to the polls was uncanny," said Dr. Heinrich Schlitz of the Democracy Institute. "He gave voice to those who surely would have supported him had they been alive."

In his previous run against Platt, Fenwick made history by winning 120 percent of the registered voters in Cobb County, Georgia, sweeping every cemetery in Pennsylvania, and garnering 100 percent of the absentee ballots in Minnesota hospice centers to clinch an upset victory.

The party's electoral hopes now rest on the well-tailored shoulders of Robbie Crowe, a billionaire descendant of the famed twentieth century industrialist Homer Crowe whose call for taxing other rich people is a centerpiece of his campaign.

"I shall not rest until we make this a fairer and more equitable nation for most of us," Crowe declared.

Out of respect for the dead, Ned waited nearly an hour following Dewey's demise to send out funeral invitations to five thousand top donors, plus a glittering roster of Hollywood celebrities, media personalities, pop musicians, union leaders, environmental activists, and social media influencers.

You're Invited!
President Dewey H. Fenwick
Funeral Gala

With Special Guest
Robbie Crowe

Sponsored by
The National Committee and Public Employees Local 299

Ticket Levels
$500. Cocktail Reception
$1,000. Cocktail Reception + Dewey Fenwick Tote Bag
$10,000. Dinner, Drinks, Dancing + Miniature Headstone
Paperweight
$25,000. All of the above + signed copy of *Just Plain Dewey*

One percent of all proceeds go to the
Make Measles Measly Foundation
End measles in our lifetime!

The invitation was accompanied by a letter from Ned.

Dear Friend of President Fenwick,

It was with a heavy heart that I witnessed the passing this morning of our beloved leader, former President Dewey Fenwick. I grieve with all Americans at the incalculable loss of a statesman, a gentleman, and a political colossus. While each of us mourns in our own way, I must tell you that the last thing President Fenwick would want is to give in to despair. He would count on each and every one of us to show our fighting spirit in the campaign to take back the White House from Roland Platt.

That is why I ask that you honor President Fenwick's memory by attending his funeral gala where we will celebrate the life of an essential man. If you cannot attend, please give what you can to our most urgent cause: supporting Robbie Crowe, President Fenwick's hand-picked successor, to lead our just and noble cause.

As President Fenwick said just last week: there is no greater threat to our democracy than our divisive president, who is the source of all anxiety in our nation today. With your help, Robbie Crowe will return our nation to civility, decency and honor by ousting the vile shithead Platt.

Sincerely yours,
Ned Witherspoon
Executive Director, the National Committee

The invitation landed in Lindsey Harper Crowe's email at her office in Miami before Marty had even left the hospital. She called him immediately.

"Funeral *gala?* Is this for real?" she asked incredulously. "I don't know whether to wear a black dress and a veil or a sequined gown."

"I'm thinking a little strapless number," Marty replied drily.

"For you or me?" Lindsey asked.

"You, obviously," Marty said. "I think mine's at the dry cleaner."

"I thought when a revered statesman dies," Lindsey said, "you were supposed to show your grief, not your dance steps."

Marty, walking through the hospital's crowded lobby, found a quiet place to sit on the ledge of a fountain. "Nobody's mourning around here," he said. "As soon as it became clear Dewey was no longer useful, he slipped into their memory hole. They didn't even notice he died."

"They're saying he died of measles," Lindsey said.

Marty cupped the phone to his mouth and spoke quietly. "They would have said he died of a hangnail if they could have hung it on Platt," he said. "Honesty is not their best policy."

"Robbie should fit right in."

There was silence on the line before Lindsey gasped. "Have you seen Platt's response to Dewey's death. I'm sending it to you now."

Marty pulled the phone away from his ear to view the bulletin.

PRESIDENT PLATT ORDERS FLAGS AT HALF-STAFF FOR 'HALF-ASSED PRESIDENT'

WASHINGTON, DC – President Roland I. Platt today ordered flags at all federal buildings to be flown at half-staff for the next thirty days to "reflect Dewey Fenwick's half-assed presidency."

"The guy was never up for the job, which should be obvious from his pathetic record," Platt declared. "Half-staff is appropriate since his half-baked staff never bothered to show up for work when he was supposedly running the show."

The president added that he gives "thanks to Almighty God for mercifully sparing the American people a second Fenwick administration, which would have been another complete disaster."

The president also announced that Friday would be a National Day of Mourning to grieve Dewey Fenwick's "terrible choice of a candidate to succeed him as his party's nominee: Robbie Crowe."

"There was no candidate easier to beat in this year's election than Dewey Fenwick, but his chosen successor is a close second," Platt said.

"Dead Dewey couldn't have made a worse choice. I knew Robbie Crowe when he was in short pants, hanging out in his father's office on Broad Street. Wee Widdle Wobbie doesn't know what he's up against."

"Wobbie?" Lindsey laughed. "I almost feel bad for him."

"No, you don't," Marty said.

"I said, 'almost,'" she reiterated. "I'm still working on it."

"I'm sure you'll have an opportunity to pity him in the next few weeks," Marty sighed. "When are you coming to DC?"

"I'm packing my dancing shoes as we speak," she said. "And my briefcase. I have an appointment tomorrow with Bennie Barbu, at his request. Not sure what it's about, but I suspect it has to do with Robbie."

"Text me when you get there and when you leave," Marty said.

"Why?"

"Bennie's a little scary." He paused. "More than a little, actually."

24. Harassed from the Past

Robbie dreamed he was Ebenezer Scrooge in *A Christmas Carol* and that Jacob Marley was rattling his chains, trying to wake him up. At last, he shook off his slumber and saw that his phone was ringing on the nightstand. He picked it up, blinked away his fog, and saw that the caller was BLOCKED.

He answered warily without identifying himself. "Hello?"

The voice on the other end said, "I thought we were friends."

Robbie sat up, suddenly on alert, his eyes darting from side to side in the darkness, as if the caller would show up any second. "Who's calling?"

"We go back forty years and you don't know my voice?" the man said. "I remember when you were just a little squirt playing under your father's desk at the Crowe Power Company in Lower Manhattan. Now you're running against me for president? Nobody would believe it."

"President Platt?" Robbie turned on the light, as if to see him.

"You're not as dumb as you sound in those statements your campaign puts out on your behalf," Platt said. "But you know, if you're going to be president someday—and I hate to burst your bubble, but I don't think that day is coming any time soon—you're going to have to take calls in the middle of the night. Crises come up every day, and you have to respond. You can't be like Drowsy Dewey, asleep at the wheel. Russia could have bombed his beach house and he wouldn't wake up."

Robbie struggled to find his voice. "I am wide awake, I assure you."

"Don't assure me," Platt replied. "Assure the American people. They're the ones you need to convince. And I don't know how you're going to do it. You've got a couple of big, big problems."

"Like what?"

"I hear you don't work past two p.m., much less two a.m.," Platt said. "This requires a hell of a lot more work than you're used to."

"I doubt that," Robbie said. "Nobody outworks me."

"The other problem is that I don't think you understand who you're getting in bed with," Platt claimed. "Those are some very bad people in your party, Robbie. Very bad. Some of the worst people in the world. That

Bennie Barbu, who runs your party? He hates our country. Do you know that? He's got some crazy grudge going back to Romania. I don't know what it is exactly, but the people who know him tell me he wants to bring communism to America. Why would you be a party to that? Your father would be mortified."

Robbie got out of bed and paced along the windows. "Communism is not going to happen on my watch," he insisted.

"That's what you don't get, Robbie. It won't be your watch," Platt said. "It will be Bennie Barbu's."

"Nobody's going to push me around," he claimed. "With all due respect, Mr. President, that includes you."

"Well, if you don't go along with them, all I can say is, 'watch out,'" Platt said. "You know how many times they tried to kill me? It turned out to be a lucky thing. Their assassination attempts made me a sympathetic person for the first time in my life. Probably got me elected. Maybe you won't be so lucky. Look at Dead Dewey. They tossed him out like yesterday's fish bones. If you don't do what they want, they'll throw you out, too."

Robbie gulped. "That's not going to happen," he said. "Everyone's been incredibly nice."

"Nice? You think those people are *nice?*" Platt laughed. "Now I know you're pulling my leg, or they're pulling yours. Do you know why Bennie Barbu pushed the party to nominate Decrepit Dewey for president? They were counting on him to die in office so Evita could take over. And you know what? I have it on good authority that's still their plan—except now it's you they expect to croak."

Robbie took a deep breath. "That's just a conspiracy theory."

"It is a theory, but it is also a conspiracy," Platt said. "You need to face the facts, Robbie. Do you have any idea why they plucked you out of your failing foundation to run for president?"

Robbie was tiring of Platt's heckling. "Mr. President, I don't think we should be having this conversation."

"No, I'm sure this makes you very uncomfortable," Platt said. "But out of respect for your father, who's not here to advise you, I'm going to tell you anyway. It's because they think you're the least deserving billionaire in America. You're a sheep in wolf's clothing, the nepo baby who has no business sitting on the kind of fortune you have. They'll pressure you to give away your money for the greater good and they'll just fork it over to their friends. It's the commie way. You watch. Taxpayers aren't the only ones they want to fleece. You're the first sheep up for shearing."

Robbie mulled that over. Would that be so terrible if he gave away a little of his dough? Maybe a few million here or there? Would such a noble gesture break through with Evita? Or would she want more?

"As Margaret Thatcher said," Platt continued, "'The problem with socialism is you eventually run out of other people's money.' You should think about that before you accept their nomination because they'll run out of your money first. But if you still want to run, don't say I didn't warn you. If you're alive in November, I'll just have to kick your ass myself."

Platt hung up, leaving Robbie holding a dead phone to his ear, peeking through the curtains to the White House, which suddenly looked more distant. He dropped the curtains, shuffled back to bed, and pulled the covers over his head.

25. A Star is Born Again

Robbie and Marty arrived at the screening room in campaign headquarters, where they found seats behind Evita, Ned, Dinda, Worth and Marius in the middle row. The house lights were brought down, the doors creaked open in the back of the theater, and Zuzanne "Zooz" de Chartres, the campaign's creative director, made her dramatic entrance. She came swooping down the aisle with flowing scarves trailing behind her and jangling jewels offering a percussive soundtrack.

"Hello, hello, *hellooo!*" Zooz said grandly as she walked in front of the screen. "Welcome to the show." She clasped her hands together and peered through her dark glasses. "Very pleased to see you all—especially the wonderful man who is the subject of our film today." She gestured toward Robbie and applauded him, prompting applause from the others.

"Before we raise the curtain, I want to remind you all of our assignment: Make Robbie Crowe's life of astonishing wealth and privilege relatable to our base, which now includes the millions of new voters our party imported from around the world. We think this film accomplished our mission by showing where Robbie started and where he is today are two very different places. He is a changed man. And it only took a week!"

All in the assembly laughed and applauded—except Robbie, who forced an uneasy grin.

"I should add that we had some unexpected good luck in producing our video," Zooz continued. "Robbie, your dear mother did us a huge favor. Believing you were destined for great things even before you were born, she thought it her duty to document your life for posterity. And so, as you know," she said, "she did what any one of us would do: she hired an Oscar-winning documentary film maker, the great Raoul Wallenberger, to chronicle your young life. Between that, AI, and an illuminating interview with Robbie, we were able to make a plausible story that shows Robbie's remarkable humanity. And who knows?" She laughed. "Some of it might even be true!" She looked at a booth in the back of the room. "So, without further ado...."

Upon the screen came the title.

RUN ROBBIE RUN
Lead Us to Victory!

A voiceover began. "Once in a generation, a special man may come along. Or maybe a woman. Or perhaps something in between. They are people who appear from the moment they are born that they cannot fail…"

The screen showed the sun rising over Lenox Hill Hospital on Manhattan's Upper East Side. Inside a private suite, a baby is born, with a peeping sun casting a halo-like glow around its head. The baby is held aloft by a doctor to the applause of the medical personnel in the room. Robbie's father, business tycoon Charles Crowe, passes out cigars to his cronies in the waiting room, and they light up in a cloud of smoke, as a nurse brings in a tray of glasses and a bottle of brandy.

"Lester Robinson 'Robbie' Crowe the Third was born to one of the most storied families in America," the voiceover continued. "His parents wanted a simple life for him, but that was not easy. The looming threat of kidnapping made it impossible to live a normal existence, with security required around the clock."

A ten-year-old Robbie, wearing a baseball uniform that said "Crowe Power" across the chest, hits a ground ball weakly up the middle, which dribbles into the outfield. Three security agents run with him as he sprints toward first base, and escort him all the way around the bases, roughly pushing aside any players on the opposing team who try to tag him out. Robbie raises his arms in triumph as he crosses home plate, and his teammates mob him.

"He developed a keen understanding of power dynamics and was immersed in America's foreign policy in his youth."

A shot of Robbie at thirteen wearing a sport coat and tie with his father at the White House was on screen. Robbie shakes hands with President Carter, who asks him, "What do you think of this hostage situation in Iran, Robbie?"

Robbie shrugs. "I think you should get off your ass and go get 'em," he says. He turns away, looks at the camera, and makes a circular motion at his temple with his index finger. "Duh," he says.

"Robbie discovered early that school was a rigged system, as he was thrust into a competitive struggle against students who sought unfair advantage by studying." The video showed eight students sitting around a table in an ornate library. All of them were studying except Robbie, who was face down in his book asleep.

"Robbie believed in the adage that 90 percent of success was simply showing up, and that he should be graded accordingly."

Robbie is seen in a prep school classroom where he and the other students from the library are taking a test. As the other students quickly mark up their test sheets, Robbie stares vacantly into space as he twirls a pencil. The teacher walks by, notices Robbie's cluelessness, smiles benignly, and replaces his test with one that is already filled out. Through the windows outside, workers can be seen building a power plant. The camera zooms in on a sign hung prominently on the chain-link fence:

A New Generation of Power
Courtesy of the Crowe Power Company

The narrator continued. "He never let exhaustion from his relentless fight to create a fairer world slow him down. He believed anyone should be able to achieve success. All we need is a little help now and then…"

Young Robbie, wearing his gown and mortarboard from college graduation, is shown into a large office at Crowe Power. He smiles broadly and shakes his father's hand. The camera pulls back to show a worker stenciling on the glass:

L. Robertson Crowe III
Vice President & General Manager
of
TBD

"Yet he also learned what it's like to fail, despite one's best efforts," the narrator says, "because the system is rigged against you," as a spinning cover of *The Wall Street Journal* comes to a stop.

**Robbie Crowe Fired by His Family
at Iconic Power Company**
Ex-wife calls Robbie's green dreams a "financial fiasco"
Harassment claims "bogus," Robbie says

The video shifted to Robbie being interviewed on camera. He sits comfortably in his suite at the Hay-Adams dressed casually in blue jeans and an open-collar shirt.

"I know how people feel when they say the system doesn't work—and it doesn't matter how hard you try," Robbie said. "Even for me, with one or two advantages in life, the dog-eat-dog nature of capitalism can grind you down. That's why I want to be president. To create a new and fairer system that affords everyone an equal chance at getting their just rewards."

A shoeshine man in front of Grand Central Terminal talks to an interviewer. "Sure, I'd vote for Robbie Crowe. From what people tell me around here, he's the kind of guy who'll give you the shirt off his back. It might have them fancy little cuffs and it's nothin' you'd wear out in public. Somebody might kick your ass. Know what I mean? But yeah. Robbie Crowe is all right."

A beautiful barista at a Commie Coffee on Wall Street writes "ROBBIE" on a cup. She smiles coyly when asked about him. "The amazing thing is that he acts just like a regular Joe. He comes in to get the coffee himself. He doesn't send an assistant like these big shots around here who think they're too big or too busy. And he doesn't just get coffee. He stops and chats 'cause he's interested in us as people, asking questions like, 'What time do you get off work?'"

Robbie is seen at a podium for a black-tie dinner. Behind him, the screen showed a photo of Robbie at his desk writing a check. The headline over the photo says:

Robbie Crowe

Human of the Year

At the podium, he is handed a trophy while the crowd rises to give him a standing ovation. Robbie holds the trophy aloft and declares. "My message to the ordinary people out there struggling to make their way: I see you! I hear you! And I get you! I've struggled too, kinda, which is why I want to create a better world!"

In the video, a contemplative Robbie is seen strolling the National Mall in Washington, DC, with the Jefferson Memorial in the distance. His voice played over the imagery.

"I envision an America where everyone—no matter what your race, creed, color, gender selection, criminal status, or sexual peccadillos—can claim their piece of the pie. If your intentions are pure, and you put the greater good above yourself, then you should not be penalized if the results fall short. Everyone should get credit for good intentions."

Robbie stopped and peered across the reflecting pool. "Whether you're a Rhodes scholar or a high school dropout, a CEO or a common thug... everyone deserves to be a winner," Robbie claimed. "If we feel good about ourselves and care more about our fellow humans, there will be no more greed, crime, poverty or injustice. We'll have the perfect world I've always dreamed of."

As Robbie turned and walked toward a hazy distance, the soundtrack concluded with an expletive-laden rap version of The Star-Spangled Banner by JizzyWizzy. "*Yo-o, say can you motherfuckers see...*"

The lights came on and the people glanced around at one another.

"Well," Zooz said, as she walked back to the front of the room. "What do we think?"

"Chills," Worth declared, flatly.

Ned nodded in agreement. "It hits our key message points, for sure."

Ned turned to Robbie, whose face scrunched as he processed what he saw. The namby-pamby BS about caring for other people seemed over the top. Especially since, truth be told, he really didn't give a shit. On the upside, his hair looked good and he appeared to have a nice tan. The big question for him: What did Evita think?

He leaned forward toward her seat. "Well?" he asked.

She spoke without looking at him as she freshened her lipstick. "I kinda hate to say this because you are who you are. But to be honest? I think you come off as kind of a douchebag."

Robbie fell back in his seat as if he'd been shot. "A... what?"

Evita winced, feeling herself out on a limb. "I don't know," she said. She looked at Ned. "What do you think?"

Ned shrugged. "Nothing wrong with that assessment. Douchebags are huge voting bloc," he said. "We could take Minnesota, for sure."

"Okay, so I'm just sayin'," Evita continued. "You have to do more than just blah-blah-blah. This pie-in-the-sky or whatever you call it isn't enough. I think to really sell Robbie Crowe to the people, you need to make a big statement."

"Like what?" Robbie asked.

"Distance yourself from all that wealth and privilege," she said, waving toward the now-dark screen. "You're a changed man. You've seen the error of your ways. Now show how you've seen the light and demonstrate it with something real." She turned to Marius. "Don't you agree?"

"Of course," he said. "But maybe it's not in the video. Maybe it's something he says from on the convention floor—you know, in his acceptance speech. Make a big, bold announcement of some kind. Could be very stirring."

Evita became more animated. "Yes! A declaration of independence! Say goodbye to all that wealth and privilege. Join the rest of us in the real world! The people will *love* you!"

Robbie swooned. Did she mean it?

26. The Emperor's New Clothes

For Robbie to become a man of the people, or at least a reasonable facsimile, Ned decided Robbie needed to look more like a regular guy. He asked Kristi to take Robbie over to a men's store near the White House for a makeover.

"I don't want him looking like a goober," Ned said. "But he needs to look like someone a goober could relate to."

As they arrived at the store, Robbie paused in the doorway. "You're kidding me. Joseph A. Bank is a clothing store?" He shook his head in wonder. "I always thought it was a bank."

"With shirts in the window?" Kristi asked, incredulously.

He shrugged. "How would I know?"

How would he know, indeed? Kristi was reminded once again that the bubble Robbie inhabited his entire life was also an airship he traveled around in. He rarely emerged to see how the other 99.99 percent lived.

After a quick perusal of the racks, Kristi picked out a pair of plain suits for Robbie to try on for the funeral and the convention, and a tuxedo for the gala. She led him to the back of the store, guided him into a fitting room, and handed him the suits.

"What am I supposed to do with these?" he asked.

"What do you think?" she asked.

Robbie squinted. "Try them on?"

"You are a quick study," she said sarcastically.

As she waited in a bay of mirrors, Kristi heard thumping against the plywood wall, a clanging of hangers, frustrated sighs, then nothing. "Are you okay in there?" she called.

"I guess so," he called back. "The pants are all fucked up."

"What's the matter?"

"They didn't finish them," he said. "The legs are a foot too long."

Kristi sighed. "They're supposed to be like that," she said. "They have to get your measurement before they hem them."

"This is an ordeal," he griped.

"Welcome to America, Mr. President," she said.

She heard more rustling of clothing, more banging against the walls, a rattling of the door, and a few muttered expletives. She looked at her watch and realized time was wasting. "Are you decent?" she called.

Robbie looked up at the space over the door frame. "Not exactly."

"Good," she said as she opened the door. She squeezed into the tight space and closed the door behind her.

"You can't come in here," Robbie said in an exasperated whisper. "What are people going to think?"

"I don't care what they think," she said. "It's not like I haven't seen the goods."

Robbie relaxed. "They're good goods, right?"

Kristi shrugged. "I might have to refresh my memory." She held up the black trousers. "Did you try these on?"

Robbie regarded them with disdain. "I did. Do they have to be so plain?" he asked. "They make me look Amish or something."

"If that's what it takes to win Pennsylvania, then I'm all for it. I'll drive you around Lancaster in a horse-and-buggy myself," she said. "But we've got to get you through Dewey's funeral and the convention first and I don't want people lookin' at you as some highfalutin billionaire—even if you are one."

Robbie put his right leg in and hopped on his right foot, then put his other foot through the left pantleg.

As he struggled to get his foot through the bottom, she said, "What in heaven's name are you doin'? The hokey pokey?"

"My foot's stuck," Robbie whined.

She bent over and pulled the pant leg up over his foot. "How long have you been dressing yourself?"

"About five years now," he said drily.

"That long," Kristi mused.

"I'm better at undressing," Robbie claimed.

"I'm not so sure about that either," she said, assessing the fit. "Turn around. I want to make sure you're not all draggedy-ass."

Robbie turned and wiggled his butt.

"Lookin' good, Mr. President," she said. "You've clearly got the background to run the country."

As he turned, Kristi said, "Maybe the foreground, too." She reached down to his crotch and cupped her hand under his balls. "How does this feel down here?"

As Little Robbie was roused from a nap, Big Robbie acknowledged, "Pretty damn good!"

She drove her hand slowly around the neighborhood, hugging every curve. "And this?"

"This store really is full service," Robbie said approvingly. "I may have to shop here more often."

Kristi pulled Robbie close to her and fell back, rattling the hanger against the door.

For the first time since his arrival in Washington, Robbie felt like he knew what he was doing. He brought his lips to hers and it was suddenly like old times, if only for a moment.

"Hmm," Kristi murmured with a frown.

"What's the matter?" Robbie asked.

"Little Robbie seems to have fallen asleep," she said, feeling around his shorts. "I must have lost my touch."

Robbie gulped. The truth was he just wasn't feeling it for Kristi in the same way since he met Evita. If anyone was going to be rifling through his new pants, it should be her.

"I'm just feeling stressed, you know?" Robbie claimed. "I, uh… I've got this speech hanging over my head."

Kristi sagged to the bench. "Right," she said, shaking her head.

"What?"

"You've fallen for her," Kristi suggested.

"I don't know what you're talking about," Robbie said.

She guffawed. "Oh yes, you do," she said. "You're head over heels for Ms. Manolo. I can see it on your face anytime she's around. You swoon! And I can tell you: it's not a good look. It's an even worse idea." She snapped her fingers. "You need to pull out of it."

Robbie slumped on the narrow bench next to Kristi. For all his interest in Kristi's significant charms, he appreciated even more her ability to cut through bullshit—maybe because she was such an artful bullshitter herself. "Why do you say that?"

She leaned over to look into his eyes to make sure she connected. "Because you need to keep your wits about you around these people," she said. "They're freakin' *ruthless*. All they're doin' is puttin' a glossy coat of paint on the same old commie crap. If you're not careful, you're going to step in it."

"I'm not a commie," Robbie protested.

"You think I don't know that?" Kristi scoffed. "But that doesn't matter. You're the guy they're counting on to sell Commie Lite to the public. And I've got to tell you: there's nothin' 'lite' about it. Push will come to shove, and you do not want to be the shovee."

Robbie absorbed that. "If it's so scary, why are you still here?" he asked.

She cocked an ear to hear whether anyone might be lurking outside their door before dropping her voice to a whisper. "I got a piece of the action," she admitted. "I'm going to get so rich I'll be cooking my food with burning cash, but they're going to own me. I gave up 51 percent of my business to the Hands Up Foundation to get my share."

Robbie looked at her incredulously. "If you needed money, why didn't you just ask me?"

She grasped his forearm. "I didn't just need money, honey bunny. I needed a livelihood," she said. "I had bills comin' out the wazoo and goin' in the wazoo at the same time. My entire wazoo was in gridlock! Linkin' in with this new program was a way to get things movin' again. But there's a downside for me and everyone else."

"What is it?" Robbie asked.

"Someone needs to keep the Barbus in check," she said. "They're taking this much further than they said at the beginning, and it's scary. They're in bed with some countries that do not have our best interests at heart. I don't know who can do anything about that except the president of the United States. And that's a maybe."

Robbie blew out his cheeks as he considered the implications. "I should just get out and leave it to Platt. He doesn't mind telling the world to go to hell."

"Are you kidding?" she said. "If Platt gets reelected, they'll go after him again. And this time, they won't miss."

"What do I do?"

She handed over the slacks. "Get your big boy pants hemmed. You'll need 'em."

27. So Long, Sports Fans

Ned drummed his fingers as he listened impatiently to his events team discuss plans for Dewey's funeral. All this academic discussion about the history of presidential funerals, and long-established protocols, and the roles of color guards and distinguished guests was missing the point. Worse, it was wasting precious time.

As a historian from the Smithsonian Institution droned on with an eye-bleeding soliloquy on what they served for lunch at FDR's funeral, Ned decided he could take it no longer. He shot out of his chair and clapped his hands.

"Thank you, Henrietta. Fascinating stuff there about those tea sandwiches," Ned said. "But in the interest of time, we're going to have to move on from watercress and dill."

Shaken by the rude interruption, Henrietta blinked her eyes rapidly and wobbled to a chair in the corner, where she plopped down and fanned herself. The nerve of that man! She hadn't even told them about Eleanor's special lemonade!

"All right. Here's the deal," Ned said. "Dewey's dead, and we're all sad as can be. Boo-hoo, wah-wah, and all that. But it's over. We need to send him packing to his next destination as quickly as possible so we can move on to Robbie."

With that guidance in mind, the team took less than three hours to complete the funeral plan. And the funeral four days later took less time than the planning session.

The cortege began in Dewey's hometown of Beachville, Maryland, where it retraced a typical workday schedule for the late president. Using special balloon tires, the hearse rolled through the sand where Dewey took his morning walks, paused along the boardwalk where he would sometimes stop and play pinball, and proceeded to the Dairy Queen drive-through, where the driver ordered a "Fenwick Fave"—a Peanut Buster Parfait.

From there, the casket was whisked by chopper to the Capitol in Washington, where it was hustled onto a caisson by US Marines. Ned declined Lady Janice's recommendation of a slow-moving twenty mule team to drag Dewey to his final destination and instead ordered quarter horses from Virginia to pull the caisson up Wisconsin Avenue at full gallop, racing past mourners lining the route, many of whom had not yet reached the curb. An honor guard then hustled the casket into the National Cathedral while legions of octogenarian senators and congressmen who had been asked to serve as honorary pallbearers were still climbing out of their cars. Even the twenty-one-gun salute was condensed, with twenty-one guns fired at once, creating a boom so loud that it sent some legislators diving back into their cars believing the nation was under attack.

Marty escorted Robbie to a room where the family gathered at the back of the church before slipping into the nave. He scanned the crowd to see if Lindsey had arrived but did not see her. He found a spot to stand behind the last pew next to a man studying the people filing in. The man leaned toward Marty and spoke quietly.

"Did you know him?"

"Who?" Marty asked.

"Dewey."

"No. Not really," he said. "I'm just a friend of the family."

"Me, too," the man said, offering a handshake. "Fred Gunderson. Jan's first husband."

"Jan? You mean Lady Janice?"

He scoffed. "She ain't no lady."

"No?"

"What kind of business do you think she was running in the back room of the salon?" he said. "It was all massages and happy endings. Just like Dewey's mom."

Marty was taken aback. If the guy was kidding, he didn't look like it. Lady Janice, a sex worker? Dewey's mother, too? "I didn't know Janice was married before Dewey," he said.

"Of course you didn't," he said bitterly. "I was written out of her script a long time ago. They spun a fairy tale that Dewey was her one and only love. It's a joke, man."

Marty absorbed the news. "Well, if you don't mind my asking: why are you here?"

Fred chortled. "I want to make sure that prick is dead," he said.

Marty nodded. "I was in the room when he passed. I can assure you: he's not walking out of here."

Fred smiled. "Then I will." He turned on his heel and vanished.

A moment later, Lady Janice appeared in the doorway, clutching Robbie's arm as she proceeded down the center aisle, smiling, nodding, winking, and waving to people in the crowd like a drunken bride rather than a grieving widow. In another break from tradition, she eschewed the traditional black suit for a bright red dress with a black print, a slit up the side, and a plunging decolletage.

"What is she thinking? *Real White Housewives of Washington, DC?"*

Marty turned to see Lindsey had arrived. She pecked his cheek.

"Glad you made it," he said. "You want to sit down?"

"Somewhere in the back, in case I have to run out and throw up," she said.

As they took their seats, a cover band in the choir loft played one of Dewey's favorite Everly Brothers songs from 1957, *Bye Bye Love*. A moment later, the casket was wheeled down the aisle followed by the contingent of aged and infirm honorary pallbearers—colleagues from Dewey's senate days, former cabinet secretaries, and the former heads of state from the UK and France. Some carried canes, others pushed walkers, while the ever-playful wheelchair-bound Senator Slim Winston gleefully popped a wheelie. Roland Platt, however, declined to attend because of a long-standing conflict: he was hosting a rodeo around the Washington Monument.

The Most Reverend Theodore Fankelfinger offered an opening prayer asking the Lord to welcome his dearly departed servant Dewey Fenwick to that great Dairy Queen in the sky, where he could be drizzled in caramel and chocolate for all eternity.

"We mourn not for our departed brother, Dewey," the rev said. "Rather, we come to celebrate him. For he led a life that was good and full of remarkable achievement based on his unwavering faith. How else could one explain his lifetime of good fortune? He always believed in his Lord, in the good sense of the people, in the one true love of his life, Lady Janice, and in himself."

Rev. Fankelfinger looked out at the crowd and knew he struck a chord, for there were many heads nodding in agreement. "And, dadgum—as he used to say—he was proven right. For he was reelected five times and ultimately elevated to the highest office in the land. As he often told me, 'You can't fool all the people all the time, but you don't have to if you're in the Senate. Once every six years is plenty.'"

Seven-term Senator Tubby Munch of Kentucky, one of Dewey's old-time drinking buddies, hobbled to the podium to offer his perspective.

"Some people see things as they are and ask why. Dewey would see things as they could be and say, 'I'll have another,'" Tubby said to gales of knowing laughter. "The Good Lord broke the mold when he made Dewey. I imagine he said, 'I don't think the world could survive two of these rascals. There'd be too much dang fun down there!'"

Next up: Iowa Congressman Dean Deefendorf, another crony. "Dewey was a great—and I mean truly, truly great—politician because he loved people," Deefendorf said. "He could strike up a conversation with anybody. It could be a doorman, a barista, a cocktail waitress. He wanted to know all about them. 'Are you going to school? Do you need a little cash? What would you think about an internship? You could sharpen pencils in my office.' He was always there to help."

An agitated Lady Janice, stung by the implication that her husband was a predator, dug her fingernails into Ned's arm, which prompted a yelp that made others turn their way. Ned carefully removed Lady Janice's hand, stood, and walked to the pulpit to deliver his remarks.

"Four score and seven years ago, four fathers brought forth a new baby, conceived in liberties, and dedicated to a proposition," Ned declared. "It wasn't clear which one of the four fathers who showed up for his baptism was his real dad, but as far as Dewey was concerned, they were all his pop. As he was growing up, his house was a lively place, and he got to know men from all walks of life who came through town spinning exotic tales of distant lands like Ohio and Kentucky. They'd leave him with a pat on the head, a new understanding about traveling salesmen, and dimes and nickels to buy ice cream cones and comic books. He learned early on that discretion could be profitable.

"I got to know President Fenwick early in his career when we worked together on legislation to extend rural electrification. He knew better than to talk about our work until we had something to show for it. As he told me many times: 'We don't need to show folks how the sausage is made. When things are firmed up, we just give 'em the sausage.'"

There were knowing nods from legislators in the crowd. "In the decades that followed, I was privileged to see the character of Dewey Fenwick up close and personal. His selflessness. His generosity. His principled leadership. It was often said of Dewey that once you bought him, he stayed bought." A murmur of approval rumbled through the crowd. "His opponents tried to use that against him, as if it were a sign of corruption. But his many allies knew it reflected his integrity—an unflinching sense of duty and obligation to those who paid the freight. He never forgot a favor. He felt it was his responsibility to return each and every one of them. As he once told me, 'Ned, my boy, when I'm gone, I want you to remind people I was a man of conviction but I was never convicted.'" Ned looked up. "He was merely charged—and all eighty-four counts were dropped."

Ned removed a handkerchief from his pocket and wiped his eyes, then composed himself for his conclusion. "If there is any solace in Dewey's untimely passing," he said, "it is that his legacy lives on in his dear friend and soulmate, Robbie Crowe. They came from two very different walks of life, yet each arrived in the same place: possessing the firm belief that a better world was possible with some well-placed moolah."

Robbie grabbed a folder with the speech Ned had written for him and walked slowly to the podium in his spanking new Jos. A. Bank suit, which tugged at his nether regions in a deeply distracting way. *How do people get around in these things?* Should he pull the old anchorman trick and drop his drawers once he was behind the podium?

Robbie cleared his throat and eyed the gathering of people from around the world, many of whom had household names. He had addressed large audiences of distinguished people many times. But to do so as the presumptive nominee for president felt unreal, almost as hard to believe as the speech he was about to read.

"I have been honored during my life to lead a great company and to chair one our world's most distinguished foundations. Yet I was never so moved as I was a week ago when I received a call from my dear friend, Dewey Fenwick, a man I long regarded as my brother from another mother. And, as we have just heard," he said as an aside, "his was quite a mother indeed." Knowing chuckles rippled through the audience.

"'Rob-O,' as he called me, 'I need to ask you a favor. I'm afraid I'm not going to make it to the finish line for my journey back to the White House. These dang measles have gotten the best of me. I don't mind dying, amigo, I really don't. I've lived a good long life, and I know none of us get out of this thing alive. But the one regret I have is we have some unfinished business as a nation. We have to remove Roland Platt from the White House before he causes any more damage. And we have to restore things the way they used to be, when honor and dignity were the hallmarks of our presidency. But I can't see it through. And that's why I'm calling, buddy. Can you do it for me? Can you finish this business for ol' Dewball?'"

Apparently, serving up this corn soufflé worked, for Robbie could hear sniffles and blowing noses in the audience. He continued, "Naturally, I accepted his challenge. How could I not? Nobody I've ever known was Dewey's equal in putting the touch on people. It could be for a vote. It could be for a donation. It could be for joining him at the Round Robin Bar at the Willard for a little tete-a-tete over a glass of beer or two or three. Nobody said no to Dewey. You just didn't want to let him down.

"So as we go forward from this place today, let us pledge to pick up his baton and take his last race across the finish line. We can surely get there if we are fueled by Dewey's indomitable spirit, warmed by his love for humanity, and inspired by his unwavering commitment to liberty and justice for all. To our beloved brother, Dewey, we say, 'So long, sports fan!'"

Trumpets sounded from the balcony.

Reverend Fankelfinger slowly walked to the podium and concluded the service with an announcement. "The family would like to invite you all to a dinner at the memorial gala tonight at the convention center. I'm told that there are plenty of good tickets still available."

As the mourners spilled out onto the streets, with the organist from the Beachville Roller Rink playing another Dewey favorite, *See You Later, Alligator*, some of the older legislators were still being excavated from their cars. Ned encountered an exhausted Senator Mary Beth Binghamton, breathlessly struggling to get out of a back seat of a Tesla with the assistance of two aides.

Ned leaned in and said, "Senator, I'm afraid it's over."

"You're telling me," she huffed.

"I mean the service."

She nodded, exhaled, and fell back into her seat. "Oh, thank God!" She looked at Ned. "You saved my life."

Part Two

Next!

28. Eureka Moment

Platt wasted no time following Dewey's funeral to take back the spotlight, issuing a news release that, as always, returned the focus on him, rallied his troops, and infuriated his opposition. The president announced that oil was discovered by construction workers building the ballroom for the bomb shelter beneath the East Wing.

President Platt Orders Drilling Rigs
To White House

WASHINGTON, DC —President Roland I. Platt said today he would commence drilling on White House grounds following the discovery of oil underneath the East Wing, and that he had enlisted Mammoth Petroleum to begin immediately.

"We will leave no stone unturned in our quest for global oil supremacy, and that includes all public lands in Washington," the president declared on his social media platform, *Plattitudes*.

"Depending on the size of the reservoir, which Mammoth scientists say is very, very big, we may consider building a platform in the Reflecting Pool."

Pushback from the Crowe campaign was fast and furious.

"We are not going to desecrate our sacred capital with drilling rigs and gas flares," Robbie Crowe declared in a statement. "A dirty, smelly, and oily business has no place in Washington, DC, other than the dirty, smelly and oily business of lobbying, which is quite enough."

The green room at the Walter E. Washington Convention Center was abuzz with Platt's latest bombshell as dignitaries gathered for a couple of pre-game belts for the gala. Robbie stood off awkwardly to the side, holding a flute of champagne as Kristi attempted to work his bow tie.

"You have your work cut out for you if you think you're going to take attention away from Roland Platt," she said. "He is to news what gas is to flames. An accelerant."

"People will get tired of it eventually," Robbie said wishfully.

"I don't know," Kristi said. "Even my friends who hate him can't wait to get up in the morning and see the latest from Platt. Outrage is what gets them going. If you beat him, they're going to be very disappointed. I don't know what they'll do all day."

Ned looked out over the gathering and called out. "Two minutes until the doors open."

Robbie sucked in his breath. "How long do I have to stand in the receiving line?"

"Until I say you're done," Kristi replied.

"How long is that?"

"After they all go through," she said. "Two thousand guests, all paying good money to kiss the ring."

"You mean my ass," Robbie corrected her.

She laughed. "You've got that exactly backward, Mr. Candidate. These are your donors. It's you who needs to pucker up."

Robbie sighed. "This sounds way too much like work."

"You want to be in politics? This is what you do. Humiliate yourself in ways you could never imagine." She patted his chest. "It will be good for you."

The always-polished Worth approached, with one hand in his pocket and the other holding a tumbler of bourbon. He apprised Robbie up and down. "I didn't know Goodwill sold tuxedoes."

Robbie muttered, "I got two for the price of one."

"Did you look at it before you bought it?" Worth asked.

"I was distracted," Robbie replied.

Worth arched an eyebrow and cast a glance at Kristi. "I bet."

The three of them filed into the lobby, where a string quartet serenaded the guests with Vivaldi's *Four Seasons: Summer*. A marine stood at attention at the front of the line with a crier at his side. They were followed in order by Ned, Kristi, Robbie, and Worth.

The crier announced, "Mr. and Mrs. Ingmar Swenson."

Kristi smiled as she greeted the Swensons and introduced them to Robbie. "Robbie, Mr. Swenson is the founder of Jiffy Gender, which I'm sure you've heard of."

"I think so," Robbie said.

"Quick-change gender centers," Ingmar said proudly. "Going gangbusters on the coasts. But we're a bit worried Platt's FDA is going to shut us down."

"I've told Mr. Swenson that you will bring more enlightened thinking to the White House," Kristi noted.

Robbie nodded vacantly. *Was this supposed to be a good thing?*

"Jiffy Gender lets you be whatever you want to be in thirty minutes or less," Ingmar boasted. "It's all about personal happiness."

"I see," Robbie said. "And what about… I don't know what you call 'em. Parts? Can you get those back if you don't like the way things turned out?"

Ingmar chuckled and leaned in. "You want your dick back? Sure. We keep your junk on ice in case you change your mind. You might even sell it to someone going the other way," he said. "And here's the guarantee. You don't like the new you? We switch your pieces around faster than you can say 'Mr. Potato Head.'"

Robbie assured him he would give the business a fair hearing.

As the Swensons moved on, Kristi leaned close. "You'll have to give it more than a hearing. Bennie has signed them up as a proud sponsor of America's Just Rewards. They've got a booth at the convention."

Robbie took a deep breath as the crier called the next guests. "General Jackson McClellan and Tiffany Childs."

"So good to see you again, General," Kristi cooed. "And nice to meet you Ms. Childs. I understand you were Miss Armed Forces last year."

Tiffany looked at her in happy surprise. "How did you know?"

"Sash kind of gives it away," Kristi said with a wink..

"Ah. Right." Tiffany looked down at her chest. *It was kind of in big letters…*

Kristi continued. "May I present Mr. Robbie Crowe, our next president of the United States?"

"Sure could!" the general enthused, offering a bone-crushing handshake.

"The general is an adviser to Smithereens, the missile maker?" Kristi advised.

"That's right, Dr. Kramer," General McClellan said. "I just want you to know, Mr. Crowe, I am here to serve you in any way I can. Have you thought about a country you want to obliterate?"

Robbie's jaw went slack. *Obliterate? Just for the hell of it?* "Not yet."

The general leaned in. "Think about an island nation—some expendable little shithole like Barboonia. We can fuckin' vaporize it in seconds. That would put the bad guys on notice, eh?" He laughed, and gently rapped Robbie's chest with the back of his hand. "They say war is not the answer? Don't believe it, buddy. A war is a piece..." He leaned close and winked. "...Of the action."

As the general moved on, Robbie leaned into Kristi. "Wow. Anything for a buck."

Kristi spoke out of the side of her mouth, "Honestly, I don't think he cares about the money. He just likes vaporizing things."

For the next half hour, Robbie was introduced to dozens of luminaries eager for facetime with the man who could change their lives. Pete Preston, chair of Vaxeenz.com, advised Robbie that an unusual disease was scheduled to hit America from Central Africa in December that, with any luck, would "make COVID look like the sniffles." Fortunately, his company had a vaccine ready to go, along with a plan to lockdown the country.

Daisy Chaney, CEO of BlowCo, the windmill maker, told Robbie her company had devised a technology to keep wind turbines twirling on windless days so that the public would be duped into thinking they were always working. And retired Senator Winthrop Vexley of Massachusetts was humping Playpens 4 Men, which offered bouncy houses as an alternative to prison for violent felons.

Robbie wearily looked down the line of supplicants. Was it possible it was growing rather than shrinking? Ned creeped up behind him and whispered. "How's it going?"

"Everyone's got their hand out," Robbie said, wearily.

"Give it another five minutes," Ned said. "You're doing great. I'm getting a shit pile of pledges at the other end." He clapped Robbie on the shoulder and grinned. "We're gonna need a bigger bag."

Ned looked over the line and saw the aged Senator Hiram Fry approaching with his dumpy wife, Hilda. A perennial presidential candidate from Ohio who finished third in the primaries after Dewey and Evita, Hiram was the last person Ned wanted to see. "Uh-oh," he muttered.

"Senator and Mrs. Hiram Fry," the announcer called.

Robbie whispered over his shoulder to Ned. "Is he okay with me as the nominee?"

Hearing no response, Robbie turned to find Ned had disappeared. Robbie turned back to find Hiram Fry staring him in the face.

"How do you do, Mr. Crowe," Hiram said. "May I introduce my bride? This is Hilda."

Bride? Robbie thought: he couldn't have hitched up this cow recently. Hilda, wearing a fat string of pearls and a hardened hairdo that looked like it could withstand a Smithereens missile attack, extended a stiff hand. "How do you do."

Hiram continued, "Forgive me for saying this, sir, but I believe your coronation is a bit premature."

Robbie took a deep breath. "How so?"

"You don't have any votes," Hiram said. "I won Iowa and South Carolina. And you've won—what? A seat on the student council about forty years ao? Or maybe you were voted king of the prom? I don't know how we can holler about Platt destroying our democracy when our candidates keep getting selected through backroom deals."

Robbie retreated quickly. "Well, you know… I didn't ask for this."

"I'm sure you didn't," Fry said. "They needed a pigeon. And that's what they got." He nodded toward the end of the line. "I want to see you in my office first thing Monday—just you and me. Tell your bagman Ned down there he can sit this one out—if you can find him."

Robbie deflected. "I'm sorry, senator. I'll have to check my schedule."

"Make time, Mr. Crowe. Or I'll create a stink on the floor in Chicago that will make the stockyards smell like Chanel No. 5."

Hiram trudged off with Hilda in tow. Robbie shook his head, exasperated. *Why was the nomination his fault?* He was just minding his own business when out of the blue he got a call to be president. *Tuh!* He felt tired of the job already and he didn't even have it yet. He could probably do this gig in short bursts—maybe twenty minutes here and there—but hours on end like this was ridiculous. He needed an escape. Maybe he could get a little down time with one of these lefty-loosey chicks that hung out at campaign headquarters. Or maybe even Evita. She must realize they still had some unfinished business.

Alas, the line of supplicants, eager to touch the hem of his discount garment, stretched out the door.

29. Couching Answers

It was near midnight when Ned stopped by the office for his laptop. As he neared the elevator, he poked his head into Dinda's cubicle and found her toiling in the darkness, her face illuminated by a computer screen.

Piles of papers, empty cups and pizza boxes, a bag stuffed with trash from Jimmy John's, and a pillow and a sweatshirt on the floor made her workstation a dump. All it lacked were seagulls picking through the steamy debris and a bulldozer plowing the mess into a pit.

"Missed you at the gala," he said.

She rolled her shoulders and winced. "I know," she said. "Way too much to do."

"Any animals living in there?" Ned asked.

"Think I saw a mouse," she conceded.

"Probably won't kill you," he said. "But you do need to get out of here."

Dinda kept her fingers on the keyboard as she glanced over her shoulder. "I can't," she said, with a grimace. "I've got to finish this candidate questionnaire for Robbie from the *Times*. And I'm stuck."

He stepped in and looked over her shoulder. "What's the question?"

"It says, 'President Platt has stigmatized minor-attracted persons as 'pedophiles.' Do you agree with this dehumanizing slur? Or do you believe that we should acknowledge they are people, too, that they are an oppressed sexual minority, and we should use a term for them that is welcoming and inclusive?'" She looked up. "I don't know how to answer that. Are we pro-pedo?"

Ned nodded grudgingly. "Yeah. Kinda."

She looked at him incredulously. "Why?"

"Could make the difference in a swing state," he said.

"Are we that desperate?"

"It's not a matter of desperation," Ned replied. "It's a matter of principle."

"What principle is that?"

"The principle that we win," Ned said. "When in doubt, always remember: we're the empathy party. We care about everybody, no matter how perverted they may be. As long as they can fill out an absentee ballot, we're good." He checked his watch. "Look, Dinda. It's late. I'm exhausted. And you can't be here all night. You can either work on your answers at home or finish them up in the morning."

Dinda reluctantly agreed and stuffed a couple files in her backpack. Ned waited for her at the elevator, and they walked out together to the deserted street.

"Goodnight," she said as she turned away.

"Wait a minute," Ned said. "You're not walking home."

"I'm just going to Dupont Circle," she said with a shrug.

"That's—what—eight blocks?"

"I need the air."

"You need a ride," Ned said.

A large black Mercedes pulled up on F Street and Dinda climbed into the cushy back seat, followed by Ned. She told the driver her address, fastened her seat belt, and laid her head back. "I could fall asleep right here," she said softly, as the car pulled away from the curb.

"Knock yourself out," Ned said, scrolling through his messages.

Dinda folded her hands over her stomach and let the gentle rocking of the car and the quiet hum of the engine lull her to sleep. Before long, she was dreaming that the convention was beginning in Chicago, but five thousand delegates could not get into the United Center because she forgot the key. Thus began a desperate search through her backpack, where all she could find were recharging cords, a hairbrush, and scrunchies.

She was jolted awake when the car came to a stop and the door opened. Groggy, she looked around to see Ned getting out of the car.

She mumbled, "What's going on?"

Ned leaned in. "I couldn't wake you. So, I had the driver drop me off first."

Dinda took a deep breath and looked up at Ned's stately three-story townhouse. "Is this your house?"

Ned nodded. "Bennie lent me one of his homes through November."

It looked like a dream castle. "Can I sleep on your couch?"

"Don't you want to go home?" he asked.

"Not if I don't have to," she said. "I... I... oh it's a long story. But I sublet space in a studio apartment. My roommate's boyfriend sleeps over almost every night and it's fucking gross. They wake up in the middle of the night and screw."

"Ah," Ned said, briefly reminiscing. "Those were the days."

"You can have 'em. I would have slept at the office if you'd let me."

He reached out a hand. "C'mon."

He helped her out of the car, and she followed him into the brownstone. "Pick any room you like," he said. "They're all empty but one."

She stumbled into the living room and flopped face down on the sofa.

"I meant upstairs," Ned said, pointing to the stairway.

Dinda didn't move. Ned walked over to a liquor cabinet, poured himself a finger of scotch, and downed it. He thought of his own early days in politics crashing on couches. Like her, he intended to change the world. Also like her, he didn't move the needle a bit. He poured two more fingers and sauntered over to an easy chair next to the sofa.

Dinda slowly rolled over on her back and looked up at the ceiling. "Where are we, Ned?"

"Georgetown."

"I mean the campaign. Where's this going?"

"Pennsylvania Avenue, *inshallah*."

She sighed. "Is that all there is? Just get to the White House? Everything else will take care of itself?" She shook her head. "I'd like to think we're trying to win for a higher purpose."

"We are," he said. "It's called a job."

Dinda sighed. "Right. And believe me, I need one—a real one, very soon. I just don't know what we're for as a party." She rubbed her forehead. "I was going through this questionnaire tonight and thinking, 'This is embarrassing. I am far, far, *far* from a right-winger, but we're on the stupid side of every issue.'"

"That's a little harsh," he replied.

"It's a little true," she said. "I joined the Fenwick campaign because I thought he seemed like a moderate, common sense kind of guy. Now it looks like he was only pushed by the committee to fool the public. Robbie Crowe, too. We've drifted into some weird space I don't understand."

"Like what?" Ned asked.

"How did we come to side with violent criminals over victims, and high school boys to beat girls in sports, and out-of-their-mind drug addicts pooping on the street. Now we have kids pretending they're dogs and cats and what do we do? We encourage them and say, 'Good, doggie.' That's nuts."

Ned shrugged. "We have a big tent."

"A circus tent! Shouldn't we check IDs at the door?"

Ned sipped his scotch. "We don't believe in IDs. Our voters are too stupid to get them."

"Then why do we want people that dumb to vote?"

"Because they're dumb enough to vote for us," Ned replied. "Look, Dinda. We're days away from the convention. This is a poor time to get religion."

"Sorry," she said. "It's just that I'm working so hard for no money and I'm starting my period, and I can't afford groceries and I'm starting to wonder why I'm even doing this anymore. I had to sneak into the men's room today to get tampons."

"I get it," Ned said. "I was in your shoes once." Ned got up, poured himself another scotch, and settled back into his chair. "I got out of grad school, hair on fire, and came to Washington ready to change the world. I took the lowest of the low-level jobs in the West Wing working on policy papers until all hours of the night. It seemed important, and I thought, 'I'm going to work harder than anyone here, including the president.' I didn't realize he wasn't working late. He was getting blowjobs in the Oval Office and treating one of my colleagues like a humidor."

He drained his glass. "It wasn't until I met Bennie Barbu that it all started to make sense. That's when I learned I was about the only person in town who wasn't feeding out of the trough. I figured I may as well dip my beak and—" Snoring interrupted his soliloquy, which told him he should get some sleep, too. It was just as well.

Dinda would learn soon enough. Politics was the art of compromising—pretty much everything.

30. A Fry in the Ointment

What to do about Hiram Fry? That question was on the table—along with waffles, omelets, and fresh fruit—at an emergency Sunday morning breakfast meeting in Bennie Barbu's office. Hiram's threat to set off a messy floor fight at the convention triggered alarms for the National Committee, which puzzled over what it would take to shut him up. A car ride had not yet been ruled out.

"All this yapping about democracy as if Robbie never got any votes," said a disgusted Eleanor Winthrop, leader of the activist group Democracy by Any Means Necessary. "That's ridiculous! *Seven people* in this room voted for him!"

She looked around the table at the inner circle: Bennie, Marius, Ned, Kristi, Worth, Robbie, Marty, and Meredith Worthington Duke from Racial Justice Now! The sour expressions on their faces indicated they were in no mood to back down based on an antiquated notion of democracy.

"It's not as if we have to hear from everybody to know what to do," Meredith noted. "We know what this party needs better than anybody."

"I don't know what to say," Ned said, rubbing his forehead. "Hiram's stuck on this idea that votes in primaries should matter. He campaigned for a year and received five million votes. Robbie got no votes at all."

"Very rude of Hiram to say so," Meredith sniffed.

Robbie winced. "This is not exactly my fault I didn't get votes. I wasn't even running."

Kristi patted Robbie's arm. "Don't worry," she said. "I'm sure you would have gotten votes if you had been on the ballot, even if somebody voted for you by accident."

"Absolutely!" Eleanor agreed. "It's not how many votes Robbie *didn't* get. It's how many votes Robbie *would* have gotten if he had actually run. Why, he might have gotten six million votes! Maybe seven! Who's to say?

To hold such a technicality against him is… What's the word I'm looking for?"

"Fascist!" Meredith said.

"There you go: fascist!" Eleanor said emphatically. She leaned over to Meredith and patted her arm. "I hadn't used that word in almost a week. I'd almost forgotten!"

Bennie fixed his gaze on Robbie. "What does our candidate have to say?"

All eyes turned to Robbie, who shifted uncomfortably in his chair. *Why is this on me?* "Well, um…" he stammered. "I always look at things and ask myself, 'Is it for the greater good?'"

"And?" Bennie asked.

"In this case," Robbie said, "I think, yeah, it kinda is."

Bennie scrunched his face. "What is?"

Robbie cleared his throat. "You know…"

Bennie fluttered his eyes and sighed. *What is he talking about?* "Ned," he said, "do you see any way we can reason with Hiram?"

"I don't," Ned said. "He keeps blathering on about party rules and procedures, as if we didn't consider that before we blew them up." Ned got more annoyed as he thought about it. "It's so aggravating, especially when you consider all we've done for that guy."

"Fucking ingrate," Worth said, shaking his head. Mulling it over, he asked, "Just out of curiosity, what have we done for that guy?"

"Well… nothing really," Ned said. "But we didn't run anyone against him in the primaries. That ought to count for something."

"I suppose," Worth said.

Marius added, "Does he ever stop to think, 'Hey, at least they didn't break my kneecaps?'"

That silenced the room as people wondered why Marius would bring that up.

Worth jumped in to save him. "Here's the bottom line, people. We've got one chance to take everything: the White House and Congress and packing the Supreme Court. If this convention doesn't go off as planned, we'll start the fall campaign in a deep hole. And if we lose the election, everyone in this room is screwed. It's four more years in exile."

Marius rubbed his fingers together. "Let's make him a deal he can't refuse. Give him a department to run. HHS. Agriculture. He'd probably love to fuck around with weeds and corn and pesticides, right?"

"I suggested that," Ned said. "He's refused. I thought he might want to play around with bombs over at Defense since he's kind of a gun nut, but he didn't go for that either."

Kristi intervened. "Robbie, you should tell Hiram you're considering him for vice president."

Robbie blushed. "But I'm not."

"What difference does that make?" she said with a smile. "All you do, darlin', is string him along like a little pull toy. It's a time-honored tradition. We'll give him a spot on Monday night to make a glowing speech about you. Then you call him first thing Tuesday morning. 'Oops! Second thoughts, Hiram.'"

Robbie shuddered. "Won't he know I'm lying?"

Worth chuckled. "He'll know you're lying when you say, 'Hello. Nice to see you.' But you've got to try."

"I don't know," Robbie said. "He seemed really pissed."

"On the rage-o-meter? Purple," Ned said with a wince. "But, you know, he's one of those straight-from-the-shoulder guys. I think he would respect your courage going in there and looking him in the eye, mano a mano, and telling him an obvious lie. I mean, that shows political leadership right there."

"And if that doesn't work," Meredith said, "I suggest you try a baseball bat. Deliver the message right between the eyes."

Eleanor reached over and patted Meredith's hand. "Now *that's democracy in action!*"

Bennie rubbed his jaw, thinking. "All right. Let's go with pretending he can be VP. But if he doesn't budge, I want Marius to handle it."

31. Fry Day

Would Hiram Fry have Robbie assassinated? Robbie considered the senator's smoldering anger and decided it wasn't out of the question. The crotchety old bastard was from *Ohio*. Didn't everyone have a gun in Ohio? Or was that Iowa? For sure, it was one of those four-letter states in the middle of nowhere with a lot of vowels and cows and sows. Anything could happen out there! They probably shoot their breakfast every morning.

Robbie fretted over the dangerous possibilities before calling Howie-Do-It. He explained that he was meeting with a United States senator who had become a problem, and possibly a threat. Robbie was taking Marty along for logistic support, but what he really needed was a body man willing to take a bullet if things got nasty.

Howie chuckled. "That ain't Marty," he scoffed. "That guy's a fuckin' pussy."

"Don't I know it," Robbie huffed. "Normally, of course, I'd handle this Fry guy myself. But I'll be wearing a suit and… you know. Could be hard to do my moves."

"Bro! You could split your pants," Howie sympathized.

"Exactly!" Robbie replied. "I don't need my manhood spilling out."

"Hide the ladies!" Howie chuckled before his voice dropped. "You want me to take out this Hiram dude?"

"No," Robbie said uncertainly. "But if things get ugly, I want you to jump in."

"Copy that, dude."

A black car picked up Robbie, Howie and Marty and headed to the Hart Senate Office Building on Constitution Avenue. The threesome navigated their way to Hiram Fry's office overlooking the back of the Capitol, where they were met instantly by the senior senator himself, who instructed his administrative assistant to get water and coffee for his guests.

"If you don't mind," Hiram said to Marty and Howie, "I'd like to meet with Robbie in private."

Robbie quivered, then leaned over to Howie and whispered, "Stay close to the door." He followed Hiram into his inner sanctum and took a seat on the sofa, facing a painting of the Battle of Lake Erie, which Hiram proudly noted was a turning point for the United States in the War of 1812.

What a fucking goober, Robbie mused. *Why would anyone fight over such a shitty lake?*

"I appreciate you stopping by," the senator said, as he leaned back in a rocking chair.

"Of course," Robbie said nervously. "I'm happy to address any reservations you may have about my candidacy."

"Reservations?" Hiram chuckled. "No, son. Oklahoma has reservations, and they're for Indians. I'm from Ohio. We just have regular ol' towns and villages. We make presidents—eight of them so far. I had the possibility of becoming number nine after Dewey Fenwick dropped out, but somebody cut the line."

Robbie took a deep breath. "You realize it wasn't my idea."

"I assumed as much," Hiram said, as he grabbed an oatmeal cookie off a platter on the coffee table and took a bite. "Whose idea was it?"

"Dewey's, of course," Robbie replied.

"Uh-huh." Hiram looked up. "I'll just pretend for a moment that Dewey made any decisions over the past five years other than when to call for someone to empty his bed pan. I might even go along with the charade that you and Dewey were old pals, though my staff couldn't find any evidence that you'd ever even been in the same room."

Hiram shifted in his chair and glared at Robbie.

Robbie gulped for air. "I don't know how your staff would know. I've been a private citizen all my life. My activities are largely out of the public eye."

"Probably better for you that way," Fry said. "But I'm not going to argue the point, Mr. Crowe. The bottom line is that you own this decision now, regardless of who put you up to it. Have you ever wondered why they wanted you?"

"Well, you'd have to look at my record to see—"

"I have," Hiram interrupted. He reached for a folder on the table behind him and brought it to his lap. "Book on you, Mr. Crowe, is that you're lazy, entitled, and you've bobbled every opportunity that's ever come your way. I wonder why you'd do anything different in the biggest job in the world. Maybe that's what they're counting on."

Robbie flushed red. "I'm not following you, senator."

"The Barbus want a stooge, Mr. Crowe," Hiram said. "The party bosses don't like me because I follow my instincts instead of their instructions. Dewey, God rest his soul, was just the sort of go-along-get-along kind of guy they like—happy to cede control to his handlers in return for perks and prestige. Problem is that arrangement caused a great deal of damage in the last go-round. While Dewey was napping in his office, his inner circle cranked up the autopen and spent billions of dollars on every cockamamie scheme they could imagine. It took a while, but voters eventually caught on. They put Roland Platt in the White House, where he's been running roughshod on every political tradition our country holds dear."

Robbie looked vacantly out the window toward the Capitol and shrugged. *How was I supposed to know this stuff?* He turned back to Hiram, who was plainly disgusted.

"Senator, I understand your frustration with the system," Robbie said. "And that's exactly why I'm running: to clean it up."

Hiram laughed bitterly and slapped the arm of his chair. "That's a good one! If you expect me to buy that horseshit, you're not the guy to put on your rubber boots and muck out the stall." He shook his head. "Sorry, son, but counting on you to reform the system is like asking Bonnie and Clyde to guard Fort Knox. You've profited from this system with your foundation that's been sucking cash off the government teat for years. You're not here to reform anything. You're here to run interference for the old gang and their crazy new scheme." He leaned forward, rested his elbows on his thighs and peered at Robbie. "Now I suppose you want me to think that you're considering me as a running mate. That's how they want you to shut me up and spare you a floor fight at the convention. Am I right?"

Robbie's mouth went dry, and he licked his lips. "Well, I don't know what anyone else might think, but you're right there at the top of my list, given your credentials and... I mean, who wouldn't want somebody with your stature to—"

"Jesus, Joseph, and Mary!" Hiram interjected. "Spare me the spin! I've seen this play before. They want you to offer me a carrot, and if I don't bite, then I get a stick. Considering the Barbus are behind this, maybe that stick's a tire iron. I'm telling you, Mr. Crowe, if you're going to be president, you're going to need to show you can stand up to a dictator."

"Absolutely," Robbie said, rubbing his hands together. "From Day One, I'm going after Roland Platt."

"Not Platt, you ninny," Hiram scoffed. "*Bennie.* He makes Platt look like Mary Poppins! You sell your soul to Bennie Barbu, I guarantee you'll never get it back."

Robbie sensed he should be very careful about what he said next; the last thing he needed was to be quoted about the Barbus. "Senator, I think you misunderstand Bennie Barbu—"

"Don't kid yourself! I understand him very well," Hiram said. "He's a virus that's attacks the weakest parts of our body politic and breaks it down. People don't notice the infection until it hurts. And by then, it's too late. You lose your arm. Then your leg. Then you're dead."

"Why do you say that?" Robbie asked.

"Because I've known Bennie Barbu since he was running money for the CIA during the Cold War. And I can tell you that his lifelong dream is to see communism take over the United States. The only reason I ran for president was to stop him." He sighed. "I didn't get it done. Now it's up to you."

Robbie took a deep breath and exhaled slowly, trying to calm his nerves. "You're not going to contest my nomination?"

"No sir."

"Then why did you want to see me?"

"I wanted to see if you could carry on the fight that I started. And I wanted to tell you something in one of the few rooms in this town that doesn't have ears."

"What is it?"

Hiram cocked his head. "How long do you think you'll be president, son? Four years? Eight?"

Robbie shrugged. "Honestly, I haven't thought that far ahead."

"Well, let me tell you something. If you select Evita Manolo as your running mate—and I suspect she's already been selected for you—then you won't need to think too far ahead," Hiram said ominously. "Your days are numbered."

"They'd kill me?" Robbie asked.

Hiram shrugged. "Possibly."

"How?"

Hiram shook his head "It could be anything."

Robbie had to admit: Bennie Barbu and his son were more than a tad creepy. What if he was just a Trojan Horse carrying Evita Manolo into the White House, where he'd roll in and plop her on the carpet? Would they whack him to put her in charge if they didn't like what he was doing?

Robbie protested, weakly, "They recruited me."

"Of course they did!" Hiram scoffed. "You don't scare half the country, like Evita does. Once she's in there? God help us."

Hiram stood up and walked over to a display case underneath the Battle of Lake Erie painting, carefully raised the lid, and removed a long-barreled pistol.

Hiram said. "Do you know what this is?"

Robbie shrugged nervously. "Pretty sure it's a gun."

"Very astute," Hiram said. "It's a flintlock pistol made at the Harper's Ferry Armory in Virginia two-hundred-and-twenty-eight years ago." Hiram nodded toward the painting of the Battle of Lake Erie. "It's what the American soldiers used in the War of 1812. I used this one myself. We had a rabid dog on the farm a few years back that threatened my children. I had one shot." He raised the pistol and peered down the sight. "Now it appears we have just one shot to save this party and you're it…"

Jesus! Was this crazy hick going to shoot him?

"Gun!" Robbie yelled.

The door sprang open and Howie came flying in. He dove across Robbie's body on the sofa, ready to intercept the bullet.

Hiram dropped the gun to his side. "What are you doing, son?" he asked.

"Don't shoot him," Howie said. "Shoot me."

"I would if I had any bullets," Hiram said drily.

Howie sat up. "Oh."

Marty arrived in the doorway to find Hiram Fry holding a gun and Howie sprawled across Robbie's lap. "Good meeting?" he asked.

32. Gut Check

A scowling Robbie emerged from the Senate Office Building to face a new dilemma: *Should he run for president or run for his life?*

"Hiram Fry said I might get whacked after making Evita my VP," Robbie muttered as he climbed into the back seat of his waiting car, with Marty behind him and Howie jumping into the front. "Somebody should have told me what I was getting into."

"Gosh, you're right! Somebody should have," Marty said as he fastened his seat belt. "Oh wait. Let me think… *I* told you last week."

"Right, but I dismissed that because you don't know what you're talking about," Robbie insisted.

"Thank you," Marty said.

Robbie flinched. "Don't act like you're hurt. Face it, Marty. Hiram Fry has been around this town a hell of a lot longer than you have."

Howie looked over his shoulder, "Man up and admit it, Marty. You're no expert on Washington DC."

Marty looked at the back of Howie's thick skull. "You didn't even know where it was, you moron."

"I'm here, ain't I? I must 'a found it."

"Any idea what 'DC' stands for, Howie?" Marty asked.

"Of course," he replied, racking his brain. "It's… 'Da Capital. Washington Da Capital."

"Of da country?" Marty turned to Robbie. "Good hire."

"Shut up. Both of you!" Robbie snapped. "I need to think."

"Never too late to start," Marty noted.

Robbie's face tensed as he considered the many ways in which the Barbus might kill him. He could go down like Lincoln, McKinley, or Garfield. Or maybe like that Egyptian guy assassinated by his own troops as he was watching a military parade. Anything could happen! His security detail would fail to note a shooter in the crowd at a rally; suddenly, there's a bullet headed straight for his nose! Maybe someone slips poison into his kale smoothie, making him die a writhing, painful death—worse, even, than drinking kale! Maybe a chandelier falls on his head, and the lights go out forever! Would he even see it coming?

"There are a million ways they could get me," Robbie said.

"Such a shame," Marty said. "Cut down in your prime."

"Fuck off, Marty," Robbie said.

"No, seriously. I think it's sad," Marty claimed. "You're not even president yet, and you're already the darkest day in our nation's history."

"Not if I have anything to say about it, boss," Howie chimed in. "I'm always ready to take a bullet for you."

"Thanks, Howie," Robbie said.

Marty reached up and clapped Howie on the shoulder. "Chin up, Howie. You still might get that chance."

Robbie stared out the window, passing one gray building after another, pondering his fate. Everyone on the street—waiting at the stoplight, standing at the curb, boarding a bus—was suddenly a potential assassin. Yet, there was one saving grace.

"I don't believe she would allow anything like that to happen."

"Who?" Marty asked.

"Who do you think?" Robbie asked bitterly. "Evita. That just seems beyond her capacity."

"Are you kidding?" Marty asked incredulously. "She's the most ambitious person on the planet. She'd hang you by your thumbs in Lafayette Park if it would help her get where she wants to go."

"Which is where?"

Marty pointed out the window at the White House. *"There!"*

Robbie growled, slapped his thigh and declared, "I can't go through with it."

"Oh please," Marty moaned. "Which part?"

"This whole thing," Robbie said. "I don't want to be the nominee."

Marty was incredulous. "You want to back out now?"

"If they're going to fucking kill me, hell yes!" Robbie said.

"They'll kill you sooner if you quit," Marty said.

"I don't care," Robbie said. "Call Ned. Tell him I'm done. I had to—I dunno. I had to go back to New York for a dentist appointment."

"Wait a second," Marty said. "You can't run for president anymore because you have a *six-month cleaning?"*

"Yeah. That's probably not enough," Robbie conceded. "Say I had a filling fall out."

"Oh, for God's sake," Marty said, shaking his head. "I'm not making that call."

"Well, I sure as hell can't call him myself," Robbie said. "He's gonna hate me." His phone rang, cutting him off. He pulled it out of his pocket and looked at the caller ID. "Shit. It's him."

"Who?" Marty asked.

"Ned! Who do you think I'm talking about?" Robbie tried handing the phone to Marty. "You answer it. Say I'm in the bathroom."

"Of the *car?*"

"He won't know that."

Marty pushed the phone back toward Robbie. "He might hear horns honking in the background."

"Tell him we're in an RV," Robbie said.

"Oh, yeah. That's believable."

Robbie scowled. "Okay. Fine. *Fine!*" He angrily punched a button, putting Ned on speaker. "Hey Ned."

"Robbie, hi," Ned said cheerfully. "How did it go with Foghorn Leghorn?"

"Who?"

"Hiram Fry."

Robbie scratched his head. "Oh, him. Pretty good, I guess. It took some doing, but I talked him out of a floor fight."

"That's great news. Did you suggest he could become your VP?"

"Didn't have to," Robbie said casually. "Once he knew I wasn't putting up with his bullshit, he just caved."

"Excellent!" Ned said. "So what did he say?"

"He complained about Evita." He glanced sidelong at Marty. "Said she was wrong for the ticket."

Ned went silent a moment. Then he said, "Evita is your running mate. Period."

"We can't change that?"

"She's ordered a special dress for the occasion," Ned said. "You want to tell her she can't wear it."

"No."

"Listen, Robbie. I know things are moving very fast. But you should be excited. Everything is falling into place. Come on down to HQ. We're about to fire up the troops."

33. Mostly Peaceful

Robbie, Marty and Howie entered the War Room that was buzzing with pre-convention planning activity. As the legion of young campaign workers recognized their anointed leader had entered, they jumped from their chairs and stood as one and cheered.

"Democracy *NOW!*" yelled one person.

"Hail to the chief!" hollered another.

The raucous demonstration restored a wide grin to Robbie's face and reminded him why he was running for president: *hot babes!* Unfortunately, there weren't any in the room. Was he representing the wrong party? He looked around at the volunteers working to elect him: a sea of highly educated young people wearing some of the ugliest clothing he'd ever seen. Who ever thought a black and white-check keffiyeh worked with a green-and-red plaid shirt and a brown knit cap? *Clash much?* And these women with the pink wiry hair and the God-awful Elton John glasses and the decorative staples in their lips? *I don't want those salami slicers anywhere near my meat!*

As the applause died down, Ned approached and offered a fist bump to Robbie and spoke to him quietly. "Feeling the love?"

Robbie looked over the room. Well… they might be ugly, but they were his peeps, and they were demonstrating their loyalty already. He turned and offered a withering glance at Marty. "That's what I call respect," he claimed.

Marty nodded in agreement. "Like trained seals."

Ned put his index finger and thumb in his mouth and whistled. "All right people!" The room grew silent as the team settled back into their seats or leaned against the walls and windowsills.

"I want to thank you all for the amazing work you're doing," Ned said. "We are making tremendous progress toward the convention next week in Chicago." He propped his reading glasses on the end of his nose and glanced down at his iPad. "We've got an all-star cast of celebrities jetting in from New York and LA to show their love for Robbie and Evita. And we've got a Who's Who of speakers checking every diversity box known to humankind—as well as the animal kingdom. Including, yes…" he said, looking up, "a keynote Monday from BowWow, *the* big dog in the furry community."

Robbie leaned over to Marty. "Is that a community?"

"More like a pound," Marty replied.

"We've also signed the rapper CheeZee Gritz to warm up the crowd before Robbie's acceptance speech. I'm sure you all know his huge hit, *Gimme Summa Dat Big Butt.*" More hollers and applause. "And," Ned continued, "nobody does street protests like Chicago." Ned let his paper drop. "We're expecting our most ferocious demonstrations ever—wilder even than the total shitshow in 1968!"

Ned's boast was met with applause and fist pumps in the air. "*Comandante* Justin and *Soldadera* Melissa: come on up here! Tell the team about the exciting week ahead."

Marty turned to see Justin, the Café Che manager from New York, goose-stepping to the front of the room. He adjusted his red-star beret at a jaunty Che Guevara-like tilt and scowled. His sad aide-de-camp, the green-haired barista Melissa, stood at his side, her revolutionary getup undermined by a booger dangling from her nose ring. Marty vaguely recalled her as the barista who mixed up his order for a Bolivian Breakfast Burrito last week. Now she looked like a terrorist with a sinus problem.

"Ned's direction to us was clear: Scare the hell out of people," Justin declared. "Make all those deplorable assholes out there understand that if they want to re-elect Platt, we're gonna light it up all across the country. They'll get four more years of chaos in the streets."

Melissa picked it up. "Our focus groups told us that little old white ladies playing kazoos don't scare them at all. And a klatch of old hippies holding candles and singing some Woody Guthrie songs didn't move them, either. What they responded to was firebombs."

"A word to the wise," Justin said. "Through a grant from the Hands Up Foundation, we're importing a few soldiers from the civil war in Sudan to help us mix our Molotov cocktails. Cheer them on, but don't approach them. They can't read, so your credential won't save you."

Justin noted that firebombings would commence at the top of the hour each evening for maximum TV news impact, and the campaign's social media team would pump out videos on all the major platforms.

"The mayor of Chicago has been absolutely fantastic," Justin said. "He's donated a couple of city buses for us to set on fire Monday and three police cars to destroy Tuesday. That builds up to our Ultimate Day of Rage on Wednesday when we blow up a police station."

Woot! Woot! The workers were ecstatic. *What fun!*

"First firebomb drops at five o'clock Monday." Melissa said to more cheers. "We just got confirmation that Dr. Abdullah Oblongata has agreed to light the first fuse." The name elicited raucous cheers. "*Ab-dull-AH! Ab-dull-AH!*"

"For those of you too young to remember Abdullah," Justin said, "he killed two cops in an armed robbery at a Philadelphia liquor store fifteen years ago. It wasn't his fault; the pigs stepped in front of his bullets. But Abdullah went on to get his GED in prison and he's now a highly respected professor of political theology at Yale."

Ned loudly cleared his throat, making Melissa nod in his direction. "Dr. Oblongata is waving his usual fee because he believes so much in our cause. We, in turn, will give him an opportunity to address the convention, and offer his new fashion line, Dullah Duds, in our gift shop."

Marty raised his hand. "This may sound like a stupid question, but our mostly peaceful protests sound suspiciously like riots. Why do we want this at our convention?" A murmur went through the assembly. *Who is this idiot?* "If our protesters hate Platt so much, why don't they go to *his* convention in August?"

Justin stepped in front of Melissa and glared at Marty "You're right," he scoffed. "That is a stupid question."

Mocking laughter rocked the room, but Marty pressed ahead. "Do you have an answer?"

"Any idiot would know — and I know from seeing you at my shop in New York you're not just any idiot — we can't do demonstrations like this in Miami. Cops down there would beat the shit out of our people," Justin said hotly. "Cubans hate *comunistas*."

"Do you think that might be based on experience?" Marty asked.

"We're not interested in their pathetic excuses," Justin said.

"The protests planned for Chicago can't wait. There's an affordability crisis out there," Melissa claimed. "I see the pain on their faces every day at Café Che. Customers can't buy a Chocolate Choice Mochaccino *and* a Figgy Pudding Cronut; they have to choose one or the other. That's Platt's America for you. It's degrading to the human condition."

Meredith Worthington Duke, the cultural anthropology professor at Columbia University, looked at Marty. "I don't recall your name, dear…"

Justin interjected, "It's Marty."

"Thank you, Justin," Marty said. "I'd almost forgotten."

"I haven't," Justin replied.

Meredith continued. "Marty, people feel a deep need to express their displeasure with Platt. The question is how do we deal with that? Do we fight fire with fire? Of course not. We need to *lean in*, to listen to people, to feel them, so that we may understand what grieves them so. What do they *really* want besides cronuts? And how do we take it from somebody like our friend Robbie here and fork it over?"

Robbie and Marty exchanged glances, before Marty replied. "So firebombings are a kind of group therapy?"

"Exactly!" Meredith said. "Someone's crying, my lord. Kumbaya… Kumbaya."

"Well said, Meredith!" Ned said, as he jumped in. "By the way, team, if you're thinking of doing a little shopping while you're in Chicago, you're in luck—and no money is necessary. The city has agreed to make certain stores on the Magnificent Mile available for looting. One-hundred percent discounts on jewelry, phones, computers, liquor, TVs, handbags— the works."

Marty raised his hand, prompting an exasperated Ned to sigh.

"What now?" Justin seethed.

"How can we claim protesters are desperate and hungry when they're stealing Gucci bags?" Marty asked. "Who eats Gucci bags?"

An awkward silence followed as sad-eyed Melissa stepped toward him. "Maybe it's to carry the baby food they steal from Walgreen's down the street," Melissa said. "Or maybe it's to carry free turkeys to the homeless shelter. We have to assume whatever they steal is something they desperately need or they wouldn't steal it."

Marty leaned over to Robbie. "Does this make any sense to you?"

Robbie looked at him vacantly and shook his head. He gulped several times, trying to catch his breath. "I gotta get out of here."

"Are you coming back?" Marty asked.

"With any luck, I'll get hit by a bus," Robbie growled.

He jumped out of his chair, dashed out the door, and vanished into a stairwell.

34. Hands Up

A panting Robbie sat on a concrete step in the stairwell, trying to slow his racing heartbeat as he considered his new reality. Here he was the leader of a party that not only tolerated riots, but encouraged them, financed them, and *staged* them. That was not only wrong, it was embarrassing, the behavior of losers. People of his class did not engage in such public tantrums to get what they wanted. They already had what they wanted! Rioting was for low-lifes beyond the moat, banging on the castle gates trying to get in—not people comfortably entrenched on the inside who never wanted to leave. Which reminded him: how was he supposed to get out of this stairwell?

He stood up and approached the door that he had entered and encountered a sign.

STAIR A

No Re-entry

Next exit: Third Floor

What kind of shithole stairwell was this? He was supposed to walk all the way down these tiny concrete steps? He gripped the stairwell railing and haltingly made his way down, where he found the entry to the third floor. He pushed the door open and saw a marble and mahogany lobby and another sign.

Welcome to

America's Just Rewards

It's About Time!

A facial recognition program on the receptionist's computer instantly identified Robbie and brought up his file. "Hello Mr. Crowe," the receptionist said. "Are you looking for Lindsey?"

Robbie was distracted by the receptionist's perfect appearance and precise diction, then noted her name badge said her preferred pronouns were "it" and "that." She was a fucking robot!

"Who were you talking about?" he asked.

"Lindsey Crowe," it said. "My records indicate she is your former wife."

"I know *that*," Robbie snapped, then caught himself. He shouldn't chew out a machine, especially in this building. It could be his boss someday. "Lindsey's here?"

The robot pointed to its right. "She is in the café."

Robbie wandered over to the employee café, where he found Lindsey sitting in a corner, dictating a message on her phone. She looked up in surprise as Robbie approached.

"Didn't expect to see you here," she said coolly.

"I kind of stumbled into it," he replied.

"Well, I have an appointment with your friend Bennie in two minutes," Lindsey said.

"He's not exactly my friend," Robbie noted.

"No?"

"I guess you'd call him a power broker."

"Hmm," Lindsey mused. "That may be exactly what he has in mind. Join my meeting if you like. I'd like to know how all this fits together."

Robbie took a deep breath. "So would I."

"Ms. Crowe?" Brandi, a well-tailored and apparently human assistant from Bennie's office appeared in the doorway. "Mr. Barbu is ready to see you now."

Lindsey nodded. "I'd like Mr. Crowe to join me if that's all right," she said as she gathered her things.

Brandi tapped her glasses, paused as she read a message, and smiled serenely. "He's more than welcome."

Lindsey looked tensely at Robbie. "Time to meet your maker." She and Robbie followed Brandi down a corridor with glass-walled offices on one side, and a warren of cubicles on the other. Every office and desk appeared to be occupied, and the expressions on faces suggested pressure was high.

"What is all this?" Lindsey asked.

"Accounting, banking, security, and sales functions," Brandi answered.

"All related to America's Just Rewards?"

"Oh yes," she said pleasantly. "At least until we build our new campus in Arlington. We plan to break ground in November."

"After the election, I take it?" Lindsey asked.

"That's the idea!" Brandi said brightly. "We're counting on Mr. Crowe's great success!"

At the end of the hallway, Brandi opened a door to Bennie's office. The ancient warrior rose stiffly to his feet and smiled benignly as he shuffled over to introduce himself to Lindsey, and to shake hands with Robbie. He asked Brandi to summon Marius from the office next door and to find a green tea for Lindsey.

"How did you know what I like?" Lindsey asked.

"That's what our business is all about," he replied.

They took seats around a small conference table and awaited Marius's arrival. Lindsey recognized Marius immediately since his grinning visage appeared regularly in gossip pages, where he was captured cavorting with movie stars, business leaders, and political figures.

After pleasantries, Bennie said, "We are in a fast-moving situation, Ms. Crowe, so I will get right to the point. The leadership committee for our party, in which I have an abiding interest, believe the people of our country have enough of all the anger, division, and chaos sown by Roland Platt. They're looking for stability and calm—and direction. That is why we are introducing America's Just Rewards, the most ambitious program of social rearrangement this nation has ever seen."

"I see." Lindsey nodded warily. "And who is going to be—as you put it—rearranged?"

"Everyone," Bennie declared flatly. "Some people will move up. Some will move down. The idea is to achieve the equality our country's Founding Fathers envisioned two-hundred and fifty years ago."

Lindsey absorbed Bennie's summary. "Perhaps my reading of history is a little different from yours," she replied. "My understanding was that they sought equal opportunity rather than equal results. 'Social rearrangement' sounds like another name for communism."

Bennie and Marius exchanged glances, before Bennie responded. "I would not get hung up on labels, Ms. Crowe," he insisted. "Communism has always required high levels of coercion. The system we have in mind does nothing of the sort. It's Americanism, based on market incentives in the great tradition of our country's consumer loyalty programs. We are simply taking it one step further: a partnership between government and selected businesses offering points for nothing more complicated than good behavior. And it will be completely voluntary, offering our people a simple proposition: Do you want the benefits we offer or don't you? You can say yes or no. It's up to each individual whether they wish to go along." He leaned over and patted Robbie's forearm. "We are very fortunate to have Robbie lead this effort for us. Who better than a scion of a great American company to show our program has deep roots in the country's most honored traditions?"

Robbie winced. *At least he didn't pat me on the head.*

"I suppose that makes it less scary to some people," Lindsey noted.

"Indeed," Bennie acknowledged.

"What happens to people who decide they don't want to be a part of your program?" Lindsey asked. "Are there penalties?"

"You'd have to suspect the motives of a person who resists such an obviously good idea," Bennie contended. "At the very least, such a person would be shunned. You'd have to question their intelligence and their attitude." He sighed. "Even so, we would offer them opportunities to see that participation in our program is in their best interests."

Lindsey was beginning to understand why some people were terrified by Bennie Barbu; all he was missing was a hairless cat on his lap. "So… what does this brave new world have to do with me?"

Bennie turned to Marius, who picked up the story. "America's Just Rewards requires the greatest data gathering effort in world history," he said. "And that requires enormous amounts of energy. We plan to add twenty data centers to our operation next year, each with the capacity to collect several billion gigabytes of information. That requires uninterrupted electricity twenty-four/seven, which is why we need a dedicated power source for every center."

"You want these centers off the grid, I take it," Lindsey said.

"Of course. The grid is simply not dependable enough," Bennie said. "We can't afford blackouts. Our data operations need to run around the clock."

Lindsey nodded. "What kind of information are you gathering?"

"Everything," Marius said flatly. "We are in the process of collecting information from all of our marketing partners to create a detailed profile of every person, every business, every community in our country. We have all the private sources we need—banks, healthcare, big tech, and so on—ready to go. All that's left is to merge their data with the government's vast stores of information. At that point, we'll know all we need to know."

"Such as?" Lindsey asked.

"Who's supporting the greater good," Bennie replied with a benign smile.

"And who isn't?" Lindsey added.

"Of course," Bennie said.

Lindsey glanced at Robbie, who was fidgeting and looking out the window as if he wanted to be somewhere else. She couldn't blame him. It was clear he was little more than a front man, the celebrity spokesperson brought on to lend respectability to an unprecedented surveillance, command, and control program. "Lovely as it all sounds," Lindsey said, "Crowe Power does not have the scalability to build twenty power plants in such a short period of time."

Marius was clearly distracted by whatever he was looking at through his glasses. Lindsey wondered: *What are those things? X-ray glasses?* She pulled her jacket close.

Bennie, awaiting his son's response, tapped his forearm. "Marius?"

"Right. Sorry," he said as he was brought back to the room. "Ms. Crowe, we don't expect you to build power plants for all the data centers. We want you to manage them. Help us find the companies that can do the work and make sure they do their jobs. You'll get a 20 percent share in the profits for each one you develop."

Lindsey's eyes widened. "That's generous."

Marius nodded. "And well deserved. We're accepting only the best of the best into our program. We expect those who are doing the hard work on the inside of this program will live very well."

"And those who aren't?" Lindsey asked.

Marius looked at his father, who shrugged. "They will struggle," Bennie said. "And then they will go away."

Lindsey processed the offer. "How did I get so lucky?" she asked warily. She pointed a thumb at Robbie. "I take it it's because of him."

"Robbie's success as a candidate is, frankly, critical to our success," Bennie said. "We know people will ask you about Robbie, and we want to make sure you're fully invested in our mission."

Lindsey rolled her head from side to side. "Invested," she mused. "Interesting word."

"This is not a charity," Bennie said. "It's a business proposition."

"Could have fooled me," she said. "It's sounds more like a bribe."

"We're not *giving* you the money," Bennie snapped. "We expect you to earn it. There will be a great deal of pressure on all our partners. But we know based on your history that you can handle it. And that's what we need to meet our goals."

"The greater good?"

Bennie and Marius said nothing. Robbie squirmed uncomfortably. At last, Bennie said, "Give yourself a day or two to think it over."

Lindsey paused as she considered the proposition. She said, "Thank you, but I don't need a day. I don't even need an hour. What I do need is to get out of here." She stood up to leave. "I appreciate your consideration, but I have to say: you and your program creep me out." She turned toward the door. "No thanks."

An embarrassed Robbie was left to face Bennie and Marius, who both glared at him. "I hope she's not going to be a problem," Bennie said, rubbing the back of his neck.

Robbie grimaced. "I'll talk to her."

Bennie raised an eyebrow. "Has that been a successful strategy for you in the past?"

"Not terribly," Robbie said.

"You might explain that it would be better for her and your children if she went along," Bennie said. "There's an expiration date for that kind of attitude."

"When is that?" Robbie asked.

"Election Day," Marius said. "November fifth."

35. Tick, Tick, Tick

In the days following Dewey Fenwick's death, the media amped up its pressure on President Platt, amplifying Ned's claim that he had killed their beloved leader through his heartless cuts to measles research.

Commentators in the know picked up the story line and ran with it, calling for Platt's emergency impeachment and removal from office, and for grand juries to consider murder charges against him. A grieving Boof and Skeeter suggested prosecutors skip the trial and proceed directly to the death penalty. The outcry among the captive media was so intense that Platt finally decided to confront the issue by sitting for an interview with star interlocutor Peg Parsons on a special edition of the FFS network's top-rated news magazine show *Tick, Tick, Tick*.

As Platt arrived at the studio with a phalanx of Secret Service agents in tow, FFS reporters and producers walked out in dramatic fashion, signaling they would not be party to the platforming of a democratically elected dictator. They made a beeline to the Old Ebbitt Grill, where they bellied up to the bar to register their objections to sympathetic bartenders. *Damn that filthy tyrant! Fetch me another gin and tonic!*

Platt walked under the white-hot blaze of studio lights wearing his traditional blue suit, white shirt and plain red tie. He took his seat across from Parsons, who was perched on the edge of a hard wooden chair with a legal pad on her lap, a pen in her hand, and an imperious scowl on her face. Peering through reading glasses perched on the end of her nose, she adopted the manner of a district attorney and bore in on the president with the sort of aggressive interrogation for which she was famous.

"Lady Janice Fenwick accuses you of causing her husband's death, Mr. President," said Parsons, looking down her nose. "How do you plead?"

Platt shrugged. "I don't plead anything. I'm not on trial."

Parsons smirked. "You are in the court of public opinion," she insisted. "And according to the polls, you're guilty. Seventy-three percent of the American public say, basically, that you stink."

Platt bristled. "That's a phony number from a phony poll. I don't buy it."

Parsons pressed. "So… no defense? You have nothing to say for yourself?"

"About what?" Platt asked.

"About murdering a great American president," Parsons said.

Platt leaned forward. "Demented Dewey was eighty-seven years old," he replied. "He was under the care of Dr. Franklin Feeley, a quack if I ever saw one. And from what I hear, his wife, Jezebel Janice, was never around to keep an eye on him to count out his pills. How am I to blame for that?"

Parsons shook her head with disgust. "The Fenwick family says your savage cuts to measles research deprived him of medications that could have saved his life. We've talked to numerous experts who agree."

Platt cocked his head as he eyed Parsons. "How do you know he died from measles?"

"*MIS-ter PRES-sident!*" Parsons yelped in dismay, as she put her right hand over her fluttering heart. "We all saw the pictures!"

Platt shook his head. "That's a total scam. Look at those measles." He ticked off points on his fingers. "First of all, they weren't the kind that kill you. Second, they weren't even measles. They were painted on with a magic marker. He had more makeup on his puss than you do. And from what I can see, that's saying a lot. Looks to me like you lay it on with a trowel."

Parsons laughed scornfully. "You have no evidence to back that up."

"I'm looking at you right now!"

"I'm talking about *measles!*"

"Measles, shmeasles. Check with real doctors, not phony ones," Platt said. "Dewey Fenwick was never diagnosed with measles. It was a fake diagnosis from the fake media that wants to blame all of America's problems on me." He angrily jabbed a finger at her. "And you're fake, too."

Parsons bristled. "How dare you!"

"Start with that cheesy wig. It's crooked," Platt claimed. "You should get some tape or a chinstrap or something. I'm very worried it could fall off. That would be very, very bad for you and for our country."

Parsons could barely catch her breath. "You sir, are no gentleman."

"And you, Pitiful Peg, are no journalist," Platt chided. "You have no idea what the hell is going on out there. You wouldn't know a measle from a zit. Everything I've heard says Dewey Fenwick cracked his head on a water bottle, and it was lights out. *Buh-bye!*" He raised his hand and offered a wave, as if to a child. "He was done and it was probably a blessing. People should be thanking me. I've spent the past four years cleaning up his mess. God forbid he had another four years in the White House. Our country would be finished."

Parsons paused and stared at Platt, who stared back.

"What?" he asked.

"Have you no decency, sir?" Parsons asked plaintively.

"Probably not the way you define it: destroying our borders, criminalizing police, handing out drugs to junkies like it's candy," Platt responded. "I don't call that nice. I call that stupid."

Parsons sputtered, "How dare you obsess over crime and borders and drugs when there are people who are suffering in this country this very day for being misgendered by people who refuse to honor their preferred pronouns."

"You want to hear my pronouns?" Platt replied. "They're I... Don't... Care."

Parsons looked like she might hit him, and she would have if her arms were long enough.

"Let me ask you a question," Platt said.

Parsons raised her chin.

"Where the hell were you and the rest of the media on Dewey's demise?"

"We were on the front lines doing our job every day!"

"No, you weren't," Platt said. "You were out giving yourself awards for phony stories about me. None of you noticed Dewey had nothing left until his handlers had to admit he was brain dead because they couldn't cover it up anymore. If that's what you call doing your job, you should be fired. You couldn't find a real story unless it dropped out of your caboose. But I'll try to give you one anyway."

Parson glared at him. "Yes?"

"Scientists working with our Department of Health and Human Services have found a cure for measles—the real kind, not the kind you get from a makeup kit," Platt claimed. "You want to talk about making measles measly? It's done. And I did it. A little credit would be good here."

"Credit for what? If fake measles killed Dewey Fenwick, as you insist, where's the cure for that?"

Platt blinked hard several times. "I'm supposed to cure fake measles, too?"

"They killed a great man!"

Platt seethed. "They could have cured it with soap and a washcloth!"

"As far as I'm concerned, you have no right taking credit for a cure," Peg said. "You cut funding."

"Right," Platt said. "Because I measure success by results, not by how much money we can blow out our ass."

Parsons gathered herself. "Mr. President. This sounds like nothing more than another cynical attempt to win voters by aggressively attacking a problem, no matter how many people you hurt in solving it. And we here at *Tick, Tick, Tick* won't stand for it!" She dramatically unhooked her microphone, stood up and walked off the set. "The nerve of that man!" she muttered.

Platt put a hand over his eyes to shield the glare from the klieg lights and looked around the studio. "Where are you going? Isn't this your show?"

The house lights went up and security was summoned to escort the rogue president off the property. An all-clear text was dispatched to reporters at the Old Ebbitt Grill that it was safe to return, since the place had been sprayed with Febreze and there was little chance they would be exposed to Platt's cooties.

With the president safely evacuated, Parsons returned to the set with a straightened wig to discuss Platt's latest outrage with *Tick, Tick, Tick* host Merton Hinkley. "Just when you think Roland Platt has sunk as low as he can go, he finds another level," Parsons charged.

"He has no redeeming qualities as a president or as a human being," Merton claimed. "Is there any light at the end of this dark tunnel?"

"I think we have to take a long, hard look at Robbie Crowe, whom Dewey Fenwick designated as his successor," Parsons said. "First of all, he has the advantage of being someone other than Platt. And second, from everything I've heard from sources close to the campaign, Robbie Crowe exhibits the sort of humility and decency we've been missing in Washington these past four years. The fact that Dewey Fenwick endorsed him tells you all you need to know."

"Indeed," Merton said. "I like what I'm hearing about Robbie Crowe. He cares less about his own interests than he does about the greater good."

Peg nodded and smiled for the first time all day. "Oh yes! It says so right on his office door in New York. The Crowe Institute for the Greater Good. That's a powerful message about what kind of man he is and what we could expect from a Crowe administration."

The media chorus that followed the show echoed *Tick, Tick, Tick's* take on Roland Platt and the handoff to Robbie Crowe, who was sanctified without further scrutiny. Any life form was better than Platt, the punditry agreed. Robbie had an amazing bloodline. An incredible resume. A deep concern for the planet. And, despite some questionable episodes in his past, he was a chastened man who had learned his lessons. Platt, on the other hand, remained beneath contempt, a divisive worm failing to address the deadly new threat posed by fake measles.

"God speed, Robbie Crowe," Merton said. "You can't get to the White House soon enough."

Part Three

Conventional Behavior

36. Hear Ye

Marty sat back in an easy chair in Robbie's suite atop Chicago's luxurious Peninsula Hotel with his feet up on an ottoman and a computer perched on his lap. He scrolled through his email, deleting hundreds of sales pitches and newsletters, before finding the draft of Robbie's convention speech, sent from Ned two hours earlier.

After looking it over, he glanced at Robbie, who was flat on his back on the adjacent sofa, his hands folded over his chest, staring into space. Was this meditation? Medication? A stroke?

"Have you read your acceptance speech?" Marty asked.

"Not yet," Robbie said, with yawn. "I don't have to give it until Thursday night."

"Right," Marty acknowledged. "But you might want to look at it before then."

"I'm busy," he contended.

"Thinking big thoughts?" Marty asked.

"Something like that." Robbie picked up his phone and began to scroll. "Jesus," he muttered.

"What?" Marty asked.

"My phone is all fucked up."

"What's the matter?"

"I keep getting ads for gay porn."

Marty shrugged. "You must have done a search for it."

Robbie blushed. "Bullshit!"

"Well, that's how the algorithms work, Robbie," Marty said. "They feed you what they sense you're looking for."

"I sure as hell didn't look for gay porn!" Robbie insisted.

"No?"

Robbie sighed. "I might have looked up 'bareback.'"

"And not in the sense of horseback riding?"

"Not exactly."

"And you couldn't figure it out without pictures?"

"I just wanted to be sure," Robbie claimed. "I heard somebody talking about it, and… I don't know."

"Don't worry about it. I'm pretty sure porn earns points in America's Just Rewards. Gay porn is probably double, as long as you don't drive a pickup truck or own a gun," Marty said. "In the meantime, you might want to spend some time with your speech. They're signing you up for all kinds of stuff."

Robbie put his phone down and sighed. "Okay. Go ahead and bore me. Like what?"

"You support furries in the military?"

"You mean those weirdos in the animal costumes?"

"Yeah."

Robbie chuckled. "I kinda like that idea," he mused. "The enemy looks across the battlefield and sees those assholes dressed up like cartoon animals? They might die laughing. We don't have to fire a shot."

Marty nodded. "Okay. I'll check that off," he said, making a note on the script. "What about mandatory gender studies starting in seventh grade?"

"Why would you need a law for that?" Robbie asked. "I didn't need any help studying girls at that age. It's pretty much all I thought about."

"This is more about boys who want to become girls, and girls who want to become boys."

"Oh. Right," Robbie said, musing over the concept. "I was just thinking about that."

"Did you come to any conclusions?"

"I did," Robbie said. "If I became a chick, I'm pretty sure I'd play with my tits all day."

"You've given this a lot of thought," Marty noted.

"It would just be something to do," Robbie claimed.

"So, you're in favor?"

"Yeah," Robbie shrugged. "I guess so."

Marty checked off that item. "What about making pork illegal?"

"That would definitely suck," Robbie said. "You ever try beef bacon?"

"I know. It's awful," Marty said. "But Ned tells me porkophobia is a big deal with a significant bloc in your base. You probably don't want to piss them off. You could lose a swing state like Michigan."

"Okay, fine. Whatever. I'll eat whatever I want anyway. I'm sure I could still get pork into the White House." He rubbed his forehead. *The stress of it all!* "Why are you bothering me with all this? I'm pretty much for anything that doesn't affect me personally. I don't care about the particulars."

"These aren't just particulars, Robbie," Marty said. "This is your agenda for the next four years."

Annoyed, Robbie propped himself up on his elbow and glared at Marty. "Nobody expects me to live up to some bullshit promises. Everyone knows politicians say stuff just to get elected."

"So, you don't care what you say?"

"Frankly? No," Robbie admitted before laying back down. "I'll be president, Marty, not some flunky. That means I oversee the whole shebang. I can't get bogged down in minutiae. I'll leave it to people like you to sweat the details."

Marty sighed. "The little people?"

Robbie admonished him with a look. "You're not so little, bub. In fact, you could lose a few pounds," he said. "I'm talking about minions. I hear Dewey had minions coming out the ass. That's why he could hang out at the beach all day sucking down ice cream cones." Robbie sighed. "Sounds to me like what this speech needs is the big picture."

"Your vision?"

"Yeah," Robbie said. "Put that in there. My vision."

Marty shrugged. "What is it?"

Robbie rolled over and faced Marty. "Oh, c'mon. You know what it is. You wrote it a million times at Crowe Power. I want a better world. Shit like that."

Marty shifted in his seat. *Didn't they go over this with Bennie?* "Better how?"

"How the hell do I know?" Robbie replied.

"If you don't, who does?" Marty asked.

"Okay, fine. *Fine!*" Robbie blew out his cheeks. "Well, I guess... Hmm. I want things nicer, for sure... More peaceful, maybe... Fairer." He waved his hand. "All that airy fairy stuff Evita says."

"You want things to be fair?"

Robbie shrugged. "Now that I think about it, no. Not really," he said meekly.

Marty sighed. "Let's try this. Close your eyes for a second," he suggested. "What do you see in your perfect world?"

Robbie rolled over on his back again, hugged a pillow over his chest, and closed his eyes. "All right. I see… trees of green… Red roses too… "

Marty sighed. "You see them bloom? For me and you?"

"Yes!" Robbie said, opening one eye and offering a thumbs up. "Write that down."

Marty wearily shook his head. "You're kidding right?"

"What?" Robbie said, sitting up again.

"That's from a song."

"What song?"

"Hello? Louis Armstrong? *What a Wonderful World?"*

"Oh, shit," Robbie said, snapping his fingers. "No wonder it keeps going around in my head. I must have heard it on the elevator."

"You may as well say you want a place where troubles melt like lemon drops away above the chimney tops?"

Robbie nodded thoughtfully. "That's not bad. Write it down."

"It's from *Somewhere Over the Rainbow*. I was making a joke."

Robbie snapped. "Then, damn it, Marty, you should say that up front," he scolded. "Say, 'Joke! Incoming!' 'Cause otherwise, I wouldn't know. I can never tell when you're sarcastic or just being a jerk."

"Probably both," Marty conceded.

Robbie sat up and looked around the suite, exasperated. "Why do I have to think up all this speech stuff myself anyway? That's why I wanted you here in the first place."

"Because it's your name, your campaign, and potentially, your presidency." Marty looked at his computer screen and returned to reading the speech. "If you leave it all up to Ned and Bennie and Marius, you're screwed. Do you want to hear what else they have in mind for you?"

"No, but I'm sure you're going to tell me anyway."

"Reading: 'Some politicians lead with their mouths. I believe the leaders of our party must lead by example. My solemn pledge tonight is that I will give away all my money by the time I leave office and—"

Robbie shot up. "Wait, wait, wait, wait. Back up. I'm supposed to give away *my* money?"

"That's what it says."

Robbie was not sure he was hearing correctly. "Not just other people's money?"

"No."

"Well, fuck that!"

Marty lightly rapped his computer screen with the back of his knuckles. "It's goes on. 'I invite every other billionaire in this country to join me in giving away our fortunes to those who are more deserving. And in return, I pledge to you: big, big points in America's Just Rewards."

Robbie glowered at Marty. "Who's more deserving of my money than me?"

Marty nodded. "Right. I mean, you almost earned it. After all, you were born…"

"And?"

Marty shrugged. "That was kind of it."

Robbie walked to the windows overlooking Chicago's Magnificent Mile. "It wasn't easy being born into this family, you know. I had to put up with a lot of crap."

"I saw the video," Marty said. "Brutal."

"Why would I offer to do something so stupid as give away all my money?"

Marty glanced back at the script. "Because, according to this, 'There's something fundamentally wrong with a system that would allow a guy like me to have so much money.'"

"A guy like me…" Robbie said, shaking his head in disgust. "I don't even know what that means. My family didn't do anything so terrible."

"What can I say? Your party hates dead white men. And they hate live ones even more."

Robbie turned back toward Marty and leaned against the windowsill. He massaged the back of his neck as he thought about the proposal. "Let's play this out a minute. Just for argument stake, let's say I agree to give all my money away. Do you think she'd go for me?"

"Who?"

"Evita."

Marty was taken aback. "You're not serious."

Robbie unburdened himself. "I can't stop thinking about her."

Marty struggled to stifle a laugh. "Well, you should try. Evita is a dead end, Robbie. To her, you are inherently evil. You're rich. You're white. And you're a man—by several generally accepted measures."

Robbie paced in front of the windows, thinking. "But… maybe I can get past all that with one big gesture," he said. "Renouncing my wealth could be all I need to win favor."

"With voters or Evita?"

"Both," he said. "All my life I've had this weird sense that people looked at me as evil because I had money. I've always wondered whether there was a way to change their mind. Maybe this is it. Just get rid of it."

Marty took a deep breath and gathered himself over this unexpected turn. "I'm shocked you're actually considering it." He'd heard of rich men who lost their minds and their fortunes pursuing a seductive paramour. But this was going way too far. "Sorry. I just don't see the attraction. She wants to steal your money."

"Right," Robbie said. "So why not just give it to her? I might get something in return."

"A boner?"

"To start," Robbie said.

"Here's how they position your giveaway in the speech," Marty said. "'For too long, Americans have been a people adrift, making decisions based on selfish desires to get ahead of other people, and unjustly take from others what should rightfully be shared. And what are the results? Competition. Rivalry. Division. America's Just Rewards will guide each of us to make better decisions that consider the needs of the many rather than the few. How many children should we have, if any? Should we drive a car or take the bus? Should we live in an inefficient small town that squanders precious resources like land and energy? Or should we live in close quarters with our fellow Americans where the cuddly, cozy blanket of collectivism offers peace and comfort and absolute certainty?'"

"Sounds like we're handing out sedatives," Robbie noted as he sat down.

"If you read this speech as is, I don't think anyone will need them. They'll all be asleep." Marty closed the laptop. "We're due at McCormick Place to see the exhibits."

Robbie shook his head. "Do I have to?"

"Do you still want to be president?"

"I'm not sure," Robbie replied.

"This will be one way to find out."

37. The Road to Redemption

Robbie rode in sullen silence in the back seat of a black SUV with Marty by his side and Howie-Do-It riding shotgun. They were speeding to the McCormick Place Convention Center, named for a right-wing newspaper publisher whose views were long ago considered taboo in progressive Chicago. Marty wondered why city fathers and mothers hadn't yet gotten around to erasing Robert McCormick's name from the massive hall but suspected it was just a matter of time.

As they pulled up to the curb, Howie-Do-It jumped out of the front seat like a paratrooper dropping into Normandy.

"I got your six, boss," Howie announced as Robbie emerged from the back seat.

Robbie shrugged. "What the hell does that mean?"

Howie looked up and squinted into the sun. "Um… I don't know exactly."

Robbie sighed as he buttoned his jacket. "Then why did you say it?"

"It's just… you know. Security talk."

Marty, climbing out of the car, intervened. "It means he's got your back, Robbie. Good luck with that."

Howie seethed as Robbie began walking toward the convention center. As he looked ahead, he stopped in his tracks. Media trucks lined the road. "What is this? They invited media?"

"That's what the walkthrough is for," Marty said. "It's a press preview of the exhibition hall."

"Why didn't you tell me? You know I can't go in there," Robbie declared.

"I thought you knew," Marty said. "It was in the memo."

"You know I don't read those damn things," Robbie said. "What if they ask me what I think? I don't even know yet."

"Maybe we'll run into Bennie and Marius and they can tell you," Marty said.

"Is that a shot?" Robbie asked bitterly. "You think I do whatever they say?"

"You're batting a thousand so far."

"You know what? Fuck it. You go in," Robbie insisted. "Tell me about it later." He turned toward the car, but Marty grabbed Robbie's upper arm.

"You can't let the media see you leaving," Marty insisted. "They'll think you're avoiding them."

"I am. So what?" Robbie muttered. "I don't like those people."

"Robbie!" Ned called.

Marty turned to see Ned and gently prodded Robbie in his direction. "Man up," Marty said quietly.

"So glad you could make it," Ned said, offering a handshake.

Robbie looked at his watch. "Actually, Ned, I'm sorry. I've got to run back to the hotel."

"Did you forget something?" Ned asked, concerned.

"Yes," Robbie claimed.

"We can send somebody to get it for you." Ned said. "What is it?"

"I forget," Robbie said.

Ned struggled to understand. "You forget what you forgot?"

"Obviously, there's a lot on my mind, Ned," Robbie insisted. He turned to Marty. *Don't just stand there! Bail me out, asshole!*

"He forgot he hates the media," Marty said.

Ned laughed. "Oh. Is that all? Well, I can tell you: they love you! Everyone's climbing aboard the Robbie Crowe bandwagon. But don't worry. We can shoo them away if they get too close."

Robbie sighed and reluctantly agreed to stay. He, Marty, Howie and Ned joined Worth, Kristi and Dinda at the door, where they were escorted past the waiting throng of reporters and the delegates eager to fill their tote bags with buttons, bumper stickers, keychains, and other campaign swag at the booths inside.

They walked past the bomb-sniffing dogs under a tufted rainbow, topped by a sign announcing the exhibit's theme.

AMERICA'S ROAD TO REDEMPTION

Robbie looked up. "What are we redeeming?"

"Your soul," a voice behind him said.

Robbie turned to see a grinning Evita, looking hotter than ever in blue jeans, sneakers and a tight white t-shirt. She moved in and gave him a hug. Robbie breathed deeply from the intoxicating scent of her perfume.

"Do you think I need redemption?" he asked.

"Of course you do!" she said with a laugh.

He leaned close to her ear. "I haven't even been bad yet."

"You might get that chance," she said, teasingly. "Then again, you might not."

Evita left Robbie with his heart pounding. So, there was still a possibility?

Marius explained as he led the group into the hall that his creative team designed an immersive experience that would take visitors through a variety of exhibits leading to an inescapable conclusion: America was a disaster under Platt, but salvation was just beyond the November horizon.

"By the time delegates reach the gift shop," Marius said, "there's one product they'll want to buy other than dashikis at Dullah Duds." He clapped Robbie on the shoulder. "And that's you, my friend."

Robbie shuddered, wondering what that meant. He took a deep breath and followed Marius into "PLATTSVILLE," a grim interpretation of Anytown USA. Using video backdrops, animated characters, and howling music suitable for a haunted house, Plattsville had hints of the nightmarish Pottersville in the movie, *It's a Wonderful Life,* and the squalid Hoovervilles that dotted America during the Great Depression.

An electronic sign overhead flashed a warning.

DIVIDED WE FALL

On one side of the street was a homeless encampment of tarps, shopping carts, and cardboard huts where junkies and mentally ill people dressed in rags were passed out on the sidewalk. Drag queens were arrested by police, and migrants were frog-marched to an idling prison bus by ICE agents.

On the other side of the street was a gated estate, "Roland Platt's Billionaire Acres." Behind armed guards, a man in a tuxedo and a woman in a gown stood on a balcony of a mansion overlooking the squalor across the street as they sipped champagne.

The entourage moseyed on to an exhibit with a sign offering "Psycho Therapy." Platt-obsessed nutjobs were invited to sit inside a two-hundred thousand dollar Mercedes G-Wagon to record a rant on a dashcam video and post it on social media for the admiration of their friends.

"Evita, do you want to show them how it's done?" Marius asked.

"Sure!" she said enthusiastically. She hopped into the front seat of the vehicle and hit a couple of buttons, before launching into a rage played on loudspeakers. "Oooh! That Platt! He makes me *sooooo* mad! I hate, hate, HATE HIM! *DIE PLATT! DIE!*" She pounded the steering wheel with her fists and finished with tears before stopping the recording. She looked out at Marius and smiled. "How was that?"

"*Magnifico!*" he replied, as the entourage applauded.

Next up was "Incarceration Station," where Marius demonstrated how delegates could create an AI video of themselves marching against the fill-in-the-blank outrage of the day. Following arrest, they were placed in paper handcuffs, booked by police, offered souvenir mug shots, and sent through the Turnstile O' Justice back to the streets.

At the end of the path, attendees pushed through a gate next to the exit that said:

LEAVING PLATTSVILLE
Goodbye, misery.

A second sign pointed with a large arrow to "*A Bold New Direction!*"

ENTERING A NEW AMERICA
Hello, happiness!

At the New America Welcome Center, with greetings posted in thirty-six languages, delegates were invited to take an America's Just Rewards card, scan for the app on their phone, or have a transponder implanted in their foreheads.

"We recommend the transponder," Marius said. "That way, you never lose it, and you never worry whether you got your points. It's as painless as an EZ Pass on the turnpike. You'll forget it's even there." He turned to the group. "Anyone want to sign up?"

Howie-Do-It pumped his fist in the air. "I'm in, bro!" he said with a grin. "I want me some points!"

Marty watched in dismay as Howie signed an application. "Are you sure there's a place to put a transponder in that cranium?" Marty chided. "Might get a little crowded next to that large brain."

Howie shrugged. "Trust me, dude. I've killed enough brain cells to make plenty of room."

Evita joined Robbie and Marty as they moved along the pathway where activists worked booths to sign up delegates for various causes. The first was the Indian Caucus, helmed by tribal Chief Five Fingers from the Two Dogs Humping Casino in Joliet. He wore a headdress and offered delegates the opportunity to relieve themselves of their guilt and their property by signing over their real estate.

Evita confided, "We offered Chief Five Fingers the entire city of Chicago since the first peoples here were Potawatomi or Watapotomi or Fighting Illini or… I don't know. I think there were a bunch of tribes here way back when. They called it Shikaakwa."

"I understand the Blackhawks are still here," Marty said.

"Really?" Evita asked. "Where?"

"Right around the United Center," Marty said. "They migrated from Canada and brought hockey with them. They beat a tribe from Detroit to win their first Stanley Cup in 1934."

"Oh," Evita said with a shrug. "I don't know what that's about. But it doesn't matter now anyway. Chief Five Fingers wouldn't take back Chicago."

"Why not?" Robbie asked.

"He said it was too dangerous," she replied. "One of our donors got him a condo on the Gold Coast overlooking the lake. We smoked a peace pipe, and he gave us a sack of poker chips."

Next door was a booth for Jiffy Gender. Boobs were on sale at introductory prices and penises were half off. "Which half?" Marty asked. Told by Ingram Swenson that it was the price that was cut in two rather than the appendage, Marty said he'd think it over.

"Do you do trade-ins?" he asked.

"Depends on the condition," Ingram replied. "Does it still work?"

"Intermittently," Marty said.

"Got a lot of miles, I'll bet," Ingram said.

"Less than you might think," Marty admitted. "It's only driven on weekends."

"Take it into one of our shops," Ingram said. "They'll give you an appraisal."

Marty winced. "Only if they promise not to laugh."

The next booth was a facsimile of an "Opiate for the Masses" safe injection clinic offering syringes, alcohol wipes, condoms, whiskey chasers, and a matchmaking service. In the back was a euthanasia clinic to be visited when the thrill was gone.

The last table, "Nobody is Illegal," asked for volunteers to house undocumented immigrants in their homes. Double points were awarded for brave souls willing to board gangbangers from Tren de Aragua. Triple points went to the heirs of families who got killed for their hospitality.

"I would do it," Robbie told Evita, "but I don't think they allow it at the White House. I mean, I'm sure the gangbangers are basically good people, right?"

"They're only here for a better life," Evita claimed.

"Hell, I'd probably join a gang myself in their situation," Robbie said.

"You are in a gang—the worst one!" Evita claimed. "The rich!"

Robbie tried to laugh it off. "Maybe I should get a dollar sign tattoo."

"Trust me," she said, with a hint of disgust, "you don't need one. It's written all over your face."

Marius gathered the media together. On a screen behind him, a video projected a model city: block after block of identical concrete apartment buildings surrounding a supertall office building.

"Welcome to our radiant future," Marius proclaimed, "where everything you need is less than fifteen minutes away. No more keeping up with the Joneses. Everyone is a Jones—equal in every way! Same living space. Same stores. Same schools. And everyone enjoys the same guilt-free existence. No more worrying whether one neighbor is getting ahead, and another is falling behind. Nobody's going anywhere!"

"Who decides what earns points?" Finn Tingleberry asked.

"We have panels of experts advising us," Marius replied.

"Wonderful!" Finn nodded. "It's time we listened to the *science!*"

"We asked them: What does an individual really need to eat?" Marius said. "What jobs are most helpful to the community, and how much should those jobs pay based on their contribution to the greater good? Do people even need to leave their apartment to work or are we all better served if they stay home and limit their greenhouse gas emissions?"

"Like breathing?" Skeeter Donlan asked.

Marius winced. "We've got way too many breathers out there."

Boof raised his hand. "What about farting?" As he noticed people turning to look at him, he added, "Asking for a friend."

"Tell your friend, Boof, we'll have community fart rooms in every building where our people can hold hands in a circle and collectively let loose and know they're doing something good. We'll turn their emissions into clean, green, renewable electricity and reduce our dependence on fossil fuels," Marius said. He glanced around at the media, which looked impressed. "Nothing goes to waste in our new America."

Robbie leaned over to Marty. "I invested in that stupid technology," he said, bitterly. "We couldn't get anyone to buy it. Now it's going to make somebody a fortune? That stinks."

"Sure does," Marty said, patting Robbie on the back. "You've always been a man ahead of your time."

Marius addressed the group. "I should remind you all that this ideal life we imagine is strictly voluntary," he reiterated. "Nobody *has* to live this way. It's only if you want social credit. If you don't want points, you're free to live a miserable existence."

"This all sounds so inspiring," Skeeter said. "What do points get for you?"

"We're emulating the Chinese system," Marius said. "Trustworthy people get deep discounts on bank loans and mortgages, no waiting time at hospitals, free electricity, and priority for school admissions. We even offer better placement in dating apps."

Marty asked, "What if you're not considered trustworthy?"

Marius turned grave. "If you elect not to adopt the collective spirit, then you've chosen to live outside acceptable social circles. We will have no choice but to restrict your travel, your access to the internet, and limit your educational choices. We're counting on the media to play a critical role in ensuring compliance, as you did with COVID."

"What can we do to help?" Finn asked.

"Public shaming, for one," Marius replied. "We will post everyone's score on our website. That should provide you a million opportunities for stories. Why were these people so stupid? What was going through their mind? And what about the people who made the right choices? How were their lives changed for the better?"

There was a murmur of general agreement from the media as Dinda and Ned walked among the throng handing out a list of key talking points about the bright beautiful future.

"There's a gift bag for each of you on the table next to the exit," Marius said. "We've got something special for you."

Marty grabbed a bag with his name on it and pulled out a fuzzy green blanket, embroidered with his initials, and a tag that said:

Replace your furnace this winter
with the warm blanket of collectivism.
—From your friends at America's Just Rewards

38. Boffo!

The media quickly coalesced around a consensus about the exhibits with opinions ranging from enthusiastic to giddy. This was, at last, the answer America had been waiting for. Opinion-makers from the mainstream media stood on the curb talking into cameras extolling the virtues of what they had just seen and heard.

"A great leap forward!" Boof declared. "America's Just Rewards will make life in this country so much easier. Gone are those nagging decisions about what to do, what to eat—"

"What to think!" Skeeter added.

"*Yes!*" Boof enthused. "There's so much misinformation out there. This rewards system will guide you. Pick the right news source—like *Boof & Skeeter*—and you get more than insight! You get points!"

Skeeter added, "As they say on Sardine Airlines, sit back, relax, and enjoy the ride. Once you see the benefits for yourself, the only decision you'll have to make is, 'Where do I sign?'"

"Woo-hoo!" Boof yelped. "With a transponder in your noggin, points are easier to get than ordering Ding Dong noodles from Wi Kow Tow!"

On a platform nearby, a special edition of *The Coven* convened to confer its blessings on the party's brilliant new initiative, with Finn Tingleberry offering the first word. "It's significant that a man like Robbie Crowe is leading this cause," he opined. "That says this isn't coming from the radical fringe or a foreign adversary. No sir! It's from the mainstream. Robbie Crowe is as all-American as baseball, hot dogs, apple pie and Chevrolet. Here is a descendant of one of the country's greatest industrial leaders saying to us: 'The old ways of my great-grandfather are over, people. Rugged individualism is out; collectivism is in.'"

"If you want to see what's coming, just look at New York City," said the rapturous host Binkie Smithers. "They know how to put the 'collect' in collectivism. First they collect taxes. Then they collect more taxes. Then they collect fines, fees, interest, and profits. And for those who don't want to cooperate? Collect their butts and lock 'em up!"

Coven panelist Yappy Hoffman, professor of Marketing Marxism at Columbia University, noted that people who go against the program won't go to jail. "They will be offered a chance to rethink their choices in a reeducation camp with their loved ones. That way, you needn't separate families."

Binkie reached over and grabbed Yappy's arm. "We're blowing up nuclear families, Yaps. Families are where kids are getting misinformation—from their clueless parents. With pre-K, three-K, two-K, and one-K, our public schools can care for children the minute they pop out of the cooch, fix 'em up with new genders, and get 'em scope rifles in case that doesn't work out."

Hoot Biddle, the token moderate hired to take daily beatings from The Coven, scoffed. "I'm sorry, but that's crazy. You're putting the loco in loco parentis."

Binkie glared at him. "It's time you faced reality, Hoot: kids are *not* learning to read. They're *not* learning to write. And there's nothing we can do about it. So, let's just create a society where illiteracy won't hold back anyone anymore. All these—quote-unquote—*'negatives'* can be positives. A nation of morons, junkies, and criminals doesn't have to be a bad thing. Only if we let it!"

Back in his hotel room, Robbie flipped through the channels with increasing despair. He was missing something, but what? The ideas that he was to champion seemed nutty, yet the commentators made them sound perfectly normal.

The needle on Robbie's moral compass was spinning in circles, failing to settle on the direction he should turn. All his lifelong assumptions about his country, its history, and its way of life were turned upside down. Success wasn't something to be celebrated. They made it sound like theft that needed to be punished. Freedoms he thought were guaranteed in the constitution were cancelled to make way for official information and monitored speech. Ancestors who once made him proud of their contributions to society were a complete embarrassment. And his government—*the Robbie Crowe administration!*—was going to codify these principles into a "voluntary" program that sounded an awful lot like a coercive nightmare.

Robbie flipped off the TV and dropped on the bed, staring at the ceiling. After living a life of first-class travel in private jets and limousines, how did he end up in the clown car? He'd never seen such people up close before. Dressed like hobos. Puffy clumps of hair in the colors of Play-Doh. Faces pinned with knitting needles. And fashions that might have been pulled out of a charity bin, accessorized by keffiyehs and face masks. He felt no connection to them or their fetishes, yet he was now supposed to give away all his money for their *shit?*

The only version of this walk on the radical side that Robbie found appealing was Evita, the "Sexiest Socialist Alive" according to the *People* magazine on his coffee table. Yes, she was a little dumb and more than a tad naive. But she was also gorgeous and self-assured and made the most lunatic ideas sound innocent and pure. All one had to do was lay their head on a government-issue air mattress and float merrily down a stream of freebies. The guilt he felt for his lifetime of extraordinary privilege, and the nagging sense that maybe he really didn't deserve it, could be assuaged by her forgiveness, consummated in a Peninsula Hotel suite. The price was extraordinary but it might just be worth it if she would absolve him of his sins.

He leaned over to the nightstand and grabbed his Magic 8-Ball for guidance. If penance must be paid for the sins of his forebearers, the question was how much. One billion? Two? *His entire fortune?* And so he posed the question: *Could he ever cleanse his soul enough to satisfy Evita?* He shook the orb and turned it over.

BETTER NOT TELL YOU NOW

Robbie sank deeper into his despair. Even his trusty ball had turned against him.

He would find the answer himself.

39. The Big Smoosh

Robbie punched the doorbell on Evita's Grand Suite down the hall from his suite at the Peninsula Hotel and rocked from one foot to the other. What excuse would he offer for stopping in unannounced? Oh yes. He wanted to know about her speech. *Remember,* he said to himself, *tell her that as if you truly give a shit.*

Evita answered the door wearing nothing but a simple white bathrobe and a sheepish smile. As Robbie reeled his tongue back into his mouth, she pulled the robe around her with one hand and pushed her hair back with the other.

"Hello there," she said. "I thought you might be the valet."

He regarded her expression. "Disappointed?"

"Kinda," she admitted. "I'm waiting for the dress I'm wearing tonight for my big speech. Come on in." She glanced uneasily over her shoulder toward the bedroom. "I should probably get some clothes on."

"Please. Not on my account," he said. "We're friends now." With any luck, that robe would slip away, and her untethered body would rise to meet him. They would wrap each other in the warm embrace of collectivism, and she would seize his means of production and go to work.

Instead, she walked him over to a sofa and sat down. "What's up?"

"I just wanted to wish you good luck on your speech," he said.

"Oh my God! I'm *sooo* excited! I've got this *great* theme. It's called…" A knock on the door derailed her train of thought, and Evita ejected from the couch. "Hold on. I bet that's the dress."

She opened the door, took a black garment bag from the valet, and brought it into the living room. "Let's see how this turned out," she said as she unzipped the bag. She pulled out a long white dress, cut low in the front, with sleeves that fell off-the-shoulder. "*Ooh* yeah…" she uttered as she appraised it up and down.

She held up the dress for Robbie to see. "Check it out," she said, excitedly. She turned it around to show the back side, which had a scrawl below the shoulders that said, "HEY BILLIONAIRE!" and a giant red lip printed across the approximate location of her buns. "Think they'll get it?"

Robbie winced. "Hard to miss."

"I'm telling 'em, 'Kiss my ass,'" she said impishly.

"Right, right," Robbie replied. "I got the point."

She hung it up on a doorframe and sat down to admire it. "You can't take it personally, you know," she said. "It's not about you, per se." She reached over and patted his knee. "You can still be saved."

"You think so?"

"All you rich guys can be saved," she said with a shrug. "All you've gotta do is pay up."

Robbie wondered how much was required. What in the eyes of these revolutionaries was enough? And what were they going to do with the money once they got it?

"Are you coming to the speech?" she asked.

"I can't. Ned said I shouldn't show up at the convention until tomorrow," Robbie said. "You were about to tell me what your speech was called."

She grinned. "The Big Smoosh."

"The big... what?" he asked.

"*Smoosh*," she said, holding up her hands and intertwining her fingers. "You know, smoosh together? It's like Lincoln said, 'a nation divided...'" She paused and rolled her head from side to side. "'Something, something...' I forget. The important thing is he said being divided kinda sucks. So, let's just smoosh everyone together."

"Lincoln said that?"

"No. That's my idea. Bring people at the top down, like this," she said as she brought her right hand to chest level. "Bring everyone from below up here," she said, demonstrating with her left hand. "Keep people in the middle almost where they are—maybe a little lower. That way, everyone's the same. Nobody's jealous. Everybody's happy. It's all good because we smooshed 'em all together into one big clump."

"We want everyone in a clump?"

"Smooshed!" she said with a big smile. "America the Smooshiful!"

Robbie raised an eyebrow. "That sounds so simple," he said. "But I don't know if people will go along. Human nature, and all..."

Evita leaned forward in earnest. "That's the problem, right? Humans. But I think they'll go along when they understand what happens when they do."

"And when they don't?"

She offered a shrug. *They'll be sorry!* "Some people I've been talking to say, 'We're going to do whatever it takes by any means necessary… blah, blah, blah. But I don't like the sound of that. I want to do this the nice way. Let's offer rich people a chance to surrender the money they basically stole from us without roundups and jail and public executions and stuff. That could get very messy. Especially if they bring in guillotines like they're talking about." She extended her arm across the top of the sofa until her fingers were almost touching his. "All I think we need is a genuine leader to sign away their fortune and get the ball rolling."

Robbie sighed. "Like who?"

She smiled beguilingly, twirled her hair, and looked into his eyes. "Didn't you read your speech?"

"Apparently you did," Robbie replied.

"I just wanted to be sure we were in sync."

"Are we?"

"That depends," she replied. "All we're asking is that you give your fair share."

"It sounds like you want me to 'give' it before you take it."

"Isn't it nicer that way?" she asked.

"How much do you want me to give?" Robbie asked.

She whirled her hand in the air, as if she were throwing pixie dust. "Just… all of it."

"And that would help smoosh everybody together?"

"It's a start!" she said. "We're gonna smoosh with gender, too. No more men's restrooms. No more women's restrooms. America becomes one big restroom. And we're going to smoosh with housing; everyone can live in our model cities they never have to leave ever again. The smooshing goes on and on and on."

Robbie watched her scoop up a handful of nuts from a bowl on the coffee table and thought: *Maybe it's true that you are what you eat.* This idea of forking over even a portion of his fortune for this sketchy program sounded idiotic. What would it get him? It was time to find out once and for all if it would win Evita's affection. "How would smooshing work in real life? Like, say, between you and me?"

She slid closer to him. "Easy," she said. "You just give it to me."

Robbie gulped. "Give what?"

"All you've got," she said, in a breathy whisper.

Was this the moment at last? Robbie's heart was pounding. "Do you mean that?"

She raised her face toward his and gazed at him with sultry eyes. "Of course, I do. Anything is possible."

Call my banker and sign me up! Robbie reached out to her but stopped suddenly when he heard a click of a door, followed by shuffling footsteps. He looked up to see Marius walking out of the bedroom, wearing a robe that matched Evita's. *Oh, fuuuuck…*

"Robbie!" Marius said grandly as he towel-dried his hair. "I didn't know you were here."

Robbie felt like someone stuck a pin in his balloon, not to mention his manhood. Everything in the room seemed to sag. *Marius and Evita were a couple?* He glanced around for a powder room where he could throw up.

"I was just…" *What was I doing?* Robbie couldn't recall. "I was just leaving."

Marius's expression suggested he knew exactly what Robbie was thinking. He couldn't help savoring the humiliation. Robbie might be at the top of the ticket, but Marius and his father were in charge.

"We were talking about the idea of wealthy people giving all their money away for the greater good," Robbie said. "I'm trying to decide whether that's a good idea."

"Of course it is!" Marius said.

"Everyone will listen to you," Evita said brightly. "You're as famous as a bagel."

Robbie bristled. "A *doughnut*," he huffed as he stood up.

"Either way, it sounds like you're a soft doughy blob," Marius chided.

"No!" Robbie said. "I'm *Krispy* Kreme. Crisp—but with a K! And pretty damn tasty, from what people tell me."

Evita roared with laughter and Robbie's embarrassment was complete. His romance with Evita was finished, and so was the idea he'd give these assholes a penny.

40. Party Favors

The warm glow of collective action lit up Chicago like a summer campground, with sporadic fires popping up in the darkness all over the city and shadowy figures dancing around the flames. Police cars and buses provided most of the kindling, but any object associated with the oppressive capitalist regime was fair game.

"What you see here tonight are protests against the Platt regime that have been, by and large, extremely peaceful," a reporter claimed on FFS, as he stood in front of a blazing furniture store. "Tempers are understandably running a little hot, given their rage over what President Platt has done to this country. But violence is the exception, not the rule."

The mayhem served as the main event at the Riot Party in the Z Bar atop the elegant Peninsula Hotel. Servers mingled among the celebrity-studded crowd, offering hors d'oeuvres and champagne. Guests basking in the reflected orange light from the streets below delighted in the revolutionary mayhem on the Magnificent Mile, where marauding looters were jumping in and out of store windows, arms loaded with treasure.

Robbie watched despondently from a window in a corner of the bar, away from the happy crowd. He noticed that Harper's, the massive department store founded by Lindsey's grandfather more than a hundred years ago, had its windows boarded up to thwart the looters, and its iconic neon marquee was turned off.

"Quite a show, isn't it?"

Robbie turned to see Lady Janice, sporting a little black dress and a glass of straight bourbon. "Not my idea of entertainment," Robbie said glumly.

She moved in closer and looked into his eyes. "Mine neither. Are you interested in a little diversion?"

Robbie regarded her eager expression run and considered her question. An escape from his predicament would be more than welcome, but he could not imagine a romp with her under any circumstances, so he pretended he didn't understand the question. He nodded toward the scene below. "I don't see how destroying a great city supports our cause."

She sighed. "Haven't you seen the news? They're not blaming us," she said sharply. "They're blaming Platt."

Robbie shook his head. "Why would anyone believe that?"

"Because they want to," Lady Janice replied.

"I don't like what it says about us," he said.

"Then stand up and tell them what you want."

He wanted to tell her to go away. "Tell who?" he whined.

"Who else? The *Barbus*," Lady Janice said, insistently. "They don't scare me, and they shouldn't scare you. All it takes is some balls, if you've got 'em, and the more I see you, frankly, the less sure I am."

"Is that right?" he bristled.

"I told them what I want in no uncertain terms," Lady Janice boasted. "And you know what? Next month, I'm moving into a house they bought for me on the water in Martha's Vineyard."

Now she had Robbie's attention. "How did you manage that?" he asked.

"I just told Bennie flat out: 'I don't accept your bullshit,'" she said. "Trust me. If you're willing to go toe-to-toe with him when he needs you, he'll back down. Bullies always do."

Robbie returned to the window. "They want me to give away my money," he said. "My ancestors worked very hard to make sure their children and grandchildren had a better life. Think how disappointed they would be to see their descendants throw it away." He shook his head. "How did Dewey handle them? Did he ever push back?"

She scoffed. "Of course not," she said. "He was a cream puff."

"Yeah, well," Robbie sighed. "They tell me I'm a doughnut."

She arched an eyebrow. "Sounds right to me. You've got a big ol' hole in the middle where your guts ought to be."

"Thanks for the pep talk," he said sullenly. "Enjoy your new house."

Robbie turned away from Lady Janice to see Comandante Justin's foot soldiers bringing in pillowcases filled with merchandise from the stores below. Party guests ignored the giant TV screens showing Evita deploring greed in her convention speech and rushed to the tables to help themselves. They grabbed all the purses, belts, athletic shoes, and puffy coats they could hold and sped off to drop the goods in their rooms.

"A different kind of booty call, eh?" Marty said, as he approached Robbie.

"A band of fucking pirates," Robbie said, shaking his head. "It's disgusting."

Marty shrugged. "You know there will be plenty more of this sort of thing when you're elected."

"I'm not going to be elected," Robbie replied.

Marty scoffed. "Polls show you up five points on Platt. You're getting a big convention bounce."

"I'm getting out," Robbie declared.

Marty's head snapped back. "Why would you do that?"

"This is not what I signed up for."

"It's exactly what you signed up for," Marty reminded him.

Robbie summoned him over to the windows. "I know they want to replace the system. Do they have to burn down the old one first? I'd be embarrassed to show my face after this."

Lindsey joined them at the windows. "Well, it's official," she said sadly. "Harper's is closed."

Robbie looked at her in surprise. "I didn't expect to see you here."

"I came in for a Harper's board meeting," she said.

"I saw they boarded up the windows for the riots," Robbie noted. "What a shame."

"It's closed for good," Lindsey said. "And not because of one riot. It's because of a riot that never ends. Shoplifting. Vandalism. Assaults in the elevators, restrooms, and stairwells. Women beating the hell out of each other with suitcases and handbags with no consequences. Louis Feinberg, our CEO, has been pulling his hair out. Five straight years of losses—and there's nothing he can do about it." She shook her head. "The cops are no help here. The mayor told them, 'Hands off.' He says the community has other needs. So they sold the building to a homeless shelter."

"On Michigan Avenue?" Robbie asked, incredulously.

Marty shook his head. "Your grandfather is rolling over in his grave."

Lindsey shrugged helplessly. "If his body is still there. His granite headstone was stolen. It's probably a kitchen counter in Lincoln Park."

Robbie sighed and started toward the door. "I am so done."

Lindsey grabbed him by the arm. "Where are you going?"

"He's quitting," Marty explained.

"Wait. *What?*" She gripped Robbie's arm harder. "You can't do that."

He glared at her. "You know, Lindsey. I'm sick of people telling me what I can and can't do." He jerked his arm away. "I'm going home."

They stood in silence for a moment as partygoers roared their approval over another haul of merchandise from the besieged Magnificent Mile. Lindsey moved closer to Robbie and pointed with her thumb toward the lootfest near the door.

"You're the only one who can stop this disaster," she said.

Marty muttered, "We're doomed."

Robbie ignored Marty and turned to Lindsey. "Let Platt take them on. He loves a brawl."

"How do you expect to get out?" Lindsey asked.

"I'm just gonna leave." Robbie nodded toward Marty. "He can make up an excuse."

"I do have a file of them," Marty acknowledged. "Bad cold is a favorite. Kid's soccer game is another. I'm sure I can find one that works."

Lindsey composed herself briefly. "Okay," she said to Robbie, "I'm not telling you what to do here. I know you have sensitivity about that. But let me just suggest as politely as I can that that is the *stupidest fucking idea I've heard all week*! And I've heard a lot of them!"

Robbie stepped back like he'd been slapped in the face. Lindsey took a step closer and got into his grill.

"Nobody just walks away from a presidential nomination this late in the game."

"Dewey did," Robbie protested.

Lindsey threw up her hands. "He was brain dead."

Marty nodded. "Pretty good excuse. I haven't tried that one."

Robbie stomped around in a little circle. "I can't get behind their agenda," he said.

"Then get in front of it," Lindsey snapped.

"I can't relate to their people," Robbie said.

"Then find your own people," she insisted.

"I don't want to give away my money."

"Then don't!" Lindsey said. "Nobody's got a gun to your head."

"...yet," Marty added.

"Okay, yet," Lindsey said. "You know what you should do—and not that I'm telling you, of course—but you need to locate your balls and swing 'em."

"Big talk from you!" Robbie whined. "You walked away from the Barbus, too."

"I tell you what," Lindsey said. "If you hang in there, I'll accept the Barbus' offer to manage the power for their data centers."

Marty was stunned. "Why would you do that?"

"It occurred to me that if I can turn on their computers, I can turn them off, too," she said. "That might be important."

"And dangerous as hell," Marty said.

"So's their program," Lindsey said. She turned to Robbie. "You've always talked about your big vision. How's this: use your speech to tell the country what's in it for them with America's Just Rewards. And put the spotlight on Bennie and Marius. They hate coming out of the shadows."

Robbie looked scared to death. "They might shoot me on stage."

"Nah," Marty said. "They'll wait at least until you get back to the hotel."

"Seriously?"

"No," Marty said, shaking his head. "Evita can't win and they know it. You're safe until January."

"And then what?"

Marty sighed. "We probably need a plan."

"Oh great," Robbie grumbled. "That's very reassuring."

"In the meantime," Lindsey said, "this is the best option you've got. Lay it all out there. If they hate what you have to say, they'll boot you off the ticket. If they love it, you're stuck a while longer."

Marty put his full glass of red wine on a waiter's passing tray and turned to Robbie. "Let me noodle around some ideas. Can you meet me first thing in the morning?"

Robbie thought through his morning schedule. First thing after rolling over and scratching his balls: hydrate. Drink some water. Order a green slime from room service. Then work into his circadian rhythms, with nothing on but low lights and boxer shorts. Have breakfast in the room alone. Suck down two cups of coffee and meet his constitutional duties. Workout with a personal trainer for twenty minutes or so. Take a hot shower, then maybe call Kristi for a few laps around the sofa. "I'm booked."

"Are you kidding?" Lindsey asked. "You have something to do that's more pressing than this?"

"I might be able to do eleven or so," Robbie said with a yawn.

Marty wearily shook his head. "Glad to see you're taking this seriously."

"My calendar is nuts!" Robbie complained.

"I'm calling bullshit," Marty said, sharply. "There's only one thing on there that matters, and it's your speech."

"All right. Fine. *Fine!*" Robbie said with a sneer. "Ten-forty-five. Happy pappy?"

41. Bottoms Up

It was two a.m. when Marty finished a revision of Robbie's speech. He still needed to massage a few passages but decided to step away from the keyboard before giving it one last read.

He slipped on his shoes, grabbed his room key and his phone, and headed to the hospitality suite down the hall. He spotted the coffee urn just inside the door but found it cold and empty. A voice behind him asked, "Want something a little stronger?"

Marty turned to see Ned holding a drink on a couch in the corner. Ned held up his glass. "There's scotch under the bar," he said.

Marty decided a few moments with the campaign director might offer just the sort of perspective that he could use to finish off the speech. He found a glass and poured a weak drink before joining Ned in the corner.

"Still on the job?" Ned asked as Marty took a chair.

"Wordsmithing Robbie's speech," Marty said. "Just about there."

Ned sipped his drink, clearly one of many this evening, given his rheumy eyes and slurred speech. "He's freaking out, isn't he?"

"A bit," Marty acknowledged.

Ned shrugged. "Yeah, well. Why wouldn't he?" He leaned back on the sofa. "I'm sure this is well outside his comfort zone."

"It's nowhere near his zip code," Marty conceded.

"Duly noted," Ned said. "What he needs to understand is that none of the crazy stuff he's seeing this week matters. The protests. The violence. The fires. The chaos. That's political theater to show our base we're going to war against Platt." He mockingly shook a fist in the air. "Down with the tyrant, and all that bullshit."

"And America's Just Rewards?" Marty asked.

"That's the *real* scary stuff, isn't it?" he said with a laugh.

Ned stood up and went to the bar, where he retrieved the bottle of scotch and brought it back to the corner. "I may as well stop pretending

I'm not gonna finish this sucker," Ned said with a chuckle. He filled his glass and topped off Marty's. "Cheers."

Marty clinked his glass with Ned's and sipped slowly. "What are we celebrating?" he asked.

Ned sat up, excited. "I signed my deal tonight."

"For what?"

"Zero-point-zero-zero-one percent," Ned said with a grin. "Doesn't sound like much, does it?"

"Depends on what it's for," Marty said.

"America's Just Rewards," Ned said.

Marty arched an eyebrow. "I'm sure that could add up."

"Ya think?" Ned laughed. "America's Just Rewards is the single greatest money-making scheme the world has ever seen. You think about the scope of this program and it's breathtaking, man. The government picks the winners and the losers in every industry and directs consumers to patronize them. If you're a corporate partner, you survive. You might even make a profit. If you're not a partner, you're dead. The Hands Up Foundation gets a slice of every transaction. You realize how much money it will make in a thirty-trillion-dollar economy?"

Marty took a deep breath. "I'd guess that's a lot."

"In precise terms?" Ned said. "A shit-ton."

Marty nodded. "How does that square with the notion of smooshing everyone together into one big clump?"

"C'mon, man. You know how it goes. There's always a top, and there's always a bottom," Ned said. "An immutable law of nature." Ned sat back on the sofa. "Commies aren't immune; they just hide it better. The Soviet Union. China. Cuba. People at the top got very rich and the people below get clumped, lumped, spindled, folded, and mutilated. Lenin was pretty blunt about it."

Marty paused, thinking. "Imagine all the people, sharing all the wealth?"

Ned shook his head in disgust. "Not *John* Lennon. *Vladimir* Lenin. Check it out sometime. He painted a rosy picture of the world he had in mind. But he knew many people weren't buying it, so he demanded 'ruthless suppression' of resisters. Hang all the wealthy peasants in public so everyone could see."

"Would Bennie go along with something like that?" Marty asked.

Ned waved his hand dismissively. "In his cold heart of hearts? He wants to see America brought to its knees like Romania was after the war. He thinks the US sold his country down the Danube. It's payback time, and he's expecting a very big check. If Robbie's elected, he'll get it. And he's not the only one."

Marty felt his heart racing. "Who else is in on this deal?" he asked.

"You didn't hear this from me," Ned said, before taking another sip. "It's everybody in our leadership group. Worth, Kristi, Meredith and Eleanor are all part of the Friends and Family plan. I even got a little piece for Dinda. She doesn't know it yet, but she's set for life."

"And Evita?"

Ned paused, thinking. "She gets the biggest slice of anybody. If things go the way they expect, she'll be a billionaire on Inauguration Day."

Marty fell back in his seat. "She says billionaires shouldn't exist."

Ned chuckled. "*Bad* billionaires shouldn't exist. Good ones are another story."

"What's the difference?"

"Who your friends are."

"So, Robbie gives away his fortune and it goes to her," Marty said.

"Not directly," Ned said, "but yeah. It eventually winds its way over to her. Why do you think she agreed not to contest Robbie's nomination? She's got the best of both worlds. She gets rich *and* she gets to be president—when the time is right, of course."

"When would that be?" Marty asked.

"Whenever it's necessary," Ned said.

Marty drained his drink and put his glass on the table. "Suppose this gets exposed."

Ned laughed. "You're kidding right? If we take Congress and we control the Department of Justice, who's going to investigate? Nobody. Our pals in the press won't touch it. They're already on the lookout for Russian disinformation."

"Is that what you're calling this?"

"If it needs to be, sure," Ned said. He poured the last of the scotch in his glass. "Did I tell you Boof and Skeeter are writing a book: 'How the Media Covered up Dewey Fenwick's Decline.' The foreword is by Finn Tingleberry." Ned roared with laughter.

"I'm sure they'll get to the bottom of it," Marty said.

Ned nodded. "They've already reached one conclusion," he said. "It was somebody else!"

Marty stood to leave, which jolted Ned out of his buzz. "I probably shouldn't have told you all this. It's the kind of stuff that gets people killed," he said. "But I think you know that."

"I do," Marty said as he turned toward the door.

"Good luck with the speech," Ned called. "Just remember what W.C. Fields said: If you can't dazzle them will brilliance, baffle them with bullshit."

Marty nodded. "Count on it."

"Which one?" Ned asked with a chuckle.

"That arena's going to smell like the State Fair."

42. Talking the Talk

Robbie knew as he entered through the heavily guarded security entrance at the United Center that this could be the day when Howie-Do-It would finally have to take a bullet for him. As a precaution, Robbie sent his trusted body man to the convention in advance of his speech to scope out any lurking dangers.

He found Howie on alert offstage, scanning the crowd with binoculars.

"How's it looking?" Robbie asked.

"So far, so good," Howie replied.

"Any threats?" Robbie asked.

"A couple bazookas pointing this way," he said, adjusting his focus.

"Seriously?"

"Check it out," he said, handing over his binoculars. "Super-hot chick in the front row of the Texas delegation."

Robbie raised the glasses to his eyes. "Uh-huh. Definitely got some long-range missiles there." He handed back the glasses and clapped Howie on the shoulder. "Good job."

Robbie proceeded to the green room, where he grabbed a bottle of water and watched the warm-up acts on a large screen.

A procession of cultural icons led the way. The celebrated singer Mutha Ta'Reesa declared that if Platt were reelected in November, she would leave America and suffer for her political conscience on her estate in Provence. The activist actor Mark Huffalott wept as he renounced his embarrassing whiteness and claimed he was going to be dipped into a vat of henna and tinted into a person of color. Still, he would selflessly refuse reparations checks for the oppression he was sure to suffer. Dr. Abdullah Oblongata followed to demand that American schools cease teaching math since it was a racist construct stolen from Egyptians or Nubians or "a mess 'o Potamians," and besides, it was "just too damn hard!" And the rapper CheeZee Gritz worked the delegates into a frenzy with his hit, *Gimme Summa Dat Big Butt,* which was so obscene the NFL signed him for the Super Bowl.

Marty approached Robbie. "How you feeling, champ? Ready to rock this joint?"

"I don't know how I let you talk me into this," Robbie muttered. "Who's on before me?"

Marty looked at his phone. "It was supposed to be the Migrant Extranational Choir. But I just got a text message that says the box truck they were riding in was pulled over by ICE. Last seen, they were singing *Guantanamera* on a bus to the airport." He looked up. "Looks like you're up next."

The arena darkened and the Robbie Crowe biographical video began on the screen, offering delegates an inside glimpse at their kind of billionaire: self-aware, ready to fork over cash for the noble cause, and on their side. At the video's conclusion, the crowd rose as one, roaring its approval, thrusting signs into the air touting Robbie as the people's choice. A voice of God over the loudspeakers announced, "Ladies... would be ladies... gentlemen... former gentlemen... and people who aren't quite sure: Please welcome our nominee for president of the United States of America. *Rob-bie Crooowe!*"

Robbie took the stage smiling and waving, as the sound system pumped out *Elected* by Alice Cooper. Robbie paused midway on his walk to the podium and gazed out at the crowd, a huge grin covering his private terror: *Who are these people?* Despite not recognizing a single face, he pointed at random delegates and gave thumbs up, mouthed hellos, and nodded his head in mock wonder as if he couldn't believe something so wonderful was happening to him.

"Run Robbie RUN!" they chanted. *"Run Robbie RUN!"*

Robbie appeared to exult in their praise, clasping his hands in a prayerful pose as he continued his slow walk to the podium. There he peered out at the crowd and noted that his flock looked more like a herd. *These were some of the fattest people he'd ever seen!* He should skip the speech and lead them in jumping jacks! He forced a grin and put his hand over the place where a heart was normally located, then offered his own applause for the people applauding him.

The crowd remained standing for another full minute to show its appreciation before people realized the hospitality suites might close before this shindig was over, and they could miss out on the last round of free booze. They piped down as Robbie motioned for quiet.

"Hello, America!" Robbie called, as more jubilant cheers rang out and air horns blared. When the crowd calmed again, Robbie offered thanks to the many people who made his nomination possible, starting with the late great Dewey Fenwick. The mention of his name launched a farewell serenade for the dearly departed. "*Dew-eeee!… Dew-eeee!….*"

Robbie shushed them. "We honor President Fenwick's memory tonight with our deep well of love, affection, and respect. We know he's with us in spirit. All of us, especially me, owe him our gratitude. He made the job of president look so effortless, I thought: Hey, maybe I can do that!" That was met with more calls of *"Run Robbie RUN!"* before he launched into his text.

"This campaign," Robbie intoned, more somberly, "is about three things. The first is love, for we all love to hate Roland Platt. That gives us our reason for getting up in the morning." Thunderous applause rained down from the arena. "The second is about being positive, for we are positive we can't stand any of our friends and relatives who voted for that jerk." More applause. "And, third, it's about claiming America's Just Rewards, a program to help us atone for the many sins of our country's past and find redemption through our good deeds in the future."

The delegates stamped their feet, loving what they were hearing.

"Let's face it," Robbie continued, "America for too long has been too successful, with the world's largest economy, its strongest military, and a dominant role in world affairs. I ask you: Haven't we had enough? Isn't it time to take our foot off the gas and let some other countries take the wheel? Leadership is exhausting—and it takes too large of a toll on our country!"

The crowd rose as one, roaring its agreement. *"Run Robbie RUN! Run Robbie RUN!"*

Robbie looked at the crowd in wonder. Weren't they supposed to be booing? He cast a glance offstage at Marty, who rolled his hand in a motion and mouthed, "Keep going."

Robbie pressed on. "Enough of the brutal competition between our people for resources like food and shelter! Enough of the hostilities with other countries! Enough with a system that produces winners and losers, haves and have-nots, a system that creates anger, resentment, and war. Look at the thousands of demonstrators in the streets of Chicago this week. Their protests turned violent only because they so desperately want peace and love!"

That hit home for the delegates, prompting more foot stomping. A few chairs were tossed in support. Robbie was again dumbfounded by the audience buying this nonsense. Still, he pressed ahead.

"I see an America," he declared, "that is no longer guided by the antiquated notion of getting ahead in life by — quote/unquote — 'working hard and doing a good job'. As if that counts for anything!" Ripples of laughter rolled through the audience, as people yelled, *"Fuck that shit!"* and *"Enough's enough!"*

"The America I want," Robbie continued, "is one where everyone is free to decide whether they want to work or play or do next to nothing all day! Why develop a work ethic when the system is so rigged you can't get past the job interview?"

TV cameras broadcasting the event panned the crowd to show a burly bearded man dressed like Little Bo Beep pounding his shepherd's crook on the floor, a tall man dressed as a cartoon dog barking approval, and a possible woman wearing a clown outfit, a curly multicolored wig, a keffiyeh, and a COVID mask.

"I see an America," Robbie continued, "where all our people can relieve themselves of their guilt — and their possessions — through America's Just Rewards. Rolling out AI data centers throughout the land will allow us to collect information from banks, stores, and hospitals and combine it with government files to make sure every one of you gets all the credit you deserve. For those critics who may call this overreach, I say: If you have nothing to hide, you have nothing to fear. On the other hand, if you supported Roland Platt… you've got some 'splainin' to do!"

The delegates chanted their approval. *"Lock them UP! Lock them UP!"*

"Yes, through America's Just Rewards, we're going to bring those nasty clingers and deplorables back into line — or there will be a price to pay," Robbie declared. "For inspiration, we looked to China's Social Credit System, a model for tracking behaviors and rewarding people accordingly. Live right, show your loyalty, earn points, and you'll be accorded the proper respect: preferential terms on mortgages and loans… priority access to healthcare, education, and housing… travel perks at airports and train stations… and exclusive discounts when shopping with our corporate partners. On the other hand, if you live selfishly, it's no soup for you! You will be denied loans, limited in your travel, turned down for jobs, prevented from accessing health care and the internet, and publicly shamed. But that's your call, since this is all about personal choice. *Let… freedom…RING!"*

The crowd roared its approval. *"Let freedom ring! Let freedom ring!"*

"Santa Claus is coming to town, people! Getting all these wonderful presents requires us to see you when you're sleeping and know when you're awake. We'll know if you've been bad or good—and so will everyone else, because we're going to post your performance scores online, on electronic signs, on billboards, and on TV. My fellow Americans: This is your chance to *shine!"*

The arena rocked again, prompting Robbie to look over at Marty, who offered a palms up shrug.

Robbie continued, "Roland Platt has viciously claimed we are a party that promotes policies that never affect our own personal lives. Tonight, I am proud to offer an emphatic rebuttal to that blatant lie," Robbie said. "Let's show Platt and the rest of America we live by the high moral principles we espouse!"

Deafening applause rocked the arena.

"I intend to rebuild the foundation of our country where it begins: with our children. There is only one way to ensure that no child is left behind, and that's by making sure no child gets ahead. By eliminating biased programs for so-called gifted students, we can ensure true equity. Schools that reach 15 percent proficiency in math are pretty damn good if you don't understand numbers! And 20 percent fluency in reading makes no difference to someone who can't read in the first place. Let's face it: reading is *overrated* anyway!"

The crowd chanted: *"O-ver-RATE-ed! O-ver-RATE-ed!"*

Robbie nodded in agreement but held up his hands to shush the crowd. "We mustn't hold our illiterate graduates responsible for leveraging the only money-making skills they have. Is it their fault they've turned to carjacking, robbery, and peddling drugs to make a living? Not just 'no'! *Hell* no! We know whose fault this is!"

"Ro-land PLATT! Ro-land PLATT!"

"That's right!" Robbie declared, as sweat dripped down his neck. "Emptying our jails of these talented youngsters gives us the opportunity to reimagine our prisons as sanctuaries for our senior citizens who are members of our second- or third-greatest generation! Staying in prison will allow them to flee the criminals we've let loose in their neighborhoods and give them a place to play pickleball in peace!"

That prompted a huge roar from the crowd. Robbie looked over to Marty. *They were definitely supposed to boo that!*

Marty shrugged. *Got me!*

"Reaching our dreams requires gobs of other people's money, of course, and we know exactly where to get it," Robbie said. "All our party has ever asked of our nation's wealthiest citizens is to give more... and then a little more... and then maybe an itty-bitty teensy-weensy bit more before we finally say, 'hell with it,' and just freaking take it! Right?"

The crowd was in a frenzy.

Robbie continued. "That is why it has been such a privilege to spend time this summer with the great Bennie Barbu and his son Marius, who have quietly worked behind the scenes to become our party's greatest benefactors. They're not some bloodsucking vampires cynically feeding off the public's hopes and dreams with unworkable schemes! They just give... and give... and give some more. And their greatest gift is about to come!"

Spotlights shined on the suite where Bennie and Marius were seated, prompting all heads to turn in their direction and applaud. Robbie noted how grim they looked as they waited to hear what Robbie would say.

"Bennie and Marius are the architects behind America's Just Rewards, which is a culmination of Bennie's lifelong dream, as a heartfelt payback to America. And tonight, I am pleased to announce that these wonderful, selfless people will do exactly what they've asked of others: Donate all their profits from America's Just Rewards to the people."

The crowd rose to its feet to salute the Barbus in their suite, where the spotlights illuminated their frozen smiles and stiff waves.

"Let them be a shining inspiration to all of us, not just to talk the talk, but to walk the walk, wherever that may lead!" Robbie shouted. "Each and every one us can be Barbus if we think of the greater good! Thank you, thank you, thank you, America! We are one of the best countries in the world! Top ten for sure!"

The band began to play a pulsating refrain from *Gimme Summa Dat Big Butt* as Evita appeared from the shadows and joined Robbie as the crowd cheered, *"CROWE-MAN-O-LO! CROWE-MAN-O-LO!"*

Robbie leaned close to Evita's ear. "I'm on to you," he said. "I know who you are."

Her eyes widened in surprise before she remembered who he was. "And I know what you're going to do about it." She pulled her face away and smirked. "Nothing."

They joined uneasy hands and raised them in unity as confetti and red, white, and blue balloons swirled in a patriotic blizzard on stage. That was followed by the release of yellow, orange, green and violet balloons representing the pride flag. Then came black, brown, light blue and pink balloons from the progress pride flag. Next came barking furries bearing various versions of the furry pride flag, followed by runners crisscrossing the stage carrying banners from various dictatorships and kleptocracies around the world. The colorful display climaxed with a dramatic presentation of the global symbol of Palestinian solidarity and resistance: watermelons, whose green, red, black and white colors matched the Palestinian flag. As drums pounded, one hundred watermelons dropped from the rafters and plopped onto the stage to the ecstatic applause of the delegates.

Robbie and Evita dodged the thudding melons and splattering pulp and jogged offstage. Robbie furiously grabbed Marty by his lapels and pulled him aside. "Thanks, you blithering idiot," Robbie seethed. "I thought they were supposed to boo me off stage."

"Yeah, well." Marty scratched his head. "That might have been a miscalculation."

Robbie fumed. "Now what am I supposed to do?"

Marty shrugged. "Run, Robbie, run—before Bennie gets here."

43. The Afterglow

A joyous after-party in the green room capped the convention, with TVs showing roundtable discussions on the major networks and cable news shows. Ninety percent of them agreed: Robbie's speech was a smashing success. Finn Tingleberry declared it the most powerful address since William Howard Taft was pelted with cabbage in 1910.

As well-wishers crowded around Robbie to offer their congratulations, Ned sought out Marty. "Where the hell did that come from?"

"The heart," Marty replied drily.

"I thought you pulled it out of your ass," Ned replied. "Well, whatever. The crowd loved it. And Platt has already tweeted that it was the worst speech since Pat Paulsen ran for president in 1968. To me, that's a badge of honor. We're off to a great start."

"How do you think Bennie and Marius took it?"

Ned growled. "I'm not going to hang around to find out."

As Ned trundled off, Howie-Do-It sidled up to Marty. "Where's the boss?"

"He's in that thicket over there," Marty said, nodding to the crowd gathered around Robbie.

"The Barbus are on their way down," Howie said, tensely.

Marty took a deep breath. "Keep an eye on our guy. And don't let the Barbus frog-march him to a car. We don't want Robbie 'disappeared.'"

"Copy that," Howie replied.

All eyes turned to Bennie and Marius as they entered the room, where they were greeted with cheers and admiring applause. The Barbus acknowledged the attention with nods and tight smiles as they made their way toward Robbie. The crowd parted around him.

Bennie dug his fingers into Robbie's upper arm. "May we have a word," he said as a command rather than a question.

"Of course," Robbie said.

They moved to a corner of the room for privacy, where both Barbus glared at their nominee. Marius looked like he might hit Robbie, who tried to remember defensive moves he learned as kid taking karate lessons. How would he fend off a blow? Maybe an *Uchi-Uke,* like the one that earned him his yellow belt?

"You're very generous with our money, Mr. Crowe," Bennie said. "But you made a serious mistake."

"You told me when we met that I was a fuckup," Robbie retorted.

"I failed to appreciate how true that was," Bennie said. "Fortunately, you've exceeded our worst expectations. We've been selling the dollar short, earning a high yield on US bonds, and making an enormous profit—all thanks to investors' complete lack of confidence in your ability to run the country."

Marius smirked. "We've made a killing."

"As long as your killing spree doesn't include me, I consider that a win," Robbie replied.

"Your problem is you're too clever by half, Mr. Crowe," Bennie said. "There won't be any profits from America's Just Rewards. It's a non-profit. Every dollar we receive over expenses is reinvested."

"You'll just never know where," Marius added.

Bennie put his arm around Robbie's shoulder and squeezed with considerable pressure. "You can fuck up your company, your foundation, your family, even our country. But don't try to fuck around with my business. It won't work. And you won't like the consequences."

"Is that a threat?" Robbie asked.

"Is that a question?" Bennie replied.

The Barbus left Robbie with a heart jumping out of his chest. Marty and Lindsey approached, noting he was in obvious distress.

Robbie stretched out his arms and looked at them. "I don't appear to be dead," Robbie noted.

"That's why you got the nomination over Dewey," Marty said.

Lindsey nodded. "You've got five months to live, easily."

"Make 'em count," Marty said.

Worth approached. "Congratulations, Robbie! You won the nomination and survived the Barbus. So far, anyway."

"Let me ask you something, Worth," Robbie muttered. "How hard would it be to hide the profits from America's Just Rewards?"

"For Bennie?" Worth laughed. "He was a cutout for the CIA in eastern Europe after the war, funneling money to the underground resistance. He's a master of untraceable money. Nobody will figure it out until it's long, long gone. He'll have his just rewards and so will America."

"I understand you get a piece of the action, too," Robbie said.

"Ah," Worth said dismissively, "just enough to wet my beak, as they say."

Robbie was numbed by it all. The whirlwind nomination. The convention. The Barbus. Evita. He had no idea what to do next. Where was his Magic 8-Ball?

"Come on out to the Vineyard next weekend," Worth said. "I'm having a little victory party at the house for everybody on the team."

Robbie nodded toward the Barbus, who were huddled with Evita. "You think they'll come?"

"Of course," Worth said, reassuringly. "Bennie suggested it."

44. A House is Not a Home

Worth's estate in Martha's Vineyard was cooled by a gentle breeze off the Atlantic Ocean on a pristine late summer day. It was a perfect setting for Crowe-Manolo campaign honchos to gather on the veranda wearing their summer whites and pastels, savor their success, and catch a break before the fall campaign cranked up in earnest.

Worth's staff offered guests a New England picnic spread of lobster rolls, bluefish pate, salads, and artisanal cheeses along with chilled Chardonnay and Riesling made from grapes cultivated on the island. Nearby, summering residents strolled the beach, while children tossed beanbags on the lawn.

Robbie leaned against a railing that perched over a sand dune, mingling with Ned, Dinda, and Kristi, but keeping his eye on Bennie and Marius Barbu, who were gathered with Evita on the other side of the deck. What fate, he wondered, did they have in mind for him?

Worth held a glistening glass of white wine by its stem as he sidled up to Robbie.

"Relax," Worth said. "I don't sense the least bit of hostility from our friends."

Ned, who had commandeered one gin and tonic for each hand lest there be a line at the bar, agreed. "Bennie and Marius understand your success is our success," he said. "If you ask me, they've not only come to terms with it, they accept it wholeheartedly."

Worth scoffed. "Their reputation for revenge is overblown." He nodded across the bay to a stately white frame mansion with a picket fence. "Look what they did for Lady Janice, even after she threw a hissy fit right in their faces. They didn't hold a grudge. They stepped up and played as nicely as could be. We're all on the same team."

On cue, Lady Janice waved to the party from across the bay. Feeley joined her and they hopped into his Mustang convertible and drove around the inlet to Worth's house. The two of them stepped onto the veranda looking as happy and relaxed as Robbie had ever seen them. Lady

Janice took a glass of champagne from a passing tray, approached Robbie wearing a satisfied grin, and pulled him away from the others.

"What did I tell you?" she said to him in a tone of enormous self-satisfaction. She nodded toward Bennie and Marius, who were engaged with Eleanor and Meredith from the foundations. "They respect a person who stands up to them."

Robbie admitted, "Your house looks great."

"It's even better inside. The wood finishes. The paint job. Nothing but top-end appliances and a sound system that would make you think Joan Jett was in the house," she replied. "It wouldn't have happened if I hadn't told them what for."

Robbie clinked his wine glass with her champagne glass. "Cheers to that," he said before taking a sip. "When do you move in?"

"Tomorrow morning," she said. "They're just finishing up the last item on their punch list now." Feeley approached and she hugged his arm. "Then it's all systems go."

Worth offered his binoculars to Lady Janice, and she eagerly looked across the water. "Amazing! It's even prettier from here," she said.

Marty couldn't resist. "Too bad Dewey couldn't have lived to see it."

"As if," she scoffed, dropping the glasses. "He'd never leave that Beachville dump." She turned to Robbie. "You want a look?"

"Sure." Robbie peered across the bay to see a picturesque home featuring a half dozen gables, shingle-cladding, and a spectacular deck overlooking the water. Two uniformed utility men emerged from the house carrying toolboxes.

"Looks like they're finished over there," Robbie said as he handed back the binoculars. "Business must be good for them."

"Why do you say that?" she asked.

"They're running."

As the workers jumped into their van and disappeared around a bend, Worth's party was rocked by a deafening boom. An explosion rattled the glass on his home, shook the shutters, and made the party plates clatter. The real damage was across the bay, where Lady Janice's dream home was engulfed in flames. *"Noooo!"* she shrieked.

Feeley put his arm around her to comfort her. "Oh, my word! Don't look, dear."

Lady Janice furiously slapped his hands away to watch the fast-burning conflagration. All the other party guests looked on in horror, except Bennie and Marius. They turned their back on the fire and walked slowly over to Lady Janice.

"My condolences, Janice," Bennie said. "Such a lovely house."

"Really," Marius said, deadpan. "It's just a darn shame."

For the first time since he had met her, Robbie thought Lady Janice looked scared. She staggered over to an Adirondack chair and sat down, burying her face in her hands and sobbing, while Feeley stood by helplessly. That left Robbie face-to-face with Bennie and Marius, who casually munched on lobster rolls.

"Somebody must have made a big mistake," Bennie said.

"I think it was the workers," Robbie suggested warily. "I saw them run from the house."

"That's a possibility, I suppose," Marius said with a shrug. "Then again, maybe somebody blew a fuse." He nodded toward Lady Janice as Bennie stepped in inches from Robbie's face. "I understand that can happen with demand overload."

As sirens wailed in the distance, the Barbus put down their plates and walked to the steps, waiting for Evita. She paused as she joined them and glanced over at Robbie. When they made eye contact, she winked, unnerving him.

Worth walked over and clapped Robbie on the back.

"Remember what I said about the Barbus playing nice?"

Robbie nodded, his jaw slack.

"Never mind," Worth said.

Worth walked away and Marty approached. "I don't think they'd blow up the White House," he said. "Unless, they were really, *really* mad at you."

"That's comforting, you fucking asshole," Robbie snapped.

They watched Bennie walk through the yard, pick up a beanbag that fell at his feet, and toss it toward a target ten yards away. It dropped cleanly through the hole, as the kids who had been playing cheered.

"Second target he's hit today," Marty noted.

"You think there's a third?" Robbie asked with a shudder.

"Nah," Marty said, clapping Robbie on the back. "He delivered his message. And he made sure it was received."

"You think it was meant for me?"

"Of course," Marty said.

Marty clapped Robbie on the back as they watched Bennie and Marius climb into their massive Suburban. The vehicle moved slowly out of the driveway.

"Politics ain't beanbag," Marty said. "But it might be cornhole."

ABOUT THE AUTHOR

Jon Pepper writes satirical novels about politics and big business. He manages a communications consultancy, Indelable LLC, and was previously a business executive, a newspaper columnist, a magazine publisher, and a radio talk show host. He and his wife, Diane, who designed the cover for this book, reside in Coconut Grove, Miami.

Run Robbie Run (2026) is the first in a new series of three novels.

Jon's first five novels were part of a series called *Fossil Feuds*:
A Turn in Fortune (2018)
Heirs on Fire (2020)
Green Goddess (2022)
Missy's Twitch (2023)
Hostile Climate (2024)

More about Jon and his novels is available at www.jonpepperbooks.com